OMEGA
AWAKENS

THE ALPHA-OMEGA WARS

C.J. HANSEN

FISHER KING PUBLISHING

OMEGA AWAKENS

Published by
Fisher King Publishing
The Studio
Arthington Lane
Pool-in-Wharfedale
LS21 1JZ
UK

www.fisherkingpublishing.co.uk

For Mika

In Loving Memory of Harold and Eileen

With special thanks to Alex Florea,
for her advice, help and patience.

Prologue

For most Londoners it seemed like a perfectly normal night, as they slept peacefully in their beds. For one six year-old girl, however, it was anything but. She tossed and turned, deep in the throes of a terrible nightmare. In her mind she was no longer in her warm bed but in the middle of a very unfamiliar landscape. The scene filled her with foreboding.

Lightning lit up the sky in every direction, bringing a large hill into sharp relief. On the hilltop, silhouetted against the momentarily silver sky, was the outline of what appeared to be an enormous, roughly rectangular rock. A bolt of lightning struck the top of the rock with a force so terrible it might have split it in two. Then there was another lightning flash, this time unlike anything the girl had ever seen. It was horizontal, almost as though the inky fabric of the sky itself were being torn apart.

Rain pelted the ground like bullets, and the hilltop was lit up by another flash. For the first time the girl made out five figures, standing round the base of the rock. They were only visible for an instant against the illuminated sky, but one of the forms stood out clearly. It was significantly larger than the others. Although it had not been possible to make out the features of any of the figures, the young girl was gripped by a sense of immense danger.

More lightning, and suddenly the briefest glimpse of a face, now close-up. She noticed nothing but the eyes. Although only for an instant, she saw them with a terrible, daylight clarity. Where they should have been white, the eyes were blood red. The irises were black as ink, surrounding pupils from which emanated a deep, dark, menacing, red glow. And those eyes were staring at her. In fact, not just at her. They appeared to be looking right inside her.

The little girl sat bolt upright in bed, sweat dripping from her hair, screaming in a voice laden with terror and emotion unnatural at her young age. The girl's mother burst into the room, her lantern forcing the darkness to retreat. She hugged the little girl tightly and tried her best to calm her.

"Don't worry my darling Anna," she whispered, "it's only a dream, nothing but a bad dream." But this had felt too real to be a dream.

"Mother, they're here. He saw me. He knows me, he knows who I am. Why is he here? He shouldn't be here. He's going to come after me. We're all in the most terrible trouble!" The words tumbled out through uncontrollable tears, themselves scarce expression of the absolute fear that had gripped her.

Her mother held her, hugged her and rocked her back and forth for what seemed like hours, until the first grey dimness of dawn began to show itself around the curtain edges. The girl's crying slowly calmed to a gentler sobbing, but one powerful feeling would not leave her: that what she had seen in her dream was real. Those figures she had witnessed, whoever they were, did not belong here. This was not meant to be. Anna had the overwhelming sense that she and everyone she knew were in the most fearful danger.

Although the grip of that fear eased a fraction as daylight filtered in slowly from outside, she remained convinced that this had not been a dream. She was certain that the man, whose terrible eyes she had seen, had also seen her. He was real and he now knew of her. Somehow he knew things about who she was. And something about the way in which he had looked right into her, told her with certainty that one day he would find her.

Even after Anna finally stopped crying and her mother left the room, the feeling did not leave her as, exhausted, she lay back down in her bed. Something awful had happened that night. Everything had changed. The world as she had known it in her short life so far would never be the same again.

A Message

The sky above was grey; a grey of the purest, deepest shade, the colour of sky for which Victorian London was famous. Anna gazed through her bedroom window, across the rooftops of the other grand houses with their splendid, tree-lined gardens and their sloping, slate roofs, topped with tall chimneys that puffed out yet more greyness into the air. Her gaze moved further out, to the trees that lined the canal a mile or more from where she sat. How she longed to be there, where she knew her friends would be, as free as the small black specks of birds that she could see circling above in the grey ocean of cloud.

In the last few years, the opportunities for Anna to leave her house and meet with her companions had become fewer and fewer. She knew that her mother loved her dearly, and she also understood that she had probably given her mother reason enough to worry about her, although through no fault of her own. Nonetheless, she could not quite manage to suppress her resentment at having almost become a prisoner in that tall, grand house of theirs.

Fate had not been kind to fourteen year-old Anna. Her 'problems' had begun to generate attention four years earlier, and from that time onwards her life had changed irrevocably for the worse. Anna understood that there were things about her which were different from other people, although as far as she was concerned, that did not mean she had 'problems'. The only problems lay with those who thought otherwise. Since certain differences had become known, she had suffered mockery and bullying by other children. At the same time, the attention and protection from her mother and the housekeeping staff had become more and more suffocating, and her freedoms had been removed one by one. She hadn't chosen to be different, and none of what had happened seemed remotely fair. But that was just life, she supposed.

As Anna sat motionless at the window with her chin resting on her folded arms, there came a knock at the door. Startled, she span around and said, "Yes, come in." For the most part Anna could live with her own company, which was just as well, but being prevented from leaving the house for so long made her grateful for any possibility of new excitement.

The door slowly opened and a tall, gangly girl, a little older than Anna, entered. Her name was Lizzy and she worked in the house as a maid for Anna's mother.

"Miss Anna, please excuse me. I'm not stopping long, and you must promise not to tell your mother or any of the staff that I've been here. Do you promise?"

Anna had always liked Lizzy, but she was also well aware that in recent times the feeling had become less and less mutual. She wondered what had prompted this sudden visit. "Yes, I promise," she replied.

"I've got a message for you from that friend of yours, Rebecca," she began. Lizzy looked as though she had to force these words out, but they were enough to set Anna's heart racing as Lizzy continued, "You know I don't much care for Rebecca. She's free-willed and headstrong, and has far too high an opinion of herself, that one. But she promised she would make it worth my while if I passed on the message, and there are certain things that she could help me with, so here I am." Her tone and demeanour suggested she was already having second thoughts.

"I probably shouldn't be here, and I know the mistress will not approve of this message I'm to give you, so you'd better not say anything and I'd better be quick." Lizzy quickly peered over her shoulder at the closed door as if expecting Anna's mother to burst in at any moment, even though they both knew she was out in town.

"The message is that Rebecca and the others in your little gang are all meeting down by the canal tomorrow afternoon for the fête. She said they're meeting in the usual place, wherever that is, around one o'clock. They hope you can make it."

Having delivered the message Lizzy turned to leave, but then paused. After what appeared to be a brief inner struggle, she evidently couldn't resist adding a thought or two of her own and she turned back.

"I really don't understand why you and them are such good friends. I mean, you're supposed to be a young lady, although heaven only knows what you ever did to deserve such a position, especially with your... condition. And those friends of yours, well they're rough, they're wild. They don't work hard to try and earn a respectable living like the rest of us. Someone in your position ain't supposed to associate with the likes of them."

Anna waited. She could tell there was more.

"And as for them, I wonder why they would go to such an effort to have a young lady like yourself for company. On the one hand you're all prim and proper and well presented, not like them at all. And then on the other you've also got your... your problems, ain't you?" There it was. Anna had guessed that was coming. "Well, I simply don't understand what you all see in each other."

Anna had no idea why some people seemed to attach a different level of worth to other people, just because of the family they were born into. That just seemed plain wrong. Surely the kind of person they were and how they behaved was far more important? For her part, she didn't feel superior to anyone. Anna always felt awkward talking about this, fearing that bringing it up might make matters worse, but she decided to try.

"Oh Lizzy, why does my friendship with Rebecca and the others have to be so difficult to understand? Why create reasons to stop people from spending time with whoever they choose? Becca, the others and I are friends because we like each other. That's just based on how we are as people, not on the family we happened to be born into or the way we look. We don't see ourselves as different from each other in the least." She paused for a moment, then continued, "Lizzy, I know you're a good person, because... well I can't explain how, but because I can see it. I wish we could be friends too."

Something in Anna's words triggered a response in Lizzy. "Don't be silly Miss Anna, we can't be friends. I didn't choose my station in life. It chose me, but I work hard and I get on with it. You don't appreciate how lucky you are. You ought to make the most of it, I'm sure I would if I were you. You should live up to your position and associate with your own kind.

"What's more," Lizzy continued, "I'm not sure I should want to be friends with someone with your problems.

I mean, I'm all for charity and for helping the sick and needy, but your problems are different. I know we're not supposed to speak about those things that people say you can 'see', but if they're true, then it ain't natural. It ain't natural at all." These thoughts had clearly been bursting to come out for quite some time and she could not hold them back.

"You just said you could 'see' what I'm like. One thing I'll say for you, Anna, is that I don't think you're no liar, and you don't seem like one of them crazies. Me and some of the others, we don't reckon that you're crazy like other people do. But if you really can see things that other people can't, then we reckon that must be unholy. Powers like that couldn't have been created by any forces of good in this world or we'd all have 'em, wouldn't we? So they must have come from somewhere else. You know what we mean by that, don't you?' Yes, Anna did understand what that was intended to mean.

"Don't take me the wrong way, Anna," Lizzy continued. 'A little too late,' thought Anna. "I don't mean to say that you're an evil person. Not exactly. But I fear that the forces of evil have given you powers, and that evil shows itself to you, makes itself known to you and makes you see things, and that can't be good. Evil knows you, and you know evil. These times are troubled enough, what with all this talk of the Beast of Highgate and I don't know what else..."

"What was that? The Beast of where...?" Anna started.

"I'm a good, honest person Miss Anna," Lizzy ploughed on before Anna could finish her question, "and I don't want no dealings with no workings of evil, direct or otherwise, simple as that."

"But Lizzy, please believe me," Anna pleaded desperately, though no longer with any great sense of hope. "I'm not evil, I'm not a bad person, and what I see isn't born out of evil either, I'm sure of it. What I can see is just the nature of people, and that nature can be good as well as bad. Indeed, there is far more good than bad in what I see, and I long to see the good in everyone." She dared not go into any more detail as to what she saw or how she did this, harsh experience having taught her that to do so generally resulted in tears – usually her own. "I promise you, I mean no harm to anyone. I am a good person, really I am!"

"I don't know what kind of person you are, I'm sure I don't. What I do know is that you have something about you that ain't natural. Sometimes when you look at me, it's like you're looking inside of me. It's frightening, it's... unnatural," Lizzy paused, then slowly began to back away.

"I knew I should never have come up here. This was a mistake. Mistress Anna, don't you tell a soul I was up here today, not a soul, nor nothing about our conversation. You promised, and I hope you'll see fit to keep to that promise. And Rebecca had better come good 'n all, asking me to come up here against my better judgement."

With that, Lizzy hastened out of the room, closed the door behind her and scuttled away down the stairs. As Anna turned towards the window to reflect on another frustrating encounter, her spirits were nonetheless buoyed by the idea that tomorrow might bring new adventure with her friends.

Little did she know, as she laid her chin on her folded arms to gaze back out into the greyness once more, the sheer magnitude of the adventure upon which she was about to embark.

Friends

The following day, London had once again outdone itself in the utter greyness of its sky. However, on this day the sky could have been clear blue, sunset orange or the most shocking of pinks for all Anna cared. For after being confined in her house under watchful eyes for longer than she cared to remember, she had managed to slip out of the house unseen. It had been a close call when Maggie, the house cook, had almost spotted her, but she had managed to avoid capture. She loved Maggie dearly, but even Maggie would have had to raise the alarm about her leaving the house on her own.

Anna hurried down the long, straight, majestic North London street that she knew so well, passing one by one the enormous, imposing houses which lined it on both sides. She did her utmost to be as unremarkable and inconspicuous as possible, which fortunately was something at which she was well practiced. Her recent life had made her want to go unnoticed through the world. But today she had an additional reason: to avoid being caught.

Anna's mother had always been overly protective, even when she was much younger. Anna was sure it was something to do with her father having died when she was little. She understood she had met her father when she was an infant, but she had no memory of him. Anna had no doubt that it was this great loss that had made her mother even more worried for the safety of her only child than a normal mother would be. Then, when her so-called 'problems' had become known, things got much worse and her freedom to leave the house became more restricted. The turning point had come one fateful Christmas, when Anna was ten.

At the heart of the trouble lay a particular ability that Anna had possessed from an early age, to see things in other people. The word that she had found to describe what she observed was their 'aura'. If she chose to focus her vision, her attention and her mind in the right way, Anna was able to see a person's aura, and she had come to understand that this was a manifestation of that person's nature, indicating things about their character and personality. The visual appearance of the aura varied from person to person, but it was usually spherical in shape, translucent, and mostly some variation of light blue in colour. A person's aura was always located near to them, usually in the space between the top of their head and their chest, but even when she focused on it, it did not entirely obscure Anna's view of the person's physical form. In an instant she could refocus her vision entirely on the physical world again. The size, surface, texture, purity and colour of the aura's were different for each person. Over time, Anna had become able to read much about what a person was like by looking at these characteristics. The only aura that she had never been able to see was her own.

For a long time, Anna had not given this ability much thought. It seemed entirely natural to her and no more unusual than being able to see physical objects, hear sounds or smell fragrances. She couldn't remember a time when she was not aware of people's auras, and her coming to see them in more detail had been such a gradual process that she had never been surprised by it.

Anna had no idea that other people could not see what she could. As a young child, she had once mentioned auras to her mother, but her mother had scolded her severely and told her that this was not something to be spoken about. Had she reflected on this it might have struck her as strange that auras were never mentioned, but Anna had assumed that it was just another of the many things that people understood but just did not seem to discuss openly, so she did the same. It was not until that Christmas four years ago that she was to learn, very abruptly, that others did not in fact see the things that she did, and worse, that they were scared of her ability.

That winter, her mother had been struck down with a serious illness with a very high fever. Anna had been terrified that she might lose her mother and so she made, with the benefit of hindsight, the grave error of telling their doctor, Doctor Evin or 'Doctor Evil' as Anna would refer to him from that day on, that her mother's aura was fading, and that she feared she was going to die. Anna had not spoken of auras since the time her mother had told her not to, but this situation was critical; she feared that if the doctor did not act quickly it could be too late. However, the doctor had started to ask questions about what she meant, and it wasn't long before he seemed to be spending more time and effort questioning Anna than attending to her mother. For her part, her mother, in delirium, uttered things about beasts and evil forces, and for reasons that were never sufficiently explained to Anna, Evin had decided that she was somehow to blame for her mother's condition. He accused her of being possessed, and that she was a danger to all those around her. It had made no sense, but without her mother's protection and with her Uncle James, an indomitable character who would surely have put an immediate stop to Evin's actions, being overseas, there was no one else able or willing to argue against the doctor's orders. Those orders were for Anna to be institutionalised, for her own good and for that of everyone else.

Anna was sent to an asylum. It was a dreadful, truly shocking place. It was an experience Anna would never forget through all her living days. The things she saw shocked her profoundly, and would, for many years, trouble her waking hours as well her dreams. It was only when her mother had recovered sufficiently from her illness that she was able to take control, fight the authorities and use the influence of her own considerable contacts to get Anna freed. By the time Anna returned home, she had been in that ghastly place for a number of days and nights. There had been absolutely nothing wrong with her, but had she stayed there much longer she felt sure that soon there would have been. Had her mother not had the necessary connections in society, in all likelihood Anna would never have been freed from that place. It was this thought above all that most disturbed Anna about the whole episode. How many others had been wrongly imprisoned and had not been so lucky?

In the meantime, word had got out, not only amongst the household staff but seemingly to everyone she knew and more, that she had been institutionalised. No matter that it had been under false pretences, and that Dr Evin was held to account for his rash actions and suspended from practising for six months, a punishment that was considered scandalously light by Anna's mother. For everyone who would not take the time to understand the details, which meant practically everyone else, there was 'no smoke without fire'. It seemed that she was now and forever more to be branded a lunatic, whilst the kindest amongst them would simply refer to her as having 'problems'.

This episode quickly taught her to avoid at all costs the topic of auras. Soon after returning home, Anna raised it with her mother just once more, but her mother told her that this was something never to be spoken of again unless she gave her permission to do so. To make a bad situation worse, these events turned her already overprotective mother into more of a jailer. The shock of almost having her daughter permanently taken away from her had no doubt had a severe effect, and Anna did understand that her mother's intentions were good, but from that time on, Anna's life became a misery.

There were no longer any reasonable excuses that Anna could use to get out of the house, so on the occasions she did leave unattended, it could only be done by deceiving everyone and slipping out and back again unnoticed. In reality this was made easier because when her mother was not giving her lessons, Anna was usually left to her own devices in her room. As long as she was safely locked in the house it was assumed that she was fine, so when she slipped out, provided she went unseen and then made it back to her room before anyone checked on her, no one was any the wiser.

Anna had successfully achieved the first step of that

day's deception, but she had to avoid drawing attention to herself if she was to maintain it. Appearing nonchalant and unhurried, her mind raced ahead of her to her destination. The canal was not far away, but not yet in sight. Doubts started to intrude on Anna's nervous excitement like unwanted clouds on a long-awaited summer sky. Was there really a fête happening along the canal today? Would her friends be there? And would Rebecca's younger brother, Timmy, be there? She allowed herself this final thought only briefly before banishing it again from her mind, but it had been enough to make her blush at the honesty of her own feelings. She did very much hope that he would be.

Anna cast all other doubts aside and focussed on her objective. There was only one major obstacle to cross between her and her destination – a large thoroughfare which ran parallel to the canal, busy at this time of day with carriages and the bustle of city life. This was the place where she was most likely to be spotted, either by one of the household staff or by one of the enemy, the Fletchers and their Marylebone Street Gang. Either of these encounters would be bad. If it were the former, that would likely guarantee her being locked up for the rest of her life. The Marylebone Street Gang on the other hand would be only too pleased to see her, for the opportunity to chase, attack, humiliate her or cause her whatever other kind of misery they could. As far as she could tell, that seemed to be the sole purpose of their existence. If any of them saw her, she would be in real trouble until she managed to reach her friends. She slowed down as she approached the corner, then nearly jumped out of her skin when she heard her name called out.

"Good afternoon young Anna, how are you? I haven't seen you in a while. Is life treating you well?"

Anna looked around desperately and saw a slightly rotund old man with lively eyes, ruddy plump cheeks framed by bushy white sideburns, and a broad, beaming smile. Anna breathed a sigh of relief. It was kindly old Mr Warwick, a long-time family friend who ran the old bookshop on the corner. Mr Warwick's clothes, from his top hat, long black coat, silver-grey waistcoat and green cravat, to his dark grey trousers and black shoes, had all once no doubt been very fine, but all now had considerable signs of age upon them. The impression was one of a man who had known the finer things in life, but for whom such things were now largely referred to in the past tense. However, he had always been very kind to Anna, showing a special interest in her and taking the trouble to find out how she was. She liked him very much. He had sometimes let her play in his shop when she was younger, in the days when her mother had still allowed her such freedoms, and the extremely pure blue appearance of his aura had always told her he was someone she could trust.

In Anna's experience, a pure sky blue aura indicated a person with a good heart. The appearance of other colours tended to suggest flaws in the person's character. It was generally the case that the less blue in the aura, the less pure that person was. The presence of any red in the aura tended to mean a bad, sometimes violent person, and usually spelt danger and trouble. Such auras tended to belong to people who caused harm to others. The size of the sphere of the aura also varied considerably from person to person, and although Anna understood less about what this meant, it seemed to correspond somehow to the strength of that person's will and character and their ability to exert influence on events and the world around them, whether that be for good or bad. Mr Warwick's aura, whilst not particularly large, had always shone with the most radiant blue colour, Anna had always felt safe in the old man's presence.

"Oh, hello there, Mr Warwick," she responded. "Yes I'm fine thank you. Been cooped up in the house for too long. I'm sorry to rush off, but I'm late meeting with my friends. Mr Warwick, I know I can trust you. If you see anyone from the house, please don't tell them you saw me!"

"Ah-ha, I see. Well I do understand that a young person needs to get out and about sometimes. But Anna, you must be careful. The streets can be a dangerous place you know. Still, I expect you know all about that. Very well, I won't breathe a word, just as long as you promise me you will take great care and avoid trouble."

"Thank you very much, Mr Warwick. I do promise!"

"Very well. Enjoy your afternoon, young Anna." With that, the old man turned away and left her to her journey.

Relieved but still on edge, Anna peered up and down the road, waiting for a gap to appear in the steady stream of carriages. There were more people about on this street, but Anna kept her head down to avoid eye contact with anyone. Even as she did so, her eye was caught by the striking headline of a newspaper being read by a man walking towards her. 'Beast from Hell Strikes in Highgate!' The headline was all she could make of it before the man had walked past her. Momentarily she recalled Lizzy mentioning something similar the previous day. What could this mean? She would ask her friends if they knew.

No time to stop and think now though, finally a small gap appeared in the traffic and she scampered across to the other side of the road as fast as she could. Once across, it was a quick right along that side of the road and then left, and she was on the narrow path sloping steeply down toward the canal towpath. On the water there were a number of working barges with faded paintwork, dirty from past loads they had carried and now laden with more, puffing smoke into the air as they moved slowly along the waterway. There was one particularly colourful barge moored to the canal side, painted in yellow with green around the windows and the top of the deck. It had the name 'Canal Queen' written in bright red letters on the bow. It was owned by a family called the Rileys, who lived on the boat and whom she had got to know well when she had spent as much time as she could by the canal in her younger years. Anna wondered if the Rileys were home, but no time to check just now. Nothing could distract her.

At last, Anna approached the darker stretch of path which lay in the shadow of the road bridge that crossed the canal. This was where she always used to meet her friends. At first she could not make anything out. With a sinking feeling in her stomach, the doubts began to flood her mind. Was she too late, or indeed had she been misled about there even being a rendezvous with her friends?

Then a voice called out, "There you are! We thought you'd never come. Thought you'd been inside so long you'd lost the use of your legs!" As her eyes grew accustomed to the gloom she could see them, sitting on the raised ridge under the bridge, and on quick inspection she could see that they were all there.

Rebecca Thompson, the leader of the gang, was two years older than Anna and several months older than anyone else in the group. The daughter of the laundry manageress, she was a pretty girl with shiny, dark hair and lively, attractive brown eyes. There were a further three girls in the group. Tessa and Tilly were the youngest and identical twins, so similar that it took Anna a while to be able to tell them apart, and Alice, who was fair-haired with the brightest of blue eyes. As was the case with Rebecca, Anna also considered Alice far prettier than herself, and like Rebecca, Alice too always seemed to be popular with the boys.

Then there were the five boys of the group. Johnny Adams, the most impetuous of the gang was the son of an ironmonger and a year older than Anna. He had a mop of curly brown hair and brown eyes, and was the most athletic of the friends. Then there was Edward, whose mother worked as a maid in one of the expensive hotels in town, and who was about half a year older than Anna. He was blond with blue eyes, and quite a bit taller than Anna. Next to him sat Alice's brother, Robert. A few months younger than Anna, he had light brown hair and eyes, and was rather good looking, or so Anna thought. Sitting next to Robert was Charlie Morgan, the over-sized and somewhat clumsy baker's son, slightly older than Anna with mousy coloured hair and blue-grey eyes.

As she arrived, both Robert and Charlie looked at

her in a way which, had she not known better, she might have mistaken for attraction. However, she knew too well that such a thing could not be possible, and she was just grateful they seemed pleased to see her. Sitting at the end of the line was the final member of the group, Timmy, Rebecca's shy younger brother. It was he that Anna had been secretly seeking out since she arrived.

As greetings were exchanged, Anna's glance met Timmy's for just the briefest moment, before they both quickly looked away again in determinedly opposite directions, neither of them focused in the slightest on whatever it was their eyes next met. The glance had been enough to send Anna's heart almost crashing through her ribcage. Brief though it was, the look was also long enough for Rebecca to notice it. She grinned at Anna, but said nothing.

Timmy always wore a bashful expression, and his long, floppy, sandy-coloured fringe made it difficult for his blue eyes either to see or to be properly seen. His clothes were always ill-fitting and not in the best of repair, but despite all that, Anna was reminded again just how handsome he was. Well, to her at least.

Many were the times when Anna, alone in her room, had wished desperately that she had been born pretty, like Rebecca or Alice. Hard as she tried, she could never find anything noteworthy in her appearance, or at least, anything attractive. Her hair was brown but lacked any richness of colour, her eyes were neither bright blue nor shiny brown but what seemed to her a muddy shade, and when she examined it, her face appeared to her out of proportion. Plain at best, unattractive at most honest, were the only conclusions she could ever reach about the girl who smiled shyly back at her from the mirror. She could never convince herself that anyone would be able to see beyond her plain exterior to discover that she was really a good person inside, someone they could perhaps one day even fall in love with. But this had never quite stopped her dreaming, not where Timmy was concerned.

The group spent time together whenever they were not expected to be at work or have errands to run. Although on the surface Anna's background was entirely different to the rest, she had been part of the group from an early age. It had been Anna's eldest cousin, Richard, who had first got to know the older members of the group when he used to spend time down by the canal, and it was he who had introduced Anna to them. Richard and his family had moved to Bath some years ago and only visited London occasionally, much to Rebecca's eternal disappointment as Anna hadn't failed to notice, but Anna had remained close friends with them all. That Anna came from a well-to-do family never seemed to make a difference to them. Although she was able to meet up less frequently than the others, especially recently, whenever she did it was as though she had never been away. In an instant she would slip seamlessly back into their banter and pranks. It was when she had the chance to run free in the streets of London with this group of friends that she was at her happiest. It was only then that she felt really alive.

"You've been away long enough, ain't you? I thought maybe you were dead. Thought they might have got tired of keeping you prisoner and decided to get rid of you all together!" joked Rebecca. "Mother been locking you up again, has she?"

"She certainly has, and it's driving me mad. I managed to slip out today, but if I get caught, your guess could still turn out to be right!"

"I think you should come and stay with us for a while," said Rebecca. "I know there's folk there who'd be more than happy to welcome you." At that point her gaze moved quickly and subtly in the direction of her younger brother, then she winked at Anna, all done so rapidly that no one but Anna noticed. Of course Anna knew exactly what Rebecca was suggesting, and she spoke quickly to avoid her face turning too red.

"Oh Becca, I wish I could, honestly I do. I can't tell you how good it would be to be free for a while. And your mother's cooking is the best I have ever tasted!"

"Well I know she'd love to have you to stay almost as much as we would. I suppose the chances of you being released aren't great though. At least in Newgate Prison you can go free when you've done your time. I don't reckon they're going to let you out until someone carts you off for their wife – and then your next life sentence will begin! I just couldn't live locked up like you are. For all your finery and comfortable house, I wouldn't swap places with you for the world."

"I would though, in an instant!" said Anna, and they both laughed as Rebecca put her arm around Anna's shoulder. "I wish someone would explain that to Lizzy though," Anna added quietly, almost to herself.

"Actually I need to speak to you about her. She's been acting a bit a strange lately. But not now," said Rebecca. Then she added in a whisper that only Anna could hear,

"Maybe that is the answer though..."

"What is?" asked Anna.

"Marriage!" Rebecca shot her brother another glance too rapid for anyone but Anna to make out, before looking back at Anna and bursting into laughter once more.

Anna blushed again but then joined in with Rebecca's laughter as the group started to move off down the canal side. Everyone started to talk to her at the same time, updating her on the various events that had happened since they had last met. It was almost impossible to hold down a conversation with so many people chipping in and talking at once, but she drank in their words like fresh spring water after a lengthy spell in the desert. It was so good to see them all again.

"Have you heard about the Marylebone Street Gang?" asked Charlie. The mention of that name caught Anna's attention above all the other voices. "We think they're getting into some right dodgy business now. We always knew they were wrong-uns, but now it looks like they're getting involved with some real criminals." Anna and her companions had had many a scrape, and even fights, with this gang, always instigated by the Maryleboners. Although Anna had long had a healthy dislike for them, she had never actually thought of them as criminals.

"Yes," joined in Rebecca, the rest of the group now quieter and focused on this conversation. "We've seen them running errands for some right dubious types, including some proper rough characters that I happen to know have spent time inside. They seem to be carrying packages for them. There's definitely something going on, and bound to be illegal I'll wager. We knew that some of the gang's older brothers were getting involved in criminal work, and it's them that's now got the gang members we know into it."

"We don't know what it is they're up to yet, but we mean to find out!" joined in Johnny, and the rest of the group murmured their agreement. Anna's mind began to race as she wondered what kind of business their nemeses were getting involved with.

"But that's not the worst of it," continued Rebecca. You know Kenny Gillespie, older brother of Billy from the Marylebone Street gang? Well him and his mate, Archie Knowles, have started threatening some of our families! He's already approached Alice and Robert's brother, Benny, and Johnny's older brother, George 'n all, trying to get them to run their errands for them and threatening them with a beating if they don't do it."

Alice, Robert and Johnny all nodded grimly. Anna was shocked. "What have they asked them to do?" she said. Johnny spoke first. "Kenny Gillespie wanted George to steal some books for him from a big old house in St John's Wood, near where you live, Anna."

"Books?" said Anna, surprised. "What kind of books?"

"George didn't talk long enough to find out. Told Gillespie to sling his hook, he did! George is pretty tough and he can look after himself all right." Johnny replied proudly. Then he added in a quieter voice, "He doesn't reckon Gillespie will leave it at that. I'm worried he's going to do something to George. Something really bad..."

Then Alice joined in, "And now Gillespie's friend, Archie Knowles, is trying to get our Benny involved. He's said he'll cause him real trouble if he doesn't do what they want. Knowles is a right nasty piece of work, and Robert and me are really worried something terrible is going to happen to him, too."

"So we're determined to find out what Gillespie and Knowles are up to," said Rebecca, "so that we can turn them in to the police and stop them harming Benny, George or anyone else. And we mean to start by finding out what the Marylebone Street Gang are helping them with. Anna, will you help us?"

"Yes, of course, I'll do whatever I can," said Anna, and she meant it. She would do anything she could to help her friends, even though she had no idea how as yet, or how she would even get out of the house to do it!

"So far we've found out that a couple of the Marylebone Gang, Davy Green and Bobby Watson, are going to be running another errand for Archie Knowles tomorrow. We've spied them coming and going from a house on the road up to Highgate. That's where they're supposed to be picking something up tomorrow around three o'clock, and this time we mean to follow them to see where they're going. We're gonna find out once and for all what they're up to. Can you come with us?"

"Yes, I'll try," replied Anna. She would need to carefully plan her escape from the house, but her mother was due to be out the next day so that should help. Then the momentarily serious mood was broken as Tilly cried out, "Looks as though the fête's going to start soon. Look, the Rileys' boat has moved off!"

Anna looked over her shoulder and saw the brightly coloured barge moving away from its moorings. It would be a short journey down the water to where the canal widened out and other barges were gathering for the fête on the canal side. Often the barge owners who lived or worked around this area of London, and any others who were there to carry cargo to and from the capital, would gather in this wider stretch of water and share food, drink, stories and music late into the night, especially when a fête was happening. Although none of the companions were from barge families, they had played alongside this particular stretch of canal for so long that they had got to know a fair number of the barge owners, and they were always made to feel welcome.

"Hello there folks," came the booming voice of the portly Mr Riley, his words thick with a broad West Country accent. He was beaming at the helm of the Canal Queen. "Good to see you all out for the gathering. Heavens, even Anna's joined us. This must be a special one!"

"Hello Mr Riley," replied Anna, "yes, sorry it's been a while. I've been kept indoors but managed to escape today. How are Mrs Riley, Bob and Jilly?"

"They're all just fine, in the best of health thank ye kindly. Gone on an errand to buy some supplies for the evening they have, but they'll be joining us shortly."

"Great, hopefully I'll see you all a little later then," Anna replied as her friends waved Mr Riley off. How late she could risk staying out was something she did not want to think about at that moment. She knew it couldn't be too long, but that was a problem which could wait for now.

The group approached the point where the canal started to widen and the boats were gathering, and one by one they started to climb the stone steps up to the road. From there, they would be able to cross the bridge to the side where, further down the canal, most of the barges would be moored. Anna was at the back chatting with Alice when she noticed that Timmy had stopped before the steps to tie up his boot laces, although curiously they didn't look to have come loose from what Anna could see. She slowed down and let Alice climb the steps first.

As soon as Alice was out of sight, Timmy peered up through his fringe, rose from his feigned lace tying, and Anna was able to look him fully in the face for the first time that day. She had been stealing the occasional heart-stopping glance at him whenever one had been there for the stealing, but now that she was able to look at him properly she got that familiar feeling in the pit of her stomach. This time it was so strong that she thought she might actually be sick. If anything though, Timmy looked even more nervous than she felt.

Knowing he had only a moment before they would be missed by the others, Timmy reached inside his ragged old coat, and to Anna's astonishment produced a small bunch of rather battered, yellow flowers. They looked a little on the wild side and considerably flattened from their concealment within Timmy's coat, but none of those things could have mattered less to Anna at that moment. No-one had ever given her flowers before, nor had the idea probably even crossed anyone's mind for a second. But now Timmy of all people, his hand trembling slightly as he clutched them, was presenting her with some!

The thundering of Anna's heart was setting the rhythm for the somersaults her stomach was now turning. In rough shape though the flowers were, to Anna they were the most beautiful thing she had ever seen. What was more, Timmy's aura was shining brightly, pure sky-blue and as radiant as she had ever seen it. That purity, and the kindness that it conveyed, was one of the qualities which had always made Timmy so attractive to Anna for as long as she had known him. At that moment, she didn't think she had ever seen anything quite so vividly blue, so completely pure and so utterly beautiful. Now this person, this boy who she had secretly dreamed about so many times whilst shut up in her room, was giving her flowers! She took them from him slowly with both hands, and on an impulse which somehow managed to bypass the conscious thoughts that would normally have made such an action impossible, she leant forward and kissed Timmy on the cheek.

They stood for a moment, both looking at each other in a state of ecstatic, if slightly awkward, shock. Timmy took a couple of steps back out of the shade of the bridge and was preparing himself to say something when the beautiful spell was suddenly broken as quickly as it had been cast.

Without any warning, Timmy was hit from above by a stream of brown, stinking muck! Not a small amount either – it covered his hat and the best part of his coat, as well as his fringe and part of his face. This was followed immediately by howls of laughter from a number of voices. Anna was momentarily stunned, and the thought flashed across her mind that this must somehow be her fault, that Timmy should not have been giving her flowers or that she should not have shown her feelings in the way she had. She felt sick again, but now in a very different way to moments earlier.

"Hey, lover boy, don't look so good now, do ya?" sneered one of the voices from above, followed by another even louder bout of laughter and heckles. Looking up at the bridge above, she could see at least five faces that she knew far better than she would have liked. It was the Marylebone Street Gang! Always out for trouble in general, and especially if that trouble involved Anna and her friends, they were in ecstasy over this direct hit, made all the more entertaining by its timing.

Timmy looked stunned and totally humiliated. Anna looked at his clothes, and the equine stench that was now starting to emanate from him confirmed her worst fears. Timmy had been covered from head to foot in horse manure!

Timmy was naturally so shy, she knew it must have taken all his courage to make that gesture with the flowers, and it had been the first time that anyone had ever done anything like that for her. It had been a wonderful thing, maybe the most special moment in her life, and to have it ruined so embarrassingly and in such a public place seemed to her crushingly unfair. Timmy's pure heart did not deserve it. In the seconds that these emotions exploded within her, something else inside Anna stirred. Or rather, it awakened. This injustice was not something that Anna was prepared to accept. A wrong had been done, and she needed to act.

Confrontation

Enraged, Anna turned and dashed up the stone steps. When she reached the road, she could see the Marylebone Street Gang, seven of them in all: Doug and Reggie Fletcher, Bobby Watson, Sally Hicks, Davy Green, Billy Gillespie, brother of Kenny Gillespie, and Mary Pike. At the same time, Anna's companions were now returning, having been alerted first by the howls of laughter and abuse, then by the sight of their bitter enemies. However, the rival gang's attention was focused entirely on Anna. Their howls of laughter had grown louder, and now turned to pure mockery at the sight of this small girl with her very proper dress, perfectly shiny shoes and carefully brushed hair coming towards them. She could not have looked more different from them if she had come from another world. Anna quickly identified the main offender, a ragged boy she recognised as Billy Gillespie. He was gleefully holding up the empty bucket which had contained the manure; he taunted her with it. However, as she fixed her stare on Gillespie, she also started to observe his aura, and as she did so his expression began to change. While his companions continued to laugh and jeer, Anna noticed, as much as she was able through her rage, a small flicker of surprise, possibly even fear, cross Gillespie's face. He quickly composed himself, and his look soon returned to its more characteristic sneer.

"Ooh, look who it is," he said in a mocking, high-pitched voice, "if it ain't little Miss Prim and Proper. Or should I say, little Miss Lunatic? Been let out of the asylum to fight your weakling boyfriend's battles for him, have you?" Then in a deeper, angrier tone, "You'd better scarper or I'll have you too, you loony!"

Gillespie's companions joined in the jeering, and it grew more aggressive. However, that increasing portion of Anna's mind that was paying attention to such details noted that for all Gillespie's threatening words he had not actually taken a step forward or in any way physically threatened her. There was something holding him back.

As Anna drew closer she began to slow her pace, every stride becoming more purposeful. It was now no longer the messages from her regular senses that were occupying her mind, but those from that additional sense which she possessed. She looked upon Gillespie's aura with an absolute, clear focus – and a far from pleasant sight it was. It did not exactly exude evil, but it was distinctly tarnished and discoloured, as well as being slightly disfigured. Anna had seen worse in adults, but it was still clear that Gillespie's aura had already suffered serious damage and that its owner was travelling down that same slippery path. It was definitely not the aura of a decent person. Its owner seemed to be losing any common decency, and with it any sensitivity and respect he may have had for the feelings of others.

Then a thought struck Anna. Could it be that it was the very act of her focusing on Gillespie's aura that was somehow restraining him? She had no idea if such a thing could be possible, but as she neared him the impression grew. In her heightened sensory state, she began to feel as though she were somehow reaching out and touching Gillespie's aura. Of course she was not physically touching it – there was nothing physical there to touch – but for the first time in her life, she felt as though she was somehow able to reach out and touch it *using her own aura*. She could not see it, but she could feel the contact.

As Anna approached, Doug Fletcher, the older of the Fletcher brothers and leader of the gang shouted at Gillespie. "Come on Billy, she's asking for trouble. Let the loony have it!"

Fletcher's words seemed to shake Gillespie back into life and he took a step towards Anna, who by now had nearly reached him. No sooner had he taken that step however than he froze again, and his power seemed to drain visibly from him. In her mind's eye, Anna had locked onto Gillespie's bruised and disfigured aura and started to push it backwards. She steadily increased the pressure she was applying, whilst manipulating the abnormalities and moulding its shape some way back towards the perfect sphere it ought to be. At that moment she knew that Gillespie's aura was at her complete mercy, to do with it anything she wished, good or bad. Indeed, had she chosen to, Anna felt sure she could easily have destroyed it beyond any chance of recovery, such were the enormous surges of mental power that she was now feeling.

Anna had no time to ponder what was happening, or what had happened inside her to make all this possible. All that could wait. Despite the odds against her, she suddenly felt in complete control. She continued to apply pressure to her foe's aura until she had restored it to a shape more closely resembling a sphere.

Refocusing her attention onto Gillespie's physical

form which was now within touching distance, she saw that he was standing completely motionless, staring at Anna through unblinking eyes with an expression which looked almost like awe. As her focus returned to her regular senses she became acutely aware of the rest of the gang, who were shouting and screaming for Gillespie to do something. Though she had absolute confidence that Gillespie now posed no threat whatsoever, her years of bitter experience had taught Anna that it was always best not to reveal to others the ways in which she was different from them and the powers she possessed that apparently they did not. It would only be moments before they realised that Anna had done something very strange to their friend, and done so without even laying a finger on him.

Acting to conceal her secret, Anna spoke at the top of her voice for all to hear, "Gillespie, that's the last time you humiliate any of my friends, or anyone else, do you understand me? I'm going to teach you a lesson, and you're going to remember it!" With that, Anna launched herself upon him physically, although still with careful measure and control. She pushed him back against the low wall of the bridge, grabbed the front of his shabby jacket by the lapel with one hand and his belt with the other, and with all her might she heaved him over the edge and sent him into the canal below! She barely had the strength to lift him, and had Gillespie offered any resistance there would have been no way she could have done it. However he had not resisted at all.

There was a loud splash followed by coughing and spluttering as Gillespie started to flounder his way to the side. None of the Marylebone Street Gang were laughing now. They all looked as stunned by what had happened as Timmy had minutes earlier when he had disappeared under his shower of dung.

"You're gonna regret this!" shouted Gillespie's girlfriend, Mary Pike, though even she looked visibly shaken. Anna faced the rest of the gang, with her own friends now squarely behind her, ready for any conflict that might follow. She looked each of the Maryleboners in the eye, and for a second time she felt her aura starting to move out from her, making peripheral contact with those of each of her opponents in turn. This time she applied a lighter pressure, but it was still sufficient to turn the tide of the encounter.

"Now's not the time," shouted Doug Fletcher, looking slightly disconcerted. "Come on, let's get Billy and get out of here. We'll get her another time. Then she'll be sorry!"

The gang turned and hurried to the stone steps to rescue their sopping comrade. "You're gonna get it, you know that. You're gonna pay, and you'll wish you had never been born, you loony," came the parting cries. They had no idea how often she had made that same wish herself!

Anna's friends instantly surrounded her and the mood changed to one of celebration, congratulations, then questions as to how it had all started. Anna updated them as briefly as possible, relaying the manure attack but mentioning nothing about the flowers that had preceded it.

After the group had chatted excitedly for a while, Anna's thoughts started to move on. During the encounter a number of things had happened that she needed time to think through, but before that she had to speak with Timmy again, and somehow needed to engineer the chance to do so alone.

Timmy had not yet emerged from the canal side. Anna led the way back down the stone steps and saw him sitting further down the bank, some distance away from where Gillespie had fallen in. Still half covered in muck he looked thoroughly miserable, and the stench was by now overpowering. He had managed to clean the worst of the mess from his hair, face and hands, but his clothes and hat remained generously covered. Seeing how downcast he looked and realising that he had apparently not even tried to clean any of his clothes yet, Anna began to worry how much this incident might have affected him.

However, it also gave her an idea. When he saw the group coming towards him led by Anna, Timmy smiled briefly before looking away in embarrassment at his condition, as though he didn't want to be seen. Noticing this, Anna slowed down a little and allowed Rebecca to overtake her.

"Well you're in a right state, ain't you? Lucky you've got Anna here to fight your battles for you, is all I can say!" she laughed. "You should've seen her Tim, she was fantastic. She faced them down and threw Gillespie straight in the canal! I couldn't believe it, it was brilliant.

"And you should've seen the rest of them. They couldn't believe their eyes neither. Scared them all off she did, before I'd even had a chance to have a go at them myself!"

It was only then that Rebecca seemed to notice that

Timmy was not sharing her joy and amusement, and to dawn on her how badly his pride must have been hit by the whole episode. That Anna, a girl after all, had fought and won his battle for him was probably the last straw. Clearly now feeling for her younger brother, she sat down next to him as the others looked on, made as though to put her arm around him before thinking better of it in his state, and said in a gentler tone, "Got you bad didn't they? Nothing you could've done about it though. You couldn't have seen them up there, and you couldn't have stopped them. Right cowardly of them it was, but you've taken it real well, not running away or nothing. Just like a real Thompson."

Timmy's expression was complex, as though partly comforted and grateful to his sister for her sympathetic words, but at the same time embarrassed at the need for her to say them at all, especially in front of their friends. The mood needed to be broken somehow, and Anna seized her opportunity.

"Well Timmy," she said, "I do hate to say this, but I'm afraid you stink! We can't have you going about smelling like a heap of manure for the rest of the day. There's only one thing to be done. You need a proper wash. The canal may not be the cleanest bath in the world," Anna peered at the dark water to her left, "but it's still an awful lot cleaner than you are. Come on, and no arguments."

Anna reached out and took Timmy's hand, concealing the thrill that went through her at its touch, pulled him up and directed him further down the canal side. "Right, on the count of three, into the water. No, there's no use taking your coat off, that's the whole point! Now, seeing as it's not fair that you are the only one who has to jump in, and also so that I don't get a reputation for forcing boys into canals as a regular hobby, I'll join you. It's only fair since I was as much a target for that muck as you were. No, no arguments!"

The others laughed and cheered them on. Timmy himself looked completely nonplussed, but then even he too offered a slight smile as she continued. "One, two – don't back out on me now Timothy Thompson, I don't want to be jumping in there on my own! One, two... three!"

Gripping Timmy's hand, she jumped into the cold canal water, with Timmy by her side. The rush of cold water was a shock, and at first Anna found it difficult to breathe as her chest muscles tightened.

However, as she reached the surface again and her body adapted slowly to the temperature, she could hear the jovial sounds of their friends on the bank. When Timmy also began to laugh and to splash water at them, Anna knew the worst was over.

"Come on, I'll race you to the other side where we can dry off," Anna said once Timmy had done his best to rub himself clean in the water. That would hopefully give her the chance she needed to speak with Timmy alone.

"All right," said Timmy, and they both swam the short distance to the other side before clambering out, dripping wet. Anna had spent many summers when younger playing in the canal with her friends and she was both a capable swimmer and perfectly able to haul herself out of the water. However, on this occasion she decided that it might aid Timmy's recovery if she ensured he got to the other side first, and then let him be seen to help her out. He did so, and she thanked him.

The others slowly started to make for the stone stairs again, presumably heading over the bridge and re-join them on their side of the canal. Anna did not have long.

"Timmy, there's something I want to say to you about today," she started.

"There's nothing about today I want to talk about," said Timmy, gloom suddenly descending on him once again. "I want to forget this day ever happened!"

"Well I don't," replied Anna. "And I never will forget it. Timmy, when you gave me those flowers, well, it was the most wonderful thing anyone has ever done for me. I will never forget it Timmy, never, and I wanted to say thank you."

She paused as Timmy silently watched the reflection of the grey sky dancing on the bobbing canal water.

"What happened with the manure... yes I know you don't want to talk about it and we don't have to, but it was nothing more than a horrible prank. I am sure we'll all look back and laugh about it one day, especially as we had the victory in the end. And I say 'we', because we are all together, a team, and any one of us would have done the same for any other. I know you would have stood up for me if the situation had been the reverse."

"Yes, I would have, you know that," said Timmy, now looking up at her earnestly.

"Yes I do know that, Timmy, of course I do," continued Anna, her heart starting to leap about like a maniac as she thought about what she was about to say, and to whom she was about to say it. "But please don't let that experience, or any experience like it, ever change you. Please promise me that you won't. It would be so easy to feel like you hate someone, or to want revenge, when someone does something like Gillespie did today. But you've got such a pure heart Timmy, I know you have because I can... well, I can sense it. Don't ask me how. It makes you the most special person I have ever met, and it's the greatest quality anyone could ever have. It's something that I love about you." There, she had said it, forcing that particular word out through a barrier built of fear and embarrassment which had always been completely insurmountable until that very moment. "So please promise me you won't change, that you won't start to do things to hurt other people just because someone has hurt you. I'm certain that's one of the things which eventually turns people from good to bad, and explains a lot about what's not right in the world. Timmy, you're a special person, and a very good one. Please don't lose that, no matter what anyone ever does."

Anna was sure that their friends would re-emerge at any moment, but for some reason she needed to hear him say the words.

"Please Timmy, promise me. Promise you will remain the same pure person you have always been and that you won't change, no matter what."

"All right Anna, well, I'm not too sure what you mean to be right honest with you, but if you mean you want me to promise I ain't going to change who I am, then I can do that. I promise, Anna. I don't think I'm really the changing sort anyway."

"Thank you Timmy," sighed Anna with a depth of

relief that even she could not fully understand. "And thank you again for the flowers. I will never forget them."

A sudden thought seemed to cross Timmy's mind and he patted the front of his coat as if searching for something, then peered over the side of the canal. Without a word, he reached over and fished out a single, very limp, very wet yellow flower.

"You put them down when you ran off after Gillespie, so I picked them up and put them back in my coat. Must've fallen out when we went swimming."

Anna found herself having to force back sudden tears, which she somehow managed to, as she took the one remaining flower from Timmy. She concealed it inside her sodden cardigan against her madly beating heart, and gave Timmy one more hasty kiss on the cheek, seconds before the others appeared.

"You feeling better now, after your little dip?" asked Timmy's sister who came into view first.

"Yes, I am actually. Much better in fact!" he replied, looking about him and grinning.

"Oh really?" answered Rebecca with evident suspicion. Though she pursued it no further, Anna was sure that Rebecca had flashed her another of those knowing smiles of hers. But this time Anna ignored it. Nothing could detract from the feeling she was floating on pure air.

An Unwelcome Visitor

The group all sat on the canal side as Anna and Timmy waited for their clothes to dry. In the absence of any sun this was taking far longer than Anna had anticipated. After a good thirty minutes had passed and her garments were still wringing wet, worry began to intrude upon Anna's internal euphoria for the first time. It could take hours for her clothes to dry completely, by which time it would be getting late and there would be a real danger of her disappearance being discovered. However, if she returned home in wet clothes there would be an equal chance of her being found out, and she would be in twice the trouble. She needed another plan, fast.

"I must get dry somehow, and quickly too. Do any of you have any ideas?" she asked the others.

"Why don't you come home with us and get dry there?" replied Rebecca. "It's the least we can offer after how you've stood up for my brother today."

"Yes," agreed Timmy, his earlier embarrassment at having been defended by a girl forgotten. "You can come home with us!"

"Becca, Timmy, that's very kind of you and I would love to, but I wouldn't want you to leave the fête early because of me. Also you do live quite a way away. By the time I get there, get dry and get back again I think it will be too late. Thank you again, but I need to do something more quickly."

It was then, in the distance beyond the other side of the canal, that she spotted old Mr Warwick. He appeared to be heading in the direction of his bookshop.

"I know, I'll ask Mr Warwick. He's always been very kind to me. And right now he's my only hope. I'll ask him to help."

With that Anna bade a fond farewell to her companions, being very careful not to show any special attention to Timmy in front of the others, and turned towards the canal bridge.

"Don't forget about tomorrow," Rebecca called out as she departed. "We've got to follow those Maryleboners to find out what they are up to. After today's little victory I'm even keener for you to join us!"

The afternoon's events had been so tumultuous that she hadn't started to think about the next day's mission, but she immediately assented. "Yes, I'll be there!"

"Are you sure you'll be able to escape again so quickly?" Rebecca asked.

"Yes," Anna replied, trying to sound more confident than she felt. "My mother will be out all day tomorrow, and... well, I will find a way!" Of that she was determined. She would do whatever was necessary to help her friends, and of course, in the process to see Timmy again.

"All right, same time, same place then! One o'clock. That should give us plenty of time to be ready to follow Green and Watson," concluded Rebecca. She caught Rebecca flashing another of those smiles in her direction.

Somehow overcoming the urge to look again in Timmy's direction, Anna turned away, bade a final farewell and headed across the bridge.

On reaching the other side, Anna focused on her next mission. She called out in the direction of the elderly gentleman. "Mr Warwick! Mr Warwick! It's Anna. I'm afraid I fell in the canal! I'm going to be in a lot of trouble unless I can get dry. Is there any chance you could help me? I'd be ever so grateful."

"Oh dear Anna, whatever have you been doing?" asked Mr Warwick, for a moment appearing quite concerned, before suddenly breaking into his customary broad smile again. "Of course I'll help. Come with me to my shop, and you'll be dry and ready for home before you know it."

"Oh, thank you Mr Warwick!" said Anna, relieved. They were outside the bookshop in no time. Above the window, a dark green sign with large white letters shadowed with black read 'Barton's Bookshop', and in smaller letters underneath, 'Seller of Rare & International Books'. Anna had no idea who Mr Barton was; she had only ever known Mr Warwick to work in the place. In a moment they were in the warm interior of the dusty old shop.

Inside, the walls were lined with shabby bookshelves, each housing a very large collection of old volumes in various states of dilapidation, some standing upright, others laid horizontally, all according to no pattern that Anna could make out. There were shorter, equally shabby-looking stands containing more battered old books dotted around the shop floor at random, a large number of crates, some of them opened and some of them yet to be so, and then further books piled willy-nilly around the floor. The only consistent feature amongst the semi-chaos was a layer of dust that evenly covered everything bar those items that had been recently touched. In short, the place was a mess. And it had always been so for as long as Anna could remember.

Anna followed Mr Warwick across the floor into a room at the back. She had never been here before, and she was immediately taken by surprise. Contrary to what she would have expected, this room was cleaner, tidier and altogether more elegant in appearance than the area open to customers. It contained polished, expensive-looking furniture, and it was lined from floor to ceiling with books that appeared far more costly and better cared for than those in the front. A polished and carpeted wooden staircase was in one corner of the room and led to the first floor which was lost in darkness.

In the middle of the back wall there was a large, roaring open fire, which helped explain the warmth of the shop behind them. Mr Warwick pulled up a big chair next to the fire and invited Anna to sit and warm herself. He disappeared briefly, then re-entered with a towel and a robe for Anna to change into.

Mr. Warwick then left the room once more and knocked before reappearing again with a hot drink, some bread and cheese and a rack on which to dry her clothes, before leaving her to change. He would be in the shop, and Anna was to come and find him when she was ready. She wasted no time in getting out of her damp clothing and wrapping herself in the thick robe which, although far too big for her was beautifully warm, before hanging her clothes on the rack in front of the fire. The yellow flower that had been concealed in her cardigan was the one thing she held on to throughout, as though if she let it go it might somehow disappear, along with the wondrous events of the day.

Anna sat down, and gazed into the flames as they danced about the hearth. Munching slowly on her food, she began to reflect on what had happened. Her thoughts naturally turned first to Timmy. As she looked at the battered remains of the yellow flower in her hand, she had to pinch herself to believe that it had all really happened. Timmy had given her flowers, she had kissed him on the cheek and she had even used the word 'love'! Above all else, it appeared as though he might just have some of the same feelings for her that she had harboured for him for so long. How could that possibly be? What could he have seen in her to make that happen? She had no idea, but the thought made her stomach turn somersaults all over again. If it turned out really to be true, it would be everything she had dreamed of.

There were other things to think about and to try to understand too. Reluctantly she dragged her mind away from Timmy, to the encounter with Gillespie. Some very strange things had happened, and Anna had felt sensations that she had never experienced before. There was no doubt that, after the dung dumping, she had been as angry as she could remember. She couldn't recall the initial thoughts which had sent her off in pursuit of their attackers. At that moment she had been in a blind fury. By the time she had mounted the steps and reached the top of the bridge to face her enemies, her condition had already changed. Anna could remember all her thoughts and emotions from that point onwards in very clear detail. Although still angry, once she faced the gang she had been in control of her rage; she had been able to channel it. Her anger had taken a clear direction and purpose. As she had advanced towards Gillespie, it had almost ceased to be anger at all, but a feeling of purposeful power, a determination to right a wrong, but in a way that would prevent it from happening again. Her thoughts had become very quick and clear, and she had felt in complete control. That was it, *control* – a feeling that she had never really experienced before. It was as though something had clicked into place, and she had taken a first step towards being the person she was meant to be. She could not explain it any better than that, but it had been a very powerful, liberating feeling.

Then there were other points – the experience of touching, pushing and somehow reshaping Gillespie's aura, and briefly touching the auras of his fellow gang members as well. Before that day, she had no idea that it was possible to manoeuvre your own aura, and certainly not to touch the auras of other people. She couldn't see her own aura, but she was in no doubt that this was what she had done. And the effect that it had! She had overpowered Gillespie, a boy older, larger and far stronger than her; she had rendered him defenceless, completely at her mercy. Not only that – she had been able to face down the whole gang, by exerting only a fraction of the power that she had been feeling and merely by nudging their auras!

This revelation had at once both excited and frightened Anna. She was shocked by the power she had felt at that moment, power over the auras of others, and she began to worry again. She knew that the aura was a representation of the very being of a person. Having that much power over the aura of another – what could that mean? And most worryingly, what was the extent of the damage she could have done to her opponents if she had really let go with the full power she had been feeling at that moment? She was immensely grateful that at the same time she had experienced such complete self-control. But what if they had been in range at the moment of initial fury when the manure had first struck, before she gained control? What might she have done to them then? She swallowed hard. This thought disturbed her greatly.

She reflected further on how careful she had been not to cause harm to Gillespie when she had engaged with his aura. She had even had the presence of mind to ensure that there were no barges visible on the canal before pushing him over the edge, and she had been confident that he would come to no physical harm. She seemed to have understood the importance of not overreacting and doing anything to Gillespie merely by way of revenge, anything that would have hurt his pride more deeply, and hence inflicted more damage to his aura as a result. In her own contact with his aura, she had actually worked to smooth and reshape it as best she could, to soothe it, rather than to harm it. What had made her think to do that? She hoped she had done some good. The awareness she had possessed and the care she had taken at that moment helped ease her worries. She hoped beyond hope that it would be the same if such a situation were ever to arise again.

Suddenly Anna remembered the time and tore herself out of her reverie. As soon her clothes had dried well enough she changed as fast as she could, concealing the flower again carefully inside her cardigan. Then she went to find Mr Warwick in the shop.

She found him some way away, buried in a particularly

large, dusty old volume. She thanked him and let him know that she would be making her way home. Mr Warwick seemed deeply absorbed in what he was reading, but finally he looked up at Anna, smiled and told her that she was most welcome.

Just as Anna was about to turn and leave, the old man's kindly gaze moved from Anna's face to the front of the shop – and his jovial expression was transformed immediately into one of sudden alarm! Anna span around, and through the shop window she saw the tall figure of a man wearing a black top hat and a long black cloak and carrying a silver-tipped cane. He was alighting from a carriage which had come to a halt on the other side of the street.

The sight of the tall figure caused a dramatic change in the old man's demeanour. Moving far more quickly than Anna had thought him capable of, Mr Warwick swept her up in his arm and whispered urgently, "Quickly, you must hide, you can't let him see you. In here, and not a sound. Not a sound, promise me!"

Before Anna had time to promise anything at all, quick as a flash the old man opened a concealed door that had looked just like a part of the dusty old bookcase until that moment, and half encouraged, half gently shoved Anna through it into a small, hidden room on the other side.

"I'm so sorry about this Anna, but it is absolutely essential that this customer does not see you. I will explain all in due course, but for now you must trust me. There could be enormous danger. Whatever you do, make no sound. Not a sound!"

Anna had no opportunity to tell Mr Warwick that she

did surely trust him and that she would be silent, because Mr Warwick had already closed the secret door again with Anna on the other side.

'I really need to get back home soon,' thought Anna to herself, but the sudden change in Mr Warwick told her that this must be something serious, and that she clearly couldn't go anywhere for now. She wondered what the old man had meant by 'enormous danger'. It must be something to do with that man. Who could he be?

The room in which Anna found herself was not lit, but neither was it completely dark. Light was filtering through the narrow cracks around the edges of the door through which she had just come. Moving very quietly forward until her eye was up against the vertical one, Anna could see a portion of the shop beyond. Someone had entered, and Mr Warwick was now addressing him. Anna noticed that he seemed back to his affable old self again, moving slowly and deliberately. Anna thought she could sense just the slightest apprehension in his voice, but there were no other traces of the suddenly more dynamic and excitable Mr Warwick she had seen but seconds earlier.

"Ah, Mr Faulkner, how very good to see you again. Welcome, welcome!" he said.

"Enough of your pleasantries, old man. You know why I'm here so get to the point. Do you have it?"

The other man stepped into Anna's line of vision for the first time. As he turned slightly towards her, she saw more clearly the man who had been outside in the street. He was tall, probably in his late thirties although Anna always found these things hard to judge, and had dark, slicked-back hair, visible now that he had removed his hat. He had a thin, black moustache which curved down around either side of his mouth. Anna's view was restricted but she was still able to make out the man's dark, piercing eyes, almost black in colour, and a stare that seemed to penetrate its target, in this case Mr Warwick, as though nothing could be hidden under its gaze. Anna supposed he was what would probably be considered handsome by many, but there was a complete absence of any kind of warmth. In fact, there was nothing in his appearance or manner that Anna could find remotely appealing or attractive.

Mr Warwick hesitated. It was clear that he felt uncomfortable in Faulkner's presence and his voice became more tremulous.

"Well now Mr Faulkner, sir. Won't you sit down and have some tea with me before we get on to business?"

"I'm warning you," replied the younger man angrily, "you've exhausted my patience. Do you have the book or not? If you have it, give it to me and I will pay you the sum we agreed, plus a little extra for your trouble. If you do not have it, even after these weeks of promising me it would be here, then I am going to get very angry. And when I get angry, bad things tend to happen. *Dark* things. Am I making myself clear?"

As the younger man was speaking, something else came into focus in Anna's mind, unbidden. She was beginning to make out the stranger's aura, despite her severely restricted view. What she saw sent a chill right through her.

That this was not a good man was immediately obvious. Indeed, although she did not yet fully understand everything she could see in a person's aura, the overwhelming impression was of a man with a greater potential for evil than anyone she had ever met. But the aura was also radically different from anything in her experience.

Firstly it was enormous, significantly larger than any she had seen before. Most strikingly though, rather than having a relatively smooth spherical surface like most people's, this man's aura was a roughly spherical ball of long, sharp, conical shapes, all stemming from a small spherical core. The overall impression was a deadly one, like an enormous, spiked ball. Its colour was also unlike any she had seen before. In stark contrast to the pure sky blue colour of Mr Warwick's aura, Faulkner's was inky black at its core, merging into crimson at the tips of the spikes. In short, Anna could not have imagined an aura that appeared more menacing, more lethal and basically more *evil* than this one. She could not imagine what could have happened to this man, or what he himself must have done, to have developed such a monstrous aura, and she shuddered as she imagined what this might mean this person was capable of.

"I'm afraid I still don't have it, Mr Faulkner sir," answered Mr Warwick hesitantly. "I'm going to require a little more time. But my contacts assure me that we will have it very soon now, and needless to say -"

Mr Warwick was cut off in mid-sentence by a sudden blow to the side of his head from the silver-tipped walking cane wielded by Faulkner. He had moved so fast that neither Anna nor apparently the old man himself had seen it coming. Despite her instinctive fear of this tall, sinister stranger, Anna felt that same sense of outrage building up inside her that she had felt earlier that afternoon. Mr Warwick was one of the kindest people Anna had ever met, and whatever this book was that was the cause of their disagreement and whatever might have been promised previously, the young man could have absolutely no justification for this attack.

Mr Warwick stumbled to one side, recoiling from the blow, and just managed to catch hold of the table to his left in time to prevent himself from falling. Suddenly Faulkner was on him and he shoved Mr Warwick hard until his back was against the bookcase on the far side of the shop, sending the table that the old shopkeeper had used to catch his balance crashing over sideways to the floor. Faulkner now had his thick black cane pressed horizontally against Mr Warwick's throat, and he was pressing heavily against it, almost choking him.

Anna had to do something. She had an intense sense of the danger this would involve and that Faulkner would probably be able to swat her away and crush her like a fly, or possibly do far worse, but she couldn't just stand by and do nothing. She felt a surge of power and purpose inside her once more. She was just about to bolt from her hiding place when she noticed something that made her hesitate. It was very slight and subtle, but something had started to happen to Faulkner's aura.

When the violent man had begun his assault, the appearance of his aura had become even more menacing than before. The spikes had become more pronounced and sharper, and their tips had turned almost scarlet. He had started to press it against Mr Warwick's far smaller, bright blue aura, just as he was pressing his cane into Mr Warwick's throat. However, as Anna was about to make her move, the surface of Mr Warwick's aura had also started to move, almost imperceptibly, in what looked like a very subtle, calming and soothing motion. She wondered what could be causing this and whether Mr Warwick was aware of it. Could it be... she caught her breath at the idea... that he was intentionally manipulating his aura, in a way somehow similar to that which she had done on the bridge earlier? If so, this would mean that there was someone else who was aware of auras! And by the looks of it, someone who already knew things that she was only just beginning to learn. Whatever the truth, the effect that this extremely subtle movement was having was noticeable. Faulkner's aura had suddenly seemed to lose something of its hardness. It remained spiked, but the tips looked to have become somehow softer, and its colour too seemed to have dulled. It was as though Mr Warwick's aura was in fact soothing Faulkner, calming his rage and aggression.

Anna now held herself motionless, gripped by the unfolding scene, fascination trumping her anger. Although she had been able to see auras for as long as she could remember, she had never seen two coming into contact and interacting in this way before. She was sure that Mr Warwick was acting deliberately to bring about this change in Faulkner's aura, in a way somehow similar to her interaction with Gillespie earlier, but with a far greater level of skill and finesse, against an infinitely more dangerous adversary. Surely this must mean Mr Warwick had the same powers that she did, or possibly far greater?

The thought sent a sudden thrill through her. Maybe she was not alone after all! And maybe this meant that he would be able to handle this situation for himself.

Mr Warwick's subtle influence on Faulkner's aura seemed to have worked. Slowly, Faulkner lessened the pressure on the stick held against Mr Warwick's throat, then finally he allowed the old man to move. Mr Warwick immediately collapsed in a nearby chair, rubbing his sore neck and panting hard for breath. Faulkner loomed large over him, without any air of regret whatsoever, but with his rage now somewhat contained.

"Old man, understand that this is your last chance. Get that book for me as you promised, or things will go very badly for you. I will not countenance further protests or excuses. I shall return soon, and you had better have it!"

With that Faulkner snatched up his hat, and with a sweep of his cloak he left the shop as suddenly had entered it. Mr Warwick said nothing more, but watched Faulkner's every movement until the younger man's carriage was out of sight. When enough time had passed to be confident that Faulkner would not return, Mr Warwick rose slowly to his feet. Holding the side of his head where he had been so forcefully struck moments earlier, he moved towards the window to make sure his assailant was gone, then made his way to Anna's hiding place.

Opening the door and letting her out, he said, "I suppose you saw what happened Anna? Please don't worry, I would have expected you to be watchful of everything, though I thank you for remaining concealed."

"Yes, I saw it. Are you hurt Mr Warwick? Would you like me to fetch help?"

"No Anna, please don't do that, it will not be necessary. I am quite a bit tougher than I may appear, and aside from a headache which will soon pass, I am fine."

"Who was that Mr Warwick? And why was he so angry over a book?" Anna wanted to know, her sense of outrage returning at what had just happened.

"Actually it is not just any old book. Far from it in fact. The book he seeks was once considered to be of the greatest importance, and the time may be coming when it will be considered so again." Mr Warwick paused thoughtfully for a moment before continuing. "His name is Faulkner, and he is not a good man, though I am sure you are aware of that." Mr Warwick had turned to look Anna directly in the eye. "Did you see his essence?"

Anna hesitated for a moment, assessing if Mr Warwick was asking her what she thought he was. "Do... do you mean his aura, Mr Warwick?" she asked in a quiet, hesitant voice, guessing that this must be what he meant, although she had never heard it referred to as an 'essence' before. But yes, that was a perfect word for it. The aura represented everything a person was – their very essence.

"Aura?" replied Mr Warwick. "Ah yes, very interesting. I can quite see why you would call it that. And yes, that is what I mean. Did you see it?"

Anna paused again, her heart pounding hard. This was the subject which had caused her so much trouble in the past, and which she had vowed through bitter experience never to discuss with others again. But now, for the first time, she believed that the person she was talking to might not think she was naughty, mad or evil, and that he might actually understand what it was that she was able to see.

He might even be able to explain things to her.

The effort it took her to reply was considerable. "Yes, I saw it. And it looked... it looked like the most evil thing I have ever seen."

"That is because it was, Anna. It was almost certainly the most evil thing you have ever seen." Then it was Mr Warwick's turn to pause for a moment, which felt like an eternity. His kindly old face, lined by time and experience which lent him more gravitas than she had previously noticed, wore the expression of someone considering his options before embarking on a course of action from which, once started, there would be no turning back.

"Anna, the time has come to share things with you. You are not the only one who can see the things that you can see. There is much that you need to learn, things about the true nature of the world, things that none but a select few have known of throughout human history but which, I believe, it has always been your destiny to understand.

"Your mother, your uncle and I have tried to protect you and keep you safe for as long as we could, until this moment. However events are now coming to a head. Today was very close, much too close, and I sincerely hope that we have not waited too long to begin your instruction. Without question, the time is upon us. I will arrange for us to meet again in the coming days, and at that time your instruction will begin, provided you agree. It will be led by your Uncle James and me."

Then Mr Warwick looked her directly in the eyes again, this time with a look so vibrant and piercing that it seemed it should have belonged to a far younger man – a man of enormous power. "Anna, tell me. Is there anything, deep inside you, telling you that you are ready to start this journey?"

The startling turn that the conversation had taken left Anna silent for a moment. She had been taken completely by surprise by some of the things Mr Warwick had just said. Yet when he had been speaking, a feeling had started to grow inside her. With a confidence unknown to her before that day but akin to the feeling she had experienced on the canal bridge, she sensed that everything that had happened in her life – the bad things, the things that had marked her out as different from other people, the things that she had thought she alone understood and all the many things that she had not yet been able to explain – had all been leading towards this moment.

Looking Mr Warwick straight back in the eye with a more powerful and unwavering gaze than she would ever have been capable of before that day, she replied simply, "Yes, I am ready."

Pursuit

Anna had managed to slip back into her tall house unnoticed, and had spent the rest of that day in a of blissful daze, exhausted but ecstatic. She was barely capable of thinking rationally about what had happened beyond thoughts about Timmy. Eventually, overwhelmed by fatigue, she retired early and slept deeply.

She woke the next morning with a start, the lines between what had happened the day before and what had been a dream becoming blurred in her mind. Anna had lived her life to that point so deep in the certainty that no-one she cared about was ever likely to bring themselves to truly feel about her in the same way, that in the cold light of day her doubts began to re-emerge. Had that miracle really occurred in the way she thought it had? Despite all her shortcomings, had the person for whom she had such strong feelings really seen beyond all her flaws and felt the same way about her? He had given her flowers, and she had kissed him on the cheek, that was true – she had relived those moments a hundred times in her mind, but each time she reached this point on that well-trodden path, the familiar, instinctive self-doubts lay in ambush. Had she read too much into it? Had she somehow taken a well-meaning but innocent gesture on the part of a friend, and then revealed too much about her own feelings, and shown them to be completely disproportionate to his? She had even used the word 'love' albeit indirectly – would that fatal moment of boldness now turn him away, once he had time to think about it? How she longed to know what it was that he had been intending to say to her just before Gillespie struck, and what he was thinking now. At least she would not have long to wait to find out more. She was so thankful that they had arranged to meet up again today. That might just save her sanity.

Anna felt emotionally exhausted by the time afternoon came around. She had successfully distracted herself a couple of times by recalling the confrontation on the bridge, what she had been able to do to Gillespie, then her conversation with Mr Warwick and the amazing revelation that he too knew about auras. At any other time these things would have commanded her thoughts, hinting as they did at questions being answered, secrets revealed, the possibility of adventure... maybe a fundamental change to her mundane life. Most of all, the idea that there was someone else who could see the things that she could see, who knew more about them than she did and who might be able to explain things to her – it was this that really excited her. On any other day, these thoughts would have been enough to transform the most troubled of moods. But on this day, even these things could not hold her for long. Her mind wandered on to the subject of Kenny Gillespie and Archie Knowles, as well as the Marylebone Street gang. What were they up to, and why were they threatening her friends' families? She vowed to do whatever she could to stop them. Would they find out more when they followed the Marylebone Gang boys that afternoon? That train of thought soon brought her mind around to meeting Timmy again, and her yearning to see him deepened. Eventually she could wait no longer and she slipped out of the house well before the agreed time.

Having successfully retraced her surreptitious tracks of the previous day, she sat anxiously under the canal bridge in the usual place for what felt like the longest time. Her journey had thankfully been uneventful. Having successfully ridden her luck again in slipping out of the house unseen, there had only been one thing out of the ordinary which had caught her eye on her way to the canal. It was a hand-written poster outside the newspaper stand on the main road which had shouted, 'The Beast of Highgate Strikes Again!' The bold headline had jumped off the paper when she had read it. There it was, that story again. Though Anna had needed to remain unseen and could not linger to investigate further, the headline had stuck in her mind. What was this all about? With all the other news and goings on the previous day she had forgotten to ask her friends about this story. This time she resolved to do so.

Anna looked longingly down the towpath. For the first time in what felt like months London had shed its leaden-grey cloak for the day, and it was a beautifully warm sunlit afternoon, just in time for the end of summer. Better late than never! She waited for an eternity for any signs her friends might be coming. There were none. The usual worries and self-doubts started to get the better of her. What if the Marylebone Street Gang were to see her before her friends arrived? They would surely be out for revenge after what had happened yesterday. Or worse, what if they had waylaid her friends, done something terrible, and were now hunting her down? She could easily be trapped and surrounded if they found her here! Sweat broke out on her brow. 'Just the heat', she told herself unconvincingly. Where had all the new-found confidence from yesterday gone? It was nowhere to be found. She glanced with increasing anxiety up and down the canal.

The minutes passed like years. Then, just as she convinced herself that she should make a run for it, she froze at the sight of some slightly scruffy forms approaching in the distance. But the fear turned to joy when she recognised the excited voices of her friends. Resisting the urge to run down the path and hug them, one of them in particular, she remained where she was and did her best to remain calm. The anticipation of seeing Timmy again forced the blood into her head with a pounding so fierce that she could feel it in her ears. She had said too much yesterday, and today she needed to remain calm. Working hard to control her voice, she called out in what she hoped sounded like a sarcastic tone, "So you've finally decided to come, have you?"

Peering into the gloom the approaching group evidently could not see her at first, but then Rebecca spotted her (it was always Rebecca), called out and ran forward to join her on the ledge. They gave each other a quick hug before being joined by the others – Johnny, Edward, Tessa, Tilly, Alice, Robert, Charlie... and there was Timmy. They were all there!

Usually Anna's instincts told her to be subtle when glancing at Timmy, but this time there was so much she needed to know, so many questions that needed to be answered. She could not stop herself from looking at him fully in the eyes for a few brief seconds when he greeted her... and the look was returned! It was still only momentary, but had been enough to suggest that he might just possibly have been feeling similar emotions himself since they last met. It was all she had dared hope for.

For the next few moments Anna nodded without hearing, and made out nothing of the gabbled conversations that were taking place all around her. Then three words uttered amongst all the others drew her back to the here and now with a snap. Turning to Johnny, she asked "Did you say 'Beast of Highgate'?"

"Anna, haven't you been listening? I was just talking about it. Haven't you heard the news?"

"Um, well, no actually. You know what it's like in my house – nothing gets in or out without permission, not even the news! All I've seen are some newspaper headlines. What's it all about?"

"I don't believe it!" replied Johnny. "You must be the only person in London who hasn't heard about the Beast. It's all anyone's talking about. There have been some terrible murders in the Highgate area in the last few days. But not only that. There's been talk of the supernatural, of some kind of unearthly beast. Witnesses have spoken of awful, inhuman cries, like the screaming of some terrible monster, right in the same areas where the victims' bodies have later been found. Two weeks ago, one man reckoned he saw this huge, black, winged creature in the distance in Waterlow Park in Highgate around twilight, attacking one of the victims who was found there later, body all savaged. Reckoned it looked like a demon from hell he did. Then last night another old woman reckoned she saw that same creature attacking another poor fella down the end of one of the big old roads which leads in the direction of Hampstead Heath, near one of them huge mansions, after it had gone dark. Never seen anything like it in all her years, she said. And sure enough, a body was found down there later last night, and a terrible state it was in too. There's lots of other accounts. It's in all the papers. The stories are enough to make your blood curdle, Anna, I tell you."

Anna did indeed feel a sudden chill in her blood as she listened to what Johnny had to say. The others in the group had also fallen silent to let Johnny update Anna, but now they all started talking at once again, giving her variations on the same theme that they had heard. Anna learned there were a variety of theories, from a crazed murderer dressed up in a disguise to hide his real identity and to terrify his victims, to Satan himself stalking the streets of London. What was clear was that no-one, including the newspapers and the police, was sure of the real explanation.

"Anyhow," Rebecca intervened in the conversation, "it's time we got on with today's mission. Those Maryleboners will be setting off on their errand before long, and we need to be there to follow them. It's a bit of a walk from here. Let's go!"

They set off in a northerly direction. For the first twenty minutes or so their conversations continued amongst the whole group, split between the themes of the Beast and what it could be, and the mission ahead of them to find out what the Marylebone Gang was up to and to get enough information to tell the police. After a while, amidst the conversations, something else was mentioned that caught Anna's attention. Once again it was Johnny who was talking when she heard the name 'Faulkner' mentioned.

"Who's Faulkner?" she asked, memories from Mr

Warwick's shop of that tall, violent, dark-haired man with *that* aura flooding back into her mind.

"Faulkner's a right nasty piece of work – the most dangerous man in London, if you believe the stories." Which naturally Johnny would, thought Anna. He had always been one for picking up stories and general gossip. "No-one knows where he came from – just appeared on the scene one day, and bought himself a big old mansion near Highgate. Dresses in fine clothes like a real gent and has the money to match, but by all accounts a man less like a gentleman you're never likely to meet.

"According to some, women find him irresistible, as though he puts a spell on them or something, and several have disappeared after having been in his company... and there's those who reckon that's because Faulkner's true identity is a vampire, and that he has killed them to drink their blood!"

Anna didn't believe in vampires, but a shiver went through her all the same, and to her left she heard Tilly gasp. Then she recalled his aura, and she wondered.

Clearly enjoying being the centre of attention, Johnny continued, "And then there's those that reckon he's into that, what do they call it? Devil worshipping and the like... the occult, that's it. Reckon he performs evil ceremonies and that kind of thing. And now this Beast has started to appear, right up there in Highgate, right near where he lives! Well, it wasn't long before people were putting two and two together and reckoning that it's actually Faulkner who's somehow been performing ceremonies to summon that Beast, straight from the pits of hell!"

This brought several more gasps from the group, as

they continued to make their way northwards. For her part, Anna was naturally sceptical about any stories of this kind, especially when the storyteller was Johnny, but she couldn't get the downright evil appearance of that man's aura out of her mind. 'Almost certainly the most evil thing you have ever seen,' Mr Warwick's words came back to her. It had to mean something. She vowed to ask Mr Warwick more about Faulkner.

"Where's Faulkner's mansion? Is it actually in Highgate?" Alice asked.

"No, I don't think so. Well I'm not actually sure to be honest," Johnny admitted, "but what they said was that it was on the edge of Highgate, between Highgate and Hampstead Heath I think. Right in the area where the Beast murdered that man last night in fact!" Johnny was able to hold his audience for a while longer with his stories, but following some further speculation about Faulkner's identity, what his role might be in summoning the Beast of Highgate (which to their credit, thought Anna, more than half the group still did not believe really existed), and whether or not they might meet him when they finally reached their destination, the discussion died down. Anna obviously couldn't tell them anything about Faulkner's aura, and she quickly decided it better not to mention that she had seen him at all. Unlike Johnny, she was very happy not to be centre of attention.

Conversations began to break out among smaller groups again. Anna noticed that Timmy had dropped towards the back of the crowd. Trying to look as nonchalant as possible, Anna slowed her own pace, and before long she was walking alongside Timmy at the back.

"So," she started, feeling her mouth going dry, "um, how have you been?" She fought to prevent her heart from leaping out of her chest.

"I've been great, thanks," replied Timmy, flashing her a quick, beaming grin. Anna felt her cheeks redden as her heart raced. Then her mind fogged over, suddenly she couldn't think of anything to say. She searched for words, but the more she thought, the drier her mouth became and the more her mind went blank! Why did this always happen, always when she most wanted to make a good impression? The more powerful her feelings, the less able she became to string a sentence together. The silence began to deepen, and with it so did Anna's sense of panic that she would no longer be able to think of anything coherent to say. She was about to ruin everything! What seemed like an endless time passed and she began to despair. But then, to her indescribable relief, Timmy managed to come up with something, and he asked her, "Did you get into any trouble yesterday? I mean after we jumped in the canal?"

Relieved to have a subject other than her emotions to focus on, Anna found some words at last. "No, thank you for asking. I didn't. Luckily Mr Warwick let me dry myself and my clothes in his shop. I made it home before it got too late, without being seen. So it was all fine."

"Good, I'm glad to hear that," replied Timmy. Trying to keep the conversational momentum going for fear that her brain might freeze over again, Anna asked, "Any more run-ins with the Marylebone Street Gang since Gillespie went for his swim?"

Timmy smiled. "Actually yes, although no more fights. Yesterday evening after the fête, Becca and I saw the

Fletcher brothers acting very suspicious, carrying some more of them packages and looking around them like they were trying not to get spotted. We followed them, and they met up with that thug Archie Knowles, who took the packages off them. But then we thought they'd seen us, and with Knowles with them we could have been in trouble, so we decided to run for it. Then this morning, Edward and Charlie saw Bobby Watson carrying another package. They reckon he saw them and then he darted down an alleyway, like he was trying to avoid being followed. So we still don't know what they're up to, but there's no doubt it's something shady. That's what we're out to find out today, now we're all here." Then, as if anticipating Anna's next question, he added "No more sightings of Gillespie though," and then he shared another smile.

The weather that day was a spectacular contrast to the weeks and months that had preceded it. Anna breathed in the air which tasted unusually fresh and clean, borne as it was by a pleasant breeze from the lands to the west of the city. The sun reflected off the leaves of the trees that lined the avenue in a way that made them shine in a dazzling collage of shades of light and dark green. The leaves rippling in the breeze appeared like a gently lapping sea of green in the air above them, with a cloudless blue sky just visible beyond through the gaps. Even the birdsong seemed louder than usual. On reaching a crossroads, the sky came more clearly into view between the tree branches, and it was indeed a beautiful, deep blue with only a few faint wisps of cloud. How long it felt since she had seen it! Anna looked behind her at the road along which they had travelled, at the trees now in their full summer finery almost touching one another above the middle of the road. At that moment London seemed a truly enchanted place. Anna felt as though she was walking on air. With Timmy's help she had successfully negotiated the treacherous terrain of early conversation, scaled the mountains of shyness and emerged into normal chatter with the boy who had filled her thoughts. She continued the conversation, enjoying it for what it was and focused for the moment on everything but the answer. "I wonder what was in those packages then?" she asked him.

"Yeah, that's a mystery for sure. Couldn't really tell, but the ones we saw were about this big," Timmy gestured to suggest a box over a foot long and a foot high. "Whatever was in them though, they looked heavy and we think they'd been stolen."

"You're probably right. That would explain why they were looking so suspicious. That wouldn't surprise me at all, if that Knowles had any part to play in it."

"Mind you," continued Timmy, lowering his voice, "a couple of people have said that the person they're running those errands for is actually the same person Johnny was talking about earlier – that man Faulkner." Anna immediately sharpened her focus. "And what Johnny said was true. I've heard some nasty theories about what might be in those boxes they're carrying. Things for his evil ceremonies, and so on. You know me though, I'm not like Johnny, I don't really believe any of that kind of thing."

"No, me neither," said Anna truthfully, but still wishing she could get the image of that huge, spiked, black and red aura out of her head.

"But whatever is in those boxes, they reckon it's actually Faulkner whose behind all these activities with Kenny and Archie, and it's him who's driving them to drag more people into their dodgy business, like Benny and George. Like we said yesterday, Becca, the others and me, we all want to find out what those Maryleboners are up to so that we can find out more about Gillespie and Knowles's business, to turn them in to the police and get them off Benny and George's backs. But then Faulkner might just send others after them. From talking more with Becca, to really end this trouble once and for all it might be Faulkner we need to get to, and to get him locked up. Trouble is, the man's a mystery. We wouldn't know where to start with him. So we're starting with the Marylebone Gang, and we'll see where it leads us."

Anna fell silent for a moment. She remembered the vicious man who had attacked Mr Warwick. He had been talking about a book too. Timmy and Rebecca could be right about him being behind the gang's underhand activities. However, unlike Timmy and Rebecca, Anna did have a means to find out more about him, through Mr Warwick. To help her friends and their brothers, Anna resolved to find out as much as possible about who Faulkner was and what he was up to. But she also feared deeply what might happen if any of her friends tried to tackle Faulkner. Who knew what a man with an aura like that was capable of?

"You will be careful though, won't you?" Anna said, before checking herself in case anyone else was listening.

"Don't worry Anna," Timmy replied, "I'll be fine – with you girls around to protect me!" They both laughed.

Their conversation came to an end as Alice and Tilly dropped back to talk to them. The group remained in good spirits, joking and playing pranks on each other as they continued their journey.

When they reached the foot of a long hill which led towards Highgate, Rebecca at the head of the group beckoned them all to follow her into a narrow side street and take cover.

"That's the house, over there," she whispered, and gestured towards a tall house on the opposite side of the street, quite some distance further up the hill. "I think we've got here in good time, so now we just need to wait and see if they show up."

The group waited in the side street out of sight of the house, carrying on their conversations in hushed tones, whilst Rebecca kept watch over the house. Anna was just wondering if their information had been right after all when Rebecca suddenly hissed, "There they are!"

Peering around the corner and taking great care not to be seen, Anna saw two figures emerge from the house Rebecca had pointed out, before starting to make their way up the long hill. Sure enough, it was Davy Green and Bobby Watson, two of their Marylebone Street enemies, and each was carrying a package! Then Rebecca said in a low voice, "Right, this time we follow them all the way and find out what they're up to, once and for all."

"Yes!" cried out Johnny, before immediately being scolded by Rebecca for making too much noise.

"But we've got to be careful, and we'd better not stay in one big group or we're sure to be seen," Rebecca added. Taking control as always, she divided them up into pairs and continued, "Johnny and Edward, you go down this street," pointing further down the road they had been waiting in, which ran at right angles to the one along which the two Maryleboners were now walking, "then turn right at the next junction and from there head up the hill towards Highgate. Go as fast as you can, try to get to the top before Green and Watson, then wait for us there and let us know where they go next. The rest of us will continue following them up this avenue in separate pairs.

"Now listen everyone," Rebecca's voice was deadly serious, "we've got to avoid been recognised. First of all, stick close to the side of the road, in the shadows of the buildings where it will be more difficult for them to see us. Secondly, each pair must keep separate, since we're less likely to catch the eye that way. Also whatever you do, don't make it obvious you're looking at them. Try to look down as much as possible. Only look up to check they're still ahead and to pick up any signals from me. That way, if they do look around they're less likely to see your faces and think you're following them. I'm determined to find out what they're doing, so no-one must give us away. Understand?"

So final were Rebecca's words that no-one would have dared to disagree. Johnny and Edward sprinted off down the side street as Rebecca had directed. Rebecca and Charlie led the way back onto the main avenue. They kept on the left hand side of the street among the shadows which were lengthening in the late afternoon sun, and headed in the direction of Highgate and their prey. Walking casually and looking at the ground and the building that they were now passing with only the very occasional glance ahead of them, Anna was impressed. No-one would have guessed they were following anyone.

Anna was grateful to Rebecca for pairing her with Timmy (she doubted that it had been chance) and they were the next to set off. Keeping a safe distance behind the first pair, they followed their tracks. After some time had passed, Anna allowed herself to steal her first secret glance up the hill in the direction of the Marylebone duo, and sure enough there they were, barely in sight now as they approached the brow of the hill. Neither was looking behind, and they appeared to be unaware that they were being trailed. 'So far so good,' Anna thought.

As soon as the Maryleboners had disappeared over the brow of the hill and out of sight, Anna heard a shouted whisper from Rebecca ahead of them. She saw Rebecca gesture to them to quicken their pace towards the top of the hill to avoid their targets escaping. Looking quickly over her shoulder, Anna could see Alice and Tessa a safe distance behind them following in their footsteps, and some way behind them, Robert had appeared and was just starting his journey together with Tilly, exactly as per Rebecca's instructions. Anna conveyed Rebecca's latest message to Alice and Tessa, who signalled back that they had received the message and would pass it on.

"I hope they don't get away," whispered Timmy as they broke into a run.

"Yes, me too," whispered Anna in reply, thoroughly enjoying herself and filled with eager anticipation at where this pursuit might lead. Finally reaching the brow of the hill, Anna saw the outskirts of Highgate before them, with Rebecca and Charlie about twenty yards ahead, and in the distance were Green and Watson, apparently still none the wiser. Casting quick glances behind her as she carried on, it wasn't long before she saw the rest of the group also appearing over the brow of the hill.

The secret pursuit continued. Just as the Maryleboners approached the end of the avenue, Timmy tugged gently at Anna's sleeve and then subtly gestured towards a large tree in the distance on the corner of the avenue and a large road that traversed its end. At first she couldn't make anything out. Then she grinned as she recognised Edward, partially concealed in its upper branches!

"I'd never have seen him if I hadn't been looking for him and Johnny," whispered Timmy, and Anna agreed, wondering where Johnny might be hiding.

At the end of the avenue, the package-carrying duo waited for a horse and cart to pass, then crossed the road before turning left and disappearing from view in front of a large old church. Rebecca and Charlie ahead of them quickened their pace again, as did Timmy and Anna so as not to lose the trail. Glancing again behind, Anna saw Robert and Tilly at the back, darting down a backstreet that Anna and Timmy had passed earlier. They had obviously decided to take a different route to intercept their prey further down the street. 'Bound to be Robert's idea,' thought Anna, hoping they would not give themselves away when they emerged.

As Timmy and Anna drew near the corner in the direction in which the Maryleboners had gone and then peered around it, they immediately saw Rebecca and Charlie scurrying down the road looking left and right, but there was no sign of their quarry. Just then, Edward approached them from behind having descended from his perch and he whispered, "They went down there!" He was pointing to the next side street on the right hand side, leading down the left side of the large church.

Returning towards them, Rebecca hissed in reply, "But we looked in that direction and they weren't there."

Then a shrill whistle filled the air. Looking all around them and then upwards, Rebecca was the first to spot Johnny, perched up behind a mini spire at the left hand corner of the church. 'How on earth did he get up there?' wondered Anna to herself, grinning broadly. Johnny was pointing again in the direction of the street beside the church, and he risked a shouted whisper of his own, "They went down here, and then left again down the next side street."

"Good work, Johnny!" whispered Rebecca. They all hastened in that direction, now forgetting all about being in pairs. Reaching the corner, Anna came up behind Rebecca, who was already leaning forward and peering around it. On tiptoes, Anna peered in turn over her shoulder. Timmy, Edward and Charlie were crowded behind them, Charlie panting somewhat, and all did their best to remain concealed as they looked on. Sure enough, there were the targets of their pursuit, walking slowly now, mounting the steps of a large, dilapidated-looking house on the opposite side of the road.

Anna took in the street they were now looking at. It was not as wide as the avenue along which they had been walking, but the houses were large nonetheless. As she gazed down from one building to the next, she noticed how much duller, darker and decrepit-looking the house that their foes stood outside appeared. It was as though it alone in the street had borne the weight of time and had reached a point of terminal decay. Anna looked around for a street name, and she saw a sign on the corner of the road opposite. 'Eagle Street' it read. She assigned the distinctive name to memory, just in case.

She watched as Watson rapped on the dull brass door knocker that looked as though it had not had the feel of polish upon it for many a year, possibly many a decade, and then waited in silence for what must have been a minute before the door slowly opened. Anna held her breath, straining to catch a glimpse of whoever was on the other side. And then she saw him. It was a tall, thin man in a long black cloak, with long, bony fingers that clutched at the edge of the black door. His face was that of an aging man, wrinkled and deathly pale, with large black bags under his black eyes and deeply gaunt cheeks, all framed by thin streaks of long, greasy, grey hair. His appearance gave Anna the overall impression of some kind of living skeleton, albeit one with its sagging, pale, leathery white skin still attached.

Anna could not make out his aura clearly, but the deadly expression on his face and the snarling downward curl of the pale sagging skin at either side of his mouth as it uttered something to the waiting boys left Anna in no doubt that this was a man of no good intent. What she could make out of his aura seemed to confirm this – she was only able to get an overall impression at this distance, but it was an impression of brown, black and red.

The Marylebone pair, usually so full of swagger and self-confidence, now had an altogether different demeanour, cowering in the presence of this cloaked man. Looking down at his shoes, Watson appeared to mutter something to the man, which the latter met with another snarling utterance before slowly opening the door wider and allowing the duo to enter the murky darkness within. The aging man pushed the second boy forward forcefully as he followed them inside. Anna's eye was drawn to the bony fingers of the man's other hand which was still clutching the door as they passed through it. It looked like some kind of hideous, bony spider. On its second finger was a ring of gold set with what looked to be a very large, black jewel of some kind, visible even at this distance. Just then, the man jutted his head outside the door again, looking first to his right, then slowly to his left, directly towards them!

The Mansion

As one, the group ducked behind the wall, each holding their breath, hoping against hope that those malicious black eyes hadn't spied them. Seconds later, they heard the distant noise of a door being closed. Holding the others back, Rebecca was the first to dare peer slowly and carefully back around the corner. Anna saw her form relax slightly, and then joined her to see that the door with its faded, flaking black paint had indeed been closed, its deathly-looking occupant nowhere in sight.

"He nearly saw us!" said Rebecca, leaning back against the wall and letting out a long breath as though she had been holding it for quite some time. Looking further down the street, they then saw Robert, Tilly, Alice and Tessa peering around the corresponding corner at the far end. They started to make as if to come down the street to meet them, but Rebecca gestured urgently for them to stop and instead return the way they had come. "Can't see nobody in the upper windows of that old house and the lower ones are shuttered, but I ain't taking no chances all the same," she whispered.

In silence, Rebecca, Timmy, Charlie, Edward and Anna retraced their steps back along the road by the church, where they were met by Johnny who had completed his descent from his observation point. They waited for their companions, who soon rounded the corner from the backstreet to join them. Then the communal silence gave out and everyone started talking excitedly.

"Did you see that scary old man?" asked Robert of

Rebecca and the others. "We'd just got there as those Maryleboners were going into the house, and then I thought he might've seen us when he looked back out again, but I think we got away with it."

"I hope for all our sakes that he didn't see you. That was one person I would not want coming after me!" replied Charlie.

Prompted by those words, Rebecca quickly went back to the corner of the road just to reconfirm that no-one was coming after them. She returned shortly to reassure them that the street was still deserted.

"You're right though," she continued, "he was an evil-looking one. I wonder what on earth Watson and Green are doing running errands for someone like that."

"Yeah," chimed in Edward, "I mean, did you see them?" They looked terrified. Not that I blame them. Didn't look like they were there for the fun of it, that's for sure. I wonder what kind of trouble they've got themselves into."

"Well whatever it is, it's their own fault," responded Johnny.

"That's as may be," said Rebecca, "but we haven't completed our mission yet. We still don't know what they're up to, or what was in those packages, and we still have nothing we could take to the police to stop Gillespie and Knowles. In fact the mystery's only got deeper."

"Let's wait here until they come out again, and then corner 'em and demand they tell us what they're up to!" cried Edward.

"Knowing them lot, they probably won't tell us though," countered Johnny. "I reckon we have to actually see what they're doing. I'm going to try to see inside the house!" he declared.

"I don't see how you can," said Charlie. "All the ground floor windows at the front are shuttered from the inside, even though it's still light."

"I know that," replied Johnny, "but I ain't talking about the front, am I? I'm going round the back!" It wasn't clear from just looking, but it seemed possible that they might be able to gain access to the back down the side of the building.

This idea created an immediate divide in the group. On one side, Robert and Edward piped up, "Yeah, we'll come with you!" whilst on the other Tilly said, "Oh no, Johnny, please don't do that," Alice began to warn her younger brother Robert that he'd better be careful and Tessa added, "Didn't you see that man? I'm scared of him."

"He'll have to catch me first though, won't he?" was Johnny's defiant reply.

Anna also had major reservations about this plan. Ordinarily, on principle, she would have opposed any idea of entering someone else's property, but she knew that Johnny wouldn't be suggesting it either if this was any ordinary house. It was clear to all of them that this place was probably either occupied by criminals, which would be one explanation as to why the Maryleboners had gone there with their suspicious parcels, or something more sinister was going on. However, Anna felt a different fear about the place. Apart from Tilly and Tessa, the others all seemed to have gotten over the appearance of the old man, but for some reason Anna could not shake a deep-seated apprehension in the pit of her stomach. Try as she might, she could not rid from her mind the image of that gaunt old man, his skeletal hands with that evil-looking ring on his finger, and the distant but malevolent appearance of his aura. Unbidden, the words 'Beast of Highgate' re-entered her mind.

Although Johnny had spoken boldly, he still lingered, waiting for Rebecca's opinion before setting out. She had not committed so far, but after a pause, she spoke.

"Well, usually I'd say we had no business poking around other people's houses. After all, that's the sort of thing the Marylebone Street Gang might do, or robbers and other criminals. But in this case it definitely ain't no normal house, and they're up to no good in there if I'm any judge. And you know what? Much as I don't like those Maryleboners, I think they could actually be in trouble. I think they may have got themselves right out of their depth this time. So now that we've come this far, I think we should find out what's been going on.

"Johnny, Edward and I will see if we can find a way around the back, and Anna, why don't you come too? After seeing how you dealt with the whole Marylebone Gang last time, you might be useful in a tight spot!"

Anna smiled sombrely. She was pleased to have Rebecca say that, but the larger part of her was still filled with foreboding that this might bring her face-to-face with that man. She was no coward though, and her determination not to let her fiends down conquered all else. Taking a deep breath she said, "All right, let's go then".

"The rest of you remain here and keep a look out at the front of the building, in case anyone leaves – or arrives for that matter," continued Rebecca. Robert, Charlie and most of all Timmy began to protest loudly, but as Alice reproached her brother, Rebecca explained, "If more than four go, we're more likely to get found out, and this way you can let us know if they leave the house, so that we can come back to follow them with you. Robert, if anyone leaves, you give one of them whistles like Johnny did before so we can come back round. If we need help, Johnny will give his whistle again. All right?"

Rebecca allowed no more protests, and Anna set off with her three companions down the road that led back towards Eagle Street. They had gone no more than a few paces however when in the distance behind them there came the sudden sound of clattering hooves. Hastily the group began walking in the opposite direction, dispersing and trying to look as casual as possible, as a carriage came careering around the corner and almost hit them! Narrowly missing Charlie as he dived to the cobble-stoned street, it continued on, then swerved left into the street where the Marylebone Gang boys had entered the house.

"Hey! What do you think you're doing?" shouted Rebecca and Johnny at the same time as the carriage disappeared around the corner, but the driver, hat pulled down low over his eyes, didn't look around or say a word.

"He was certainly in a hurry, wasn't he?" said Charlie gingerly, dusting dirt from the road off himself after Johnny had helped him to his feet.

"Yeah, and I bet I know where he was going!" replied Rebecca, rushing back to the corner of the street again. The rest joined her to see what was going to happen next, remaining concealed as best they could. Sure enough, the carriage had come to a halt outside the house into which the Marylebone Street boys had entered.

The driver jumped down from the carriage, bounded up the steps and rapped loudly on the door. "He really is in a hurry, isn't he?" whispered Timmy to Anna, who nodded silently. She was certain she was about to see that old man again and she shrank back slightly, watching on in grim anticipation.

Moments later the door opened, but this time it was not the old man. It was a younger-looking man carrying two boxes which looked the same size and shape as the packages the two boys had taken to the house. He was a rough-looking type, but not as downright evil as the other man. Glancing left and right, he moved forward out of the doorway. He was followed by first one, then the second Marylebone Street boy. Both looked even more downcast than they had when they arrived, and Anna thought Green even looked as though he might have been crying. And then, *he* appeared in the doorway behind them. The old man, looking just as pale and deathlike as the image that was already etched in Anna's memory. He was holding a silver-tipped black walking cane with what looked like a silver skull at the top, around which his skeletal fingers were wrapped like knobbly white vines. And there again was that hideous, black-jewelled ring.

At that moment, Green tried to make a run for it, darting past the younger man, around the other side of the driver and down the rest of the steps towards the street. No sooner had his feet touched the pavement than the black-caped figure of the old man was upon him, having sprung from the stairs above. Landing on the boy's back like a giant black spider, he knocked him clean to the ground, then raised his cane before bringing it crashing down on the poor boy's back. Green howled with pain as the hideous old man raised his withered hand and then struck his victim again, then a third time, his lank, greasy hair slapping against the side of his face as he did so. Anna and the others stayed frozen to the spot, shocked by the speed and ferocity of the old man's attack. Anna saw Watson struggling forward to try to help his friend, but he was held back by the powerful younger man who had momentarily cast the boxes he was carrying to one side.

Then the old man spoke in a hissing voice which contained sufficient anger and venom to carry clearly to where Anna and her friends were hiding. "You would try to escape, would you boy? You think you can get away? Well let me tell you, there is no escape from us! No escape! You hear me?" Crouching over him, he reached down with his horrible bony hands and lifted his victim a foot from the ground by the lapels of his battered jacket. He brought the boy's face to within an inch of his own. With his deathly black eyes piercing those of the now limp youth, his curled, snarling mouth continued, "You belong to us now, do you understand?" Green hung lifeless and completely defenceless as the old man's voice rose, "Do you understand? You come and you go when we tell you that you can, but even when you are away, you will never again be free from our will. Now that you belong to us, we will always be able to find you wherever you go – there is nowhere you can hide. Nowhere! The only choice remaining to you now is to do exactly as we tell you. And in our service you may indeed flourish and have all your desires fulfilled..." The old man paused, smiled thinly, then continued, starting in a slightly quieter but even more deadly tone, before it rose to a terrible, shrieking crescendo as he completed the sentence, "But I warn you boy, you dare to cross me one more time, just once more, and I will kill you with my bare hands!"

With that he thrust him roughly back onto the pavement and stepped away, gesturing to the driver who hoisted up his limp form and dragged him into the carriage. Green offered no more resistance. Watson was already inside the carriage; any thoughts he might have harboured for his own escape had clearly been extinguished. The younger man retrieved the boxes and their contents, a number of old-looking books which had spilled out, and he entered the carriage. With one final glance around at the deserted street, the odious old man then climbed in himself, slammed the door shut and rapped audibly on the carriage ceiling as a signal to the driver to depart. The latter instantly did as instructed, quite possibly for fear of a fate similar to that of his young passenger, and geed up the horses to leave at a pace equal to that at which they had arrived. The carriage swerved around the far corner of the street, and they were gone.

Anna and her companions looked on for a moment in silence, none of them able to speak. It was not just that Green had been subjected to such a brutal, albeit thankfully brief, attack – it was the nightmarish image of that old man which had left them all temporarily rooted to the spot. This time it was Anna who was the first to react, sensing even more keenly than the others the severe danger their former foes were now in. There had been something in Green's response to the attack, or his lack of response, that was disturbing her deeply.

"Come on," she shouted to the others, "we have to help them. I think they're in terrible danger."

"But I want to look inside the house and see what those good for nothings were up to," Johnny was the next to speak.

"No, Anna's right," responded Rebecca sternly. "They may be our sworn enemies, but right now those two are in way over their heads, and their own friends ain't around to help them. You saw what just happened. This could be really serious and we're the only ones who can help them, we've got to try."

There was no more dispute and the group took off as one down the street in which they had just witnessed the frightening scene. Rounding the corner, Anna was fearful that travelling at such a speed, the carriage would soon be out of sight and they would then never be able to trace it. Running up the road though they were, it was still some time before they reached another broad avenue with a view down the hill. The friends looked frantically left and right, but Anna could see nothing.

"Look, down there!" cried Timmy, pointing into the distance beyond the far end of the avenue, to a wide gap between two large-looking houses on the road that crossed the end of the one they were on. Sure enough, there was the black carriage being driven at great speed, only briefly visible before it disappeared behind the next house.

"It's heading in the direction of the Heath," shouted Johnny, running forwards to climb on a nearby wall for a better view. Joining him, they all watched as the carriage, which now looked quite minuscule, continued at breakneck pace towards its destination. From their vantage point, they had a good view down the hillside into an area of greenery interspersed with enormous houses which were connected by the road down which the carriage was travelling. Finally it slowed as it came to a large set of gates, swerved to the right and then passed through them. Accelerating once more along what looked like a curving driveway to the right, it disappeared from view behind the green foliage of the trees.

"I've got no idea what that place is, but it looks like the driveway to a house, so if we can find those gates then we may still be able to find them!" said Rebecca.

"That must be a good mile away, probably two, and it will be getting dark before long," responded Charlie, looking a little reluctant, not to mention hot and tired.

"Then we've got no time to waste, have we? Come on, let's go!" cried Rebecca. The friends hared off down the street. They sprinted at first, and then gradually slowed to a more sustainable run as they got further down the hill. On the way they passed two separate groups of policemen, presumably in the area on account of 'the Beast'. The policemen all looked on inquiringly as the gang sped past them, but they did not say anything. Their business was clearly too serious to concern themselves with the comings and goings of children. However Anna called out to the others to stop, and when they had all gathered she proposed that they tell the police what they had seen, and get their help in rescuing the two Maryleboners. "I think this is serious, not to mention probably dangerous, and I think we should try to get all the proper help we can."

"Yes Anna, good idea," Rebecca replied, "and then if we do uncover what the gang's up to, the police will already be on hand to capture any criminals. We could be halfway to achieving our mission to stop the gang for once and for all before the day's out!"

Following a quick discussion, it was agreed that Anna and Rebecca should go and do the talking, since between them they had the best chance of being believed.

"Excuse me constable," Rebecca called out on nearing the closest group of three policemen. "We have just seen two boys about our age being attacked and dragged into a carriage. We think they've been kidnapped and taken to a house down there." She gestured in the general direction of the gates they had seen in the distance.

The policemen looked at each other momentarily, then one of them asked, "All right, who kidnapped them? What did he look like?"

"It was a horrible old man, he looked more dead than alive, with long white fingers, like a skeleton," Anna chipped in trying to lend support, using the first words she could find to describe the image that still burned in her mind. It was only after she had spoken that she realised how they must have sounded.

But it was too late. "Dead-looking? Like a skeleton you say? Here in Highgate in broad daylight? From Highgate cemetery, was he? Suppose you've been hearing stories about the Beast, and thought you'd come up here and make mischief, did you? Did they put you up to it?" said the policeman, nodding his head in the direction of their companions who were looking on from some distance away.

"No sir. I'm sorry, I didn't mean..." Anna stammered.

"She didn't mean he was actually a skeleton," Rebecca intervened. "She just said that he looked a bit like one. Look, he had long grey hair, and he had a big black ring on his finger. He attacked the two boys and took them off in his carriage along with an accomplice. Now please, can you help them?"

"No, we're not going to help them, because I don't believe there are any boys. Now listen here you two, I'm sure you've been put up to this by your friends, but you ought to know better than to waste valuable police time. My colleagues and I are in the middle of a double shift, ain't been home for fourteen hours we ain't, and we don't take kindly to having our time wasted by young tearaways. Even properly spoken ones," he added, looking disapprovingly at Anna. "We've got important matters to deal with, what with the murders 'n all, and we don't need the likes of you coming up here making mischief about it. Now clear off before we take you home to your parents for a good hiding!" Anna and Rebecca needed no second telling. They apologised and left the irate constable as fast as they reasonably felt they could. As soon as they were out of earshot, Anna whispered under her breath to Rebecca, "I'm so sorry about that. That was the first time I have actually spoken to a policeman and I think I must have panicked. I hadn't meant to say-"

"I know, Anna, listen, don't worry about it," Rebecca reassured her. "It doesn't matter, and I don't think there was anything we could have said that would have made a difference. These policemen are too busy with their investigations of the Beast, and there was no chance that they were going to listen to a group of children like us. We were just wasting our time. When we do get proof of what the gang's doing, we'll need to go to the police with some grown-ups, probably some of our parents."

Reaching the group again, Rebecca updated them, "The police ain't interested, too busy they reckon. We're on our own, so I suggest we get on with it ourselves."

Deeply grateful to Rebecca for relaying the conversation, Anna joined her friends in running down the hill. They continued for another five minutes before Tessa, who was panting at the back of the group, was the first to shout to the others, "Stop, please, I can't keep up."

Johnny and Timmy, who were by now in the lead, slowed down until everyone had caught up. "All right," said Rebecca, breathing heavily herself, "let's get there as fast as we can, but whatever happens, we mustn't get separated. We must stay together."

All agreed. Everyone was hot and sweating as it was still a warm and humid day. When they set off again it was at more of a brisk walk. They reached the junction of the road along which Timmy had seen the carriage passing, and they proceeded straight down it without stopping. This was a narrower road with increasingly large houses spaced further and further apart on either side.

"Doesn't feel like we're in London any more, does it? Look at that place!" cried Johnny, looking up to his left at a huge white mansion, set back from the road with a curling drive leading up to its pillared porch.

"And what about that one?" Charlie joined in, looking down the hill to their right at another magnificent, even larger building, with even more pillars and a beautiful flower garden flowing down the slope towards it.

"I thought you lived in a palace, Anna, but it's quite pokey compared to these," Rebecca quipped. "Bet it makes you feel right poor, doesn't it?"

"Yes, I'm shocked!" responded Anna in mock horror, before continuing slightly more seriously, "although it doesn't necessarily mean they're happy, just because they live in big houses."

"Hmm," mused Rebecca, "well I'm sure you're right, Anna... But still, I do think it would help!"

They passed the last of the houses, then there were nothing but trees lining the road. Anna noticed the first signs of darkness, and the worry which had been lurking at the back of her mind for some time moved to the forefront. It was getting late and she was nowhere near home. There was no question her absence was going to be found out this time. However, there was no way she could consider abandoning her friends and leaving the mission now. She would just have to hurry home as soon as they were done, and accept the consequences.

"We're not too far from Hampstead Heath now, I think," said Alice, and then added after a short hesitation, "Wasn't it around here that the Beast of Highgate was supposed to have attacked that man last night?"

The group fell silent as that thought sank in. After a long pause, Johnny spoke in a quieter voice, "Yeah, actually you're right, it was. In fact I think it was exactly round here. Why aren't there any coppers about, instead of them all being back there on the high street?"

No-one had an answer. The silence resumed as they pushed on through the gathering gloom, each consumed with their own thoughts, all on the same fearful subject. Then, at last, they came upon the gates through which the carriage had passed.

Now that they were close to them, the gates were even larger and more imposing than they had looked from up the hill. Indeed they were intimidating, hinged as they were on huge stone pillars, with a large wall stretching into the distance behind the trees on either side. Atop each pillar, carved out of stone was a statue of a hideous-looking winged beast. They reminded Anna of those gargoyles she had seen in some of the older churches in London, but somehow they seemed more sinister and threatening in this setting. 'Very welcoming!' she thought to herself.

"I wonder what this place is?" she pondered aloud, her voice sounding somehow smaller and more timid than before.

There were trees directly ahead, but now they were nearby, in the failing light they could see through the gaps the shape of an enormous house in the middle distance, slightly below them down a slope, with a high roof topped by at least a dozen tall chimney stacks. At the left hand end of the building rose a short tower with what appeared to be battlements on the top of it.

"Looks more like a castle than a house," said Johnny. "Wait a minute. I wonder if this is where that man Faulkner lives. They said it was a big old place, and this must be right around the area where they said it was. Right near where..." Johnny's voice tailed off, then silence enveloped them once more.

Anna had started to feel that same sense of foreboding that she had felt outside the decrepit old house in Highgate earlier, but this time it was more intense. She glanced at her companions and could see how on edge they all looked. In fact in all the time she had known them, she couldn't remember seeing them look so apprehensive. Even the usually indomitable characters like Rebecca and Johnny seemed suddenly quiet and reserved. Everyone was hesitating as they looked through the growing darkness at the imposing gates, down the driveway which curved round to the right before disappearing behind the trees, and then back to the ominous-looking mansion that lay beyond, through the branches below.

"Has anyone noticed how there are no birds singing here?" asked Alice. "No natural sounds at all, come to that. I know night's coming, but there have been no sounds of any kind since we came near this place. Something doesn't feel right." Silence descended again, as if to emphasise the point.

Anna was lost deep in thoughts of her own. It was clear that everyone was thinking about the 'Beast' and what it might be. She sensed that in this eerie place they were all beginning to fear something beyond the world of their experience – even something 'supernatural'. Anna felt it too, but she simply refused to believe in supernatural monsters. People in the area had recently been killed, so whatever it was that people referred to as the 'Beast of Highgate' was clearly some kind of killer, but surely it must be a person, rather than some kind of beast or demon? Had they not heard a man threaten to kill Davy Green with their own ears that very afternoon? That evil old man in Highgate. From what she could make out of his aura, it certainly looked damaged and evil enough to belong to a murderer. And the last time the Beast had struck, last night, had been right around this place, where they had seen the vile old man enter but an hour ago. The very place they were in now. And there was something else about that man that had been disturbing Anna most of all, ever since she had witnessed the events outside the house in Highgate town – the effect he had seemed to have on Green...

As Anna slowly put the pieces together in her mind she shuddered, to the point that Timmy moved closer to her and put his arm around her shoulder. Without any thoughts of concealment from the others any more, Anna leaned her head against his. Whether it was brought on by fatigue from the long, hot journey they had been on or whether it was due to the tension that lay so thick on the humid air they could almost touch it, one by one the companions sank to the ground on the grassy bank outside the gates, paralysed in silence. Everyone was waiting for someone else to make a move, either forward or back. Gradually, all started to look towards Rebecca, as they always did when the time came for important decisions. However, so far she had not spoken.

Timmy whispered, "I wonder how Watson and Green are doing. They looked pretty terrified even before they went into that house earlier. Goodness only knows what they're going through down there, after Green tried to escape."

"Yes, and he got hit pretty hard by that horrible old man, didn't he?" responded Robert in a similarly hushed voice. "He didn't hold back at all in whipping him with that stick of his. But did you see how lifeless Green looked after that? He took a hiding all right, but not on his head or nothing, so I don't reckon he was unconscious. But he could barely pick himself up, like he had suddenly turned to rubber or something. It was almost like he was under a spell."

Anna said nothing, but it was the same thing that she had noticed. Unlike the others though, she did have an idea of what it might have been, and it was exactly this that had been troubling her most about the whole episode. To her it appeared to be the same as the effect on Gillespie on the canal bridge, when she had touched his aura and rendered him powerless. The more she thought about that evil-looking old man, the more convinced she was that he too must possess the same ability that she and Mr Warwick had. But the idea of someone like that, with so much evil red in their aura and such evidently evil intent, possessing the ability to see and to manipulate other people's auras... that was a truly horrific prospect. He might not be a supernatural beast, but he could very well be a human monster.

That alone had been cause enough to worry her deeply. But was there something else? Involuntarily she found her eyes drawn to the gargoyles atop the gate pillars. They were little more than large, hideous winged shadows now, in the half-light, but if anything they looked even more ominous. Almost as if they might be alive. Try as she might, she could not escape the feeling that there was something wrong here. Something that was beyond the actions of mere men...

The silence that surrounded the companions was once again absolute. It was as though nature's regular inhabitants did not want to come here – or had fled. She looked at each of her friends. They appeared unable to move. Someone needed to make the first move. In truth, Anna's forebodings about this place probably ran deeper than those of any of the others but, slowly, her spirit began to stir. No matter what Green might have done in the past, the attack by that terrifying old man in Highgate and the threats he had made were surely far more than even that wretched boy deserved. She imagined him and Watson now locked in that house below facing who knew what terrors. Her mind went back to her own terrifying incarceration in the asylum when she was younger. She remembered how frightened she had been and how desperately she had longed for someone to come and help her. However, what of the danger they themselves would face if they went down there? Her memory moved to the previous day, and the attack by Faulkner on poor old Mr Warwick. The image of the old man bravely facing the aggressive and far stronger Faulkner and somehow escaping more or less unscathed came to her mind. If he could overcome such dangers, so could she. She knew the time had come to act, and act bravely, for if they did not the consequences for Green and Watson could be fatal. She was, however, deeply concerned about the danger that her friends might be about to enter. So Anna chose her words carefully, when it was she who stood up and finally broke the silence.

"Everyone, I want you to know that I care about you all dearly, and it would break my heart into pieces if harm came to any of you. I have a strong feeling we are already in great danger, just by being here, and if we go ahead through these gates and try to save Green and Watson, that danger could become grave indeed. A large part of me would like to beg you all to leave and to return to the safety of your homes. However, that is a choice that each of us must make for ourselves. As for me, I will not leave those two boys alone to their fate. I came to this house to try to help them, and that is what I intend to do." This time her voice did not sound timid, and it did not waver.

Even in her heightened state of tension, Anna felt her heart skip a beat as Timmy slowly stood up by her side and said, "If Anna goes, then I go too." His voice too was strong and unwavering. Shifting her focus momentarily, Anna saw his aura shining strongly and brightly, and as pure blue in colour as she had ever known it. Anna felt a surge of pride for him, in spite of the situation.

Silence engulfed the group once more, as all eyes turned again towards Rebecca. And this time, at last, she spoke.

"Well, this is it then. I'm sorry to all of you that it's taken me so long to make my mind up about this. I have a feeling that Anna's right – since we came near this place I've also been feeling danger in the air. So I've been torn, because I know you sometimes look to me to decide what we should do, and that means I've got a responsibility not to lead you all into trouble. Well, not too much trouble anyhow!" That prompted one or two chuckles, as Rebecca tried to lighten the mood a little. "But I have to admit that first Anna, and then me own little brother have gone and put me to shame! They've shown all of us the right way to act, to put our own fear for ourselves behind us, and to do the right thing.

"Now that we're here, I can't deny that this place looks a bit, well, daunting. In fact, and this is something I don't reckon you've ever heard me admit before, but I won't deny that I'm more than a little scared of what may lie ahead of us in that big, dark old house down there. Now that it comes to it, I suppose we're all feeling a bit nervous, and maybe we don't really feel like going through them gates. But we came up here to find out what the gang are up to, and I'm sure we're close to finding out something really important. We also said we'd help Green and Watson, and that's what we're going to do. If we think we're frightened, then just think what it must be like for them, and they've got no-one else in the world who can help them now, only us." Anna shifted her focus again to look at Rebecca's aura, and found it too to be brighter and bluer than she had ever seen it before, as Rebecca continued, "So come on, we're done thinking and talking. We're going in!"

With that, Rebecca led the way as, in the twilight, the group moved through the imposing cast iron structures, and on into the silent grounds that lay beyond.

The Beast of Highgate

At first they moved in silence, Rebecca leading the way, not down the driveway which led off to the right but straight ahead to the trees, through which they could now only dimly make out the house. The slope leading down to the house was not heavily wooded, but there were trees dotted right down to the wide stretch of driveway that passed in front of the house before it swept round the left-hand side and behind the huge building. Unlike the other houses they had passed on their way, there were no flowers here, just long grass and undergrowth.

The house itself was enormous, with lines of windows on two storeys and wings of the building on both the left and right side, protruding out from the main building towards them. The tower that Anna had seen earlier rose up from the left-hand end of the building. The main entrance contained a large double wooden door with a pillared porch roof and a long, wide flight of steps leading up to it from a lower portion of the driveway. Dividing these steps from a drop to the driveway on either side was a low wall. Some way to the right of the door was a very large window spanning both stories of the building, suggesting that some kind of large hall lay within. Despite there being so many windows, there was barely any light emanating from the building at all, which in the current twilight made it impossible to make out any further details at this distance, but did serve to add to the dark, brooding presence of the huge structure. The only light visible came faintly through a window above the main door, but even that was scarcely visible. "Almost looks like no-one's home," remarked Tilly, although no-one believed that to be true.

"Right, so what's the plan then?" asked Johnny, who, having crossed the threshold into the grounds now seemed to have recovered some of his bravado.

"Well," started Rebecca, who appeared still to be formulating the plan as she spoke, "first I think we should wait until it's properly dark, which won't be long now. We're going to have a right job on our hands as it is, without letting them watch us strolling in. Then, I suggest we move down the slope in stages, moving from tree to tree for cover. Once we get to the building, we'll need to move right around it, looking for a way in more secret than that big front door down there... We're not exactly the types who ordinarily go breaking into people's houses and none of us have done this before, but I'm sure we'll find a way in somehow. With all them windows, surely one will be unlocked!

"Once we're in, we've got to be real quiet and find out where Green and Watson are being held. Once we know what's going on in there, we'll make another plan then."

It wasn't exactly a sophisticated scheme but it sounded reasonable enough, and no-one had any better suggestions. However Johnny then added, "Becca, do you think a couple of us should go first, to check the lie of the land and seek out the best places to try and get in? The fewer of us there are, the less likely we'd be to get caught I reckon. That's what the army infantry does from what I've read. I'd be happy to go."

Rebecca paused in thought for a second before

responding, "Johnny, I know what you mean. But overall, now that we've all decided to do this, I think we should stick together. What I'm worried about is that if we split up and one or two of us get caught, the rest might not even know about it in this light, and we might still be waiting while they're being done in. We'll be dealing with adults here, and some pretty nasty-looking ones at that too – if it comes to a fight I think we're going to need all the help we can get. It's not like there are loads of us and we should still be able to avoid being seen, so I say we all go together."

There was general agreement. Then all there was to do for the time being was to wait for it to become completely dark. They waited quietly for a time, then Johnny spoke up in a hoarse whisper, just loud enough for the group to hear. "Do you think that old man is somehow connected with the Beast of Highgate? Or do you think the Beast could even be him somehow, all dressed up or something? He certainly looked evil enough to be a murderer, and we saw him come right here, right near where that murder was yesterday."

"You know I've been wondering the same thing," Rebecca whispered in response. "Anna, I'm sure you've been working on a theory! What do you reckon?"

Anna was taken by surprise, and she hesitated for a moment. She had never spoken to her friends about auras, and to their credit they had never asked her about the rumours of what she could see. However, now was not the time to begin talking about such things. Choosing her words carefully, she replied, "Well, yes, I have had the same thought, I do really think it could be him. What I'm in no doubt about is that he is both evil and dangerous, and it does appear to be an unlikely coincidence that such a man should now be here, so close to where that murder took place yesterday."

"Johnny, do you think that man is the same one as you mentioned earlier, who they said does evil ceremonies to summon demons and the like?" Alice joined in. "You know, the man you said might live in this house..."

"Faulkner? No, I don't think he can be Faulkner," Johnny responded straight away. "Faulkner's a younger man from what I've heard, and attractive to women too. I can't imagine anyone being attracted to that old monster we saw in Highgate – not even you!"

"Ha ha!" Alice screwed up her face in mock scorn. "You're right, I'd forgotten about that. But I wonder what his connection with Faulkner is then, if, as you say, Faulkner lives here."

"Yes, that's a good question," said Rebecca.

"I don't know, but there's obviously some connection. I bet they'd make a right charming couple!" Johnny tried to joke again, but no-one was laughing now, not even Johnny.

'Yes there must be a connection, but what is it?' Anna pondered to herself. She did not understand what it all meant. She had certain pieces of the puzzle, but the picture still eluded her.

"I wonder if that old man's actually still here right now though," said Edward. "Apart from that one light it don't exactly look like there's many people at home."

"Well if he ain't, and if those Maryleboners ain't either, then we've got nowhere else to look, apart from back at that old house in Highgate town," was Rebecca's response. "But I don't fancy going all the way back up there until we've searched this place first. And I think the time for that has come."

By now it was almost dark, and Anna could see a beautifully clear, star-lit sky above them, although as yet there was no moon visible. Rebecca rose to her feet and told everyone to execute the plan discussed earlier and to run from tree to tree until they reached the last ones between them and the house. Having got that far, they were all to wait until Rebecca gave the signal to run to the house wall, from where they would begin to move around the house in a clockwise direction, looking for a way in.

"All right, let's go!" she hissed, and with that she hurried forward down the bank to the next tree, behind which she concealed herself. One by one the others followed, Tilly and Tessa choosing the same tree as each other, the rest each going for one of their own. When it came to Anna's turn to run, all the nearest trees were taken so she had a long way to go to get to one. Her state of nervous tension had been made worse by the thought of who they were running towards, and by the time she passed the most advanced of her companions she was running at full speed through the undergrowth. Just as she approached her target tree, her foot caught on a root in the darkness. Suddenly she was tumbling, before crashing down just short of the tree. For a moment she was completely dazed, and then the fear swept over her that she might have given herself away to anyone watching from the house, or even worse, given away her friends. Hauling herself up behind the tree and now wet from the evening dew on the grass, she kept herself completely concealed for a moment before braving a quick look around the side of it in the direction of the house. It remained just as dark and mysterious as before, and to Anna's immense relief there were still absolutely no signs of life.

"Are you all right, Anna?" whispered Timmy urgently, running up to join her from a tree not far behind. "Yes, I'm fine. I'm so sorry," Anna replied, "but thank you."

"I hope nothing happens to you, Anna. I don't know what I'd do if it did. I don't think I could stand that."

"Thank you Timmy. I feel the same." That was all that was said, but to Anna it meant everything.

The rest of the secret descent down the slope to the final trees was uneventful, and once there, they all waited for Rebecca's instructions to move down to the house.

"Everyone," said Rebecca in a whispered shout, "when I count to three, I want Johnny to make a run to that corner over there, at the end of the house on the left. It's closer to us than the other end and it looks even darker there than everywhere else, so it's as good a place as any. When you get to the corner, just go round it and find somewhere close where we can all hide, wave to us to let us know it's all clear and then wait there, all right? Don't go far on your own though – remember, we all need to stay within sight of each other. If anything does happen, give your whistle signal if you can, or else just shout if you need to and we'll all be right there. Then, one by one, I want each person from left to right to do the same and run to join Johnny on my count. Then when you're all there, I'll go last. All right?

"All right, one, two ..." and then she stopped dead.

For just at that moment, somewhere ahead of them in the darkness, there came the sound of a horse and carriage starting to move across gravel. The group ducked down low and then froze, waiting with breath held for what was going to happen next.

The sound grew louder, and then in the dim light shed by the brilliant but distant stars, Anna saw a carriage slowly rounding the wing of the house on the left-hand side, on the very wide driveway which wound in front of them and then away up the slope to their right. Although it was impossible to tell in the darkness, certainly from its shape it looked like it could be the same black carriage that had nearly run them down in the street near the old house earlier that day, before whisking away the two boys. It was moving at a far gentler trot now, in the direction of the front door of the house. 'That really was close', thought Anna, 'it came from exactly the direction we were about to run in!'

As the carriage approached the steps to the front door, it slowed, then came to a gentle halt in front of them. The driver climbed down, mounted the long flight of steps and gave the door a knock which was just audible from where they were hiding. He stepped back and waited as the group looked on with bated breath, straining to see who would emerge.

After a few moments passed, one of the two large doors swung slowly open, revealing a man standing, holding a lantern. In its glow, Anna could just make out the man's features; she was certain it was the younger man they had seen earlier leaving the decrepit old house in Highgate. The man took a brief moment to look outside to check nobody was about before turning back to open the door wider. And then they saw them – the two Marylebone boys they had come to rescue!

It was impossible to tell at this distance and in this light what kind of condition they were in, but at least they were alive and able to stand. Evidently they were about to be shipped off somewhere else, which would mean that the group's chances of being able to follow them and find them again would be slim at best.

Anna looked desperately around at her companions. Rebecca had evidently had exactly the same thought, and she hissed a new order to them all. "We can't let 'em take them away from here. It's now or never. We've just got to rush in and take our chances. We all go together, we do whatever we must to get them boys free, then we scarper out of here as fast as we can. Everyone's got to look out for everyone else, mind – make sure no-one gets left behind and we all get out safe. Let's meet up again by them gates at the top, and then we get back down St John's Wood as fast as we can. If we do get split up and can't meet around here, then we all gather in the usual place back home. Clear? Right, when I say, we all run at them together, but keep as quiet as you can so they only see us as late as possible."

While Rebecca had been whispering, the door had closed again with the boys on the other side of it. However, it soon opened again, and the man began to push the boys forward towards the long flight of steps leading down towards the carriage.

"Now!" hissed Rebecca, and the companions broke cover as one and began to tear through the darkness towards their target, though still trying to keep the noise from their feet to a minimum. At first Anna didn't believe they would be able to cover the wide expanse of driveway before the boys were forced into the carriage, but when the trio were midway down the steps, they stopped again and looked back towards the house. It was a relief to see them stop as it allowed the group more time to intercept them, but the relief was short-lived when she saw the reason. A fourth figure had appeared in the doorway to speak to them, and it was the old man! Anna was sure he would notice them as they ran, but it was dark and he seemed to be focused on what he had to say to those who had just left the house. Perhaps the sound of his voice was drowning out the unavoidable sound of their footsteps.

As they burst forward, the fastest runners, Johnny and Timmy, were moving ahead of the rest, followed by Edward and then Anna. The leaders were halfway across the wide expanse of driveway to the carriage when something else unexpected happened. Another figure, a young man Anna thought, suddenly became visible, carrying a large stick and sprinting down the driveway from the right hand side, running in the direction of the staircase. 'Who can that be?' wondered Anna, although neither she nor the rest of the group slowed down or changed direction at all. Whoever he was, friend or foe, help or hindrance, they were now committed and would have to deal with it when they got there.

The young man was closer than they were and he was running even faster. He reached the steps of the house before they had reached the carriage, and was the first to attract the attention of the group gathered on the steps.

The old man was the first to see him, and he yelled an order to his young henchman to get him. The younger man did as he was told, darted past the Maryleboners and met the new intruder head-on at the base of the stairs. The old man leapt forward, dropping his walking cane in the process, grabbed both boys by the shoulders and began to manhandle them back towards the door of the house. This time both boys resisted desperately, broke free from his grip for a time and delayed him for a few vital seconds, sufficient for Johnny, then Timmy, then the rest of them to reach the steps. The old man howled with startled but terrible rage on seeing this hoard descending upon them, and scrambled back to grab his cane. At the same time he shouted orders at the coach driver to stop them.

Events then followed so rapidly that Anna could barely take them all in, as her main focus was on the two Maryleboners and getting them safely away. She was vaguely aware of the driver springing down from the carriage behind her and making it part way up the steps, only to be hit from the side by a combination of Rebecca, Robert, Tilly and Tessa, who, through their combined momentum and the element of surprise, were able to manhandle him over the side of the stairs into the darkness below. Anna heard his cry as he landed, followed by groaning and cursing. It sounded like he had fallen badly.

Meanwhile, ahead of her, Johnny and Edward had grabbed the Marylebone duo by their arms and were pulling the startled pair down the stairs, when several more things happened at once. Out of the corner of her eye, she could see that the young intruder had been using his stick and had gained the upper hand over the old man's younger henchman. Leaving him sprawled face down on the ground behind him, seemingly unconscious, the young man was now haring up the stairs. He swiftly shoved Edward to one side and grabbed the arm of one the Maryleboners – Green she thought – but Anna was no longer focused on that.

Her attention had been drawn to the old man, his face lit up by the lamp that had been discarded on the steps. That face was now twisted into a hideous, venomous snarl as he leapt forward, cane in hand, in pursuit of those who would dare try to escape him. In his glistening, terrifying eyes, Anna clearly glimpsed his intention to fulfil the promise he had made earlier that afternoon – to kill them. However, as he bore down on them, Timmy had leapt into his way and had knocked him momentarily sideways against the wall on the side of the steps. Doubly enraged, the vile old man swung his cane with all his force and connected with a blow to the side of Timmy's head. Timmy let out a brief, sickening cry before slumping forward, motionless, onto the steps.

All thoughts of the Maryleboners or anything else left Anna's mind. Following her instincts she shifted her focus to the old man's aura, and she was appalled at what she saw. It was very large but hideously disfigured, with a surface covered in crater-like pockmarks. It was black at its core, but had dark brown marks and particularly large streaks of crimson across its surface. Anna's worst fears about the man were realised - sure enough, his aura was already upon Timmy's pure blue one, and it was beginning to squeeze the life out of it!

"No!" screamed Anna at the top of her voice. She

visualised her own aura being thrust forwards with all her might towards that of the old man. Though she could not see her own aura, she could see its impact well enough, as it smashed that of the old man to one side, away from Timmy's.

For a second the old man looked utterly stunned. Even the snarl was momentarily wiped from his ugly features, replaced by an expression of disbelief as he looked at the child who had just hit his aura so hard. But the look of menace was gone only for an instant, before being replaced by an even more hideous one of pure evil as he transformed the shape of his aura into a terrible spike. He stabbed it forward hard towards Timmy's aura, as though intent on killing it, and ending Timmy's life once and for all. All the while he was staring unblinkingly at Anna.

Anna thrust her own aura forward desperately, in between Timmy's and that of his attacker, flexing it as hard as she could in her mind to resist the oncoming thrust, as though she were placing a rock in the path of an oncoming blade. She made it just a split second before the awful blow struck. And a terrible, mighty, piercing stab it was indeed. It felt to Anna for all the world as though someone were pushing a physical spike right through her chest. She stumbled forward onto her knees, and for an instant slipped to the edge of consciousness. She had never felt pain like it before, and she had never experienced the very life force ebbing out of her as it was now. Her consciousness slipped further away, she was dimly aware that this was it, and that if she did lose consciousness now that would certainly be the end, for her and surely for Timmy. It was that last thought that held her, on the brink of oblivion. She would not let him be killed, not by that hideous creature, nor by anyone else.

Through searing pain, her consciousness began to return. She forced herself to look at the attacking aura, and she could see that the vile black, brown and red spike which was still inching forward had almost reached the beautiful blue sphere that was Timmy's aura. Almost, but not quite – not yet. She knew that it must be her own aura that still lay between them. With all the remaining power she could muster, she mentally clenched her aura as though it were a fist wrapped around the evil, malformed spike, and pushed against it with all her will. She could not actually move it backwards, but she was able finally to arrest its progress forwards. As she gripped the spike hard, she was also able to lessen her own pain to a degree. Both auras remained where they were, motionless, locked in a lethal stalemate as their owners tried in vain to gain the upper hand.

Then something happened which stopped every one of the crowd of combatants in their tracks. The air was rent by the single most horrific, unearthly sound that any of those present had ever experienced. It resembled an ear-splitting human scream, only far more terrible – and more terrifying. It was a sound so overwhelming that all fighting momentarily ceased, and even the hideous old man lessened his attack slightly to look upward. Still desperately retaining her grip on his aura, Anna followed his gaze almost hypnotically up to the roof of the old mansion. There, set against the clear stars of the night was the horrific outline of an enormous winged beast, its horned head raised, its jaws open and its talon-tipped wings spread wide. "The Beast of Highgate!" someone yelled from below.

The creature appeared to crouch for a moment, then launched itself from its lofty perch, and the bright, clear stars disappeared one by one, as the dark, winged silhouette slid before them, momentarily blocking them out. Anna watched, rooted to the spot, as the creature swept over the site of the melee on the steps. It dived towards the young intruder who had by now reached the driveway again and was making good his escape, taking Green with him. As the demonic beast descended upon him, it once again let out that soul-piercing shriek that nothing born of this world could have created, and this time it was immediately followed by the altogether more human and utterly terrified scream of the young man, who fought to stave it off.

Anna was marginally quicker to recover her senses than the old man, who, although still thrusting forward with his deadly aura, was looking on hungrily at the terrible scene that was now unfolding below them. Seizing the initiative, she summoned her remaining strength and pushed back with all her might at the old man's hideous aura – and this time it moved! Moving fast, she briefly released her grip, mentally clenched her own aura and then smashed it against her enemy's, knocking it sideways with all the force she could summon. At the same time, she lunged at his physical body and shoved his chest as hard as she could. She became aware that below her the old man's legs were also being lifted up – by Timmy, who had risen to his knees, driving the old man upwards with all his might. The old man reacted, but just too late to prevent this three-pronged attack from forcing him over the side of the stairs and into a long fall into the darkness below. There was a heavy thud, then no further sound.

Anna urgently helped Timmy to his feet, gave him a quick hug of pure relief, then swiftly turned her attention back to the scene below. To their right, as they looked down the stairs, Rebecca and the rest of their group had been running to help Anna and Timmy in their fight with the old man, but they were now turning and shouting for Anna and Timmy to follow. Ahead of them was Watson, who was now leading the charge away from the house towards the darkness of the trees and the upward-sloping bank beyond the drive. Further along the driveway, some distance to the left of the foot of the stairs, Anna could make out the young stranger lit dimly by the lamps from the carriage. He was engaged in a desperate battle for his life with the huge, winged creature that was now towering over him while lashing out with its enormous talons. As Anna looked on, desperately assessing what she should do next, she saw the young man finally manage to break away into some space, grab his walking cane in both hands, pull them in opposite directions and unsheathe a concealed sword! Its blade flashed in the dim lamplight as he took swings at the hideous beast. The creature hissed and growled between ear-piercing shrieks, as it lashed out again and again. It appeared to lacerate the left sleeve of the young man's coat. Despite his sword, surely the young intruder had no chance against such a monster.

By now both Anna and Timmy were running down the stairs in the footsteps of their friends, Anna still clutching at her chest following the attack moments before. She noticed the figure of Green in the darkness just beyond the battle. He appeared to be cowering slightly but not running away, he watched his would-be saviour's deadly combat. Having seemingly steeled himself, he made a move towards the battling pair in an attempt to tackle the huge beast as best he could. However, he got to within no more than two feet, before he was batted aggressively away by one of the creature's wings, and fell painfully to the ground.

"No Davy, stay back!" yelled the young man with the sword, lunging forward once more at the monster. This time his blade appeared to make contact, causing the beast to let out a terrible roar. Anna knew there was no time to spare, and leading Timmy, she darted in the direction of the fallen boy. Racing past the raging battle, they reached Green, got a hand under each of his arms, and despite the pain that Anna was still feeling, hauled him to his feet.

"Come on, we've got to leave now," Timmy yelled at him desperately. "We've got to get out of here!"

"No, I can't. That's my brother and we can't leave him!" responded the boy, half shouting, half crying.

Anna and Timmy looked towards the dispersing figures of their friends, who no doubt assumed that they were just behind them, and then exchanged desperate glances. Each knew that to intervene in the battle ahead of them would almost certainly end in disaster, but at the same time neither was prepared to leave Green and his brother to their fate in the claws of that monster.

"He's right, isn't he?" shouted Timmy to Anna. She didn't need to reply. They both understood as one what they must do.

Turning back and bracing themselves for what was likely to be their final act, the trio moved back in the direction of the beast. At that moment it let out another of its ear-shattering shrieks and lunged forward at the young man, this time its deadly fangs plunging into the man's chest. Then the monster closed its talons tightly around the man's body, leaned forward, and with a beat of its mighty wings, it lifted off the ground. Even as Anna and her companions broke into a run towards them, she could feel the wind and dust in the air from the creature's beating wings as it took flight and slowly gained height, ascending back towards the roof of the house like some kind of demonic carrion bird, carrying its prey away to its stinking nest. There was a loud clatter as the sword that had been brandished so valiantly by the young man just moments earlier crashed to the driveway in front of the house, having fallen from his now limp, lifeless hand. The dark form soared into the air above the roof of the house, and was gone from sight.

"No! No!" repeated Green, his voice breaking into a terribly cry, as the trio came to a halt again on the drive. They all knew this battle was lost.

"I'm so sorry," said Anna, taking Green in her arms in an effort to console and comfort him as much as she could. They waited for a time as Green's initial grief began to sink in, both Anna and Timmy at the same time fearfully aware of the great danger they could still be in if they did not leave soon.

"Come on you two, we've got to get out of here before that thing comes back again!" came a shout from behind them. It was Rebecca and the others, who, having retreated as far as the trees before realising that Timmy and Anna had not followed, were now running back towards them.

"Come on, there's no reason to stay in this awful place a moment longer. Let's get out of here," said Timmy.

Sobbing violently, Green seemed to be only dimly aware of what was going on. Apparently operating on survival instincts alone, he ran with the others toward their friends, who were once again running back towards the trees on the grassy bank that led up to the main gates.

It was then that all their worst fears were realised. The air behind them was suddenly rent once more by a hideous, deathly scream. Glancing back over her shoulder, her eyes now fully accustomed to the dark, Anna made out the shadowy form of the beast, high up above the house, beating its mighty wings and beginning to swoop back in their direction!

Looking to where she was running and redoubling her speed, Anna yelled to her companions for all she was worth, "It's coming! The Beast is coming back! Run for it!"

She could see the others ahead of them, who had all reached the trees and were looking round desperately as they plunged forward into cover. All now realised what was happening, and the scrambling became more frantic as the realisation entered every head that they could be the Beast's next victim. Anna's chest and legs began to burn as she and her two companions ran on in a desperate bid to reach the bank. They were on the brink when something seemed to stop Green in his tracks. He span around to face the creature above them, opened his arms in a defiant gesture and shouted at the top of his voice, "Come on then, come and take me if you can! I'll get you for Robbie if it's the last thing I do! I'll have you!" He continued screaming at the top of his voice and clenching his fists. At this, the creature appeared to adjust its direction and to begin a steeper dive directly towards him!

Before Anna could do anything, Timmy ran back to Green, grabbed him against his will and manhandled him forward to the grassy bank. Green tried to fight him off at first, but Timmy was stronger, and helped by Anna he half dragged, half carried the still yelling boy the remaining feet to the tree cover.

They reached the trees without a second to spare. By the time they darted for cover they could hear the beating of wings and the hissing of the creature in the air just above them. As they reached concealment, they could hear the sounds of the fast-dispersing group ahead of them as they scrambled desperately through the undergrowth.

Grabbing hold of the nearest tree, Anna looked above her in desperation, preparing herself for her final battle should the Beast decide to descend through the foliage onto her or any of her friends. At that moment the demonic creature clipped the tree she was holding onto as it swept overhead, and she caught a glimpse of it as it passed. It was still clutching the body of the young man, and appallingly sad though that sight was, it was also the one thing that might just have saved their lives – the Beast could not properly attack anyone else whilst it still held onto its first prey, and seemingly it did not want to let that go.

The Beast swooped up again and disappeared from view, obscured by the trees, and the air was filled once more with another of its blood-curdling screams. The powerful sound of its wings suggested that it was now sweeping in an arc over the trees, before another shriek, a little further away this time, indicated that it might be heading back in the direction of the house. Peering through the trees behind them, Anna could just make out its evil shape against the night sky – and it was indeed moving away from them! Still clutched in its claws was the limp form of Green's brother. The beast finally disappeared from view over the far side of the roof of the house.

"I think it's gone," whispered Anna to Timmy who was by her side and looking in the same direction into the darkness above the mansion.

"You may be right, but it could still come back at any time. Let's get out of here," was Timmy's response. He was right, and Anna needed no second telling. By now the sounds of their escaping friends running for their lives had grown distant, each probably having lost track of where the others were. As Anna and Timmy were looking back to where the creature had been, Green had bolted somewhere into the darkness ahead of them. However, now that the immediate danger had passed and he was physically safe for the moment, albeit no doubt deep in shock and grief, there seemed no purpose in pursuing him further against his will. "I should think he probably wants to be alone," said Timmy, and Anna guessed he was right.

All that was left to do was to run for it themselves. Sticking close together they scrambled up the bank through the trees and then, panting hard, they sprinted along the gravel driveway, through the huge iron gates and into the darkness of the road beyond. Fatigue burned painfully in Anna's legs and she thought her lungs might burst at any moment, but she kept running. Even though they were beyond the railings and no sound of the Beast could be heard, Anna continued to look anxiously behind and above her for any signs of it. Mercifully, there were none.

Desperately short of breath and their muscles hurting, Anna and Timmy continued to pound along the road past the large mansions they had seen earlier. It was only when they reached the junction of the road with the main thoroughfare that, for the first time, they allowed themselves to stop for breath. Anna collapsed to the ground, hidden under the trees a short distance from the road. There was no sign of any of their companions, nor the two Marylebone Street boys, which was much to Anna's relief. "They must have understood it's far too dangerous to wait around those gates, or anywhere near that mansion," she panted, to which Timmy nodded, "we just have to hope they all get safely back to the canal as agreed."

As she rested and the acid slowly worked its way out of her muscles, Anna felt again at her chest, where mercifully the physical pain from the aura attack had now subsided. As for what it had done to her aura, she had no way of knowing. Then Anna was overtaken by a wave of exhaustion, and tears began to well up in her eyes. "That poor man!" she stammered, "if it wasn't for him, the rest of us might have been hurt, even killed."

Timmy drew her close, put his arm around her shoulder and hugged her tightly. "I recognised him when he came running down the driveway. It was Robbie Green, Davy's older brother. He was another of them that was usually up to no good, just like most of the Marylebone Gang's elder brothers. But when it came to it, he did the right thing tonight. He was brave and gave up his life to save his brother. He deserves all our respect and more for that."

"Yes," Anna replied, trying to stem her tears before falling silent again. After what seemed like a safe time had passed and they had both recovered their breath, Anna and Timmy returned to the main road and began their long journey back south and west. It was well into the evening, and having only been thinking about the terrible events that had just taken place and whether or not all her friends had made it to safety, Anna now spared a thought as to what might be waiting for her at home. No doubt her mother and the rest of them would be beside themselves with worry, and that would soon be transformed into anger once they had found she was safe. Still, somehow that did not hold quite the fear for her that it would have done. Not after what they had faced that evening. But first, before returning to her home, she had to go with Timmy to the meeting place to make sure everyone had got back safely.

And so it was that Anna and Timmy plunged through the dimly lit streets of north London, back towards the familiar territory of St John's Wood. The euphoria that would ordinarily have accompanied such a nocturnal adventure with Timmy was all but wiped out by the terrifying and ultimately tragic events of the evening, but Anna was nonetheless greatly comforted by his presence. Being with him felt so natural – she felt safe, as though she never wanted to be parted from him again.

After a considerable time they finally reached the

familiar street which ran alongside the canal, past Mr Warwick's shop and down the towpath to the bridge under which the friends always met. As they approached, Anna's heart began to race again. What would they find? Would they all be there? And what news might they have? She hoped against hope that everyone was all right. They had been the last to make it off the driveway and into the trees, and they had seen the Beast return to the house, so surely they would all be fine.

As they entered the gloom under the bridge, Rebecca's voice was the first thing they heard emanating from the darkness.

"Oh thank God you're both all right!" she cried out, rushing forward and hugging her brother, quickly followed by Anna. This time there was none of the usual sarcasm in her voice, just deep relief. They were immediately joined by the others, and Anna tried to work out as fast as she could who had made it back. Alice, Robert, Charlie, Tilly, Edward, Tessa, they all seemed to be there... apart from one.

"Where's Johnny?" Anna asked over the group's grateful greetings, deep concern taking her over once more.

"He still ain't made it back yet. We all got split up into small groups when that monster came flying back at us. I stayed with Tessa and Tilly to make sure they were all right, and then we all made it back here by different routes."

"All right everyone?" suddenly came a familiar voice, and there was Johnny rounding the corner from the opposite direction! They all rushed over to him and Anna was the first to give him a hug, just as she and Timmy had been welcomed moments earlier.

"Everyone here all right then?" he asked, looking around anxiously as his eyes slowly grew accustomed to the dark.

"Yes, we're all here now!" replied Rebecca in a triumphant tone. Anna imagined that Rebecca had been worrying even more than anyone that someone might not make it back safely.

Anna remained with the group for a while longer as they discussed the events of the night, excited, shocked and sad by turns as they went over their encounter with the Beast and the different scenes that had unfolded.

"Who'd have thought we'd actually see the Beast when we set off for Highgate this afternoon?" said Johnny, disbelievingly. "Who'd've believed it was actually a real monster? It weren't that horrible old man after all, or someone else just dressed up. For all my talk, I didn't actually believe there'd be a real beast, but it was real all right!"

"Did you see that thing?" chimed in Edward. "What was it? Looked like some kind of demon, it did. I couldn't believe what I was seeing. And that noise it made, have you ever heard anything like that?" Everyone agreed they had not.

"Poor old Robbie Green," added Alice. "And poor Davy. I don't care what that gang has done to us in the past, he must be so distraught, and I wouldn't wish what happened to his brother on anyone." Anna became aware of a quiet sobbing sound coming from the direction of Tilly and Tessa, and suddenly she had to struggle to contain a similar reaction herself. She went over to try to console them.

"You're right, Alice," Timmy said. "Davy was brave. I mean that Beast was fiercer than anything I've ever seen, but he went back to try to help him, even though he had no hope of rescuing the lad."

"And you two were even braver for going with him," added Rebecca. "A part of me wants to give you a right scolding and tell you never to do anything so stupid again, my little brother. But in the final reckoning, we may still not know what the gang are up to, but I think we can all look each other in the eye and say we did the right thing tonight, to help those Maryleboners and to help each other."

There was a murmur of agreement from everyone. The others continued to exchange views about the evening and express their disbelief at what had occurred, but Anna no longer wanted to talk. This was partly because she felt suddenly exhausted, and partly because she needed to get home before it got any later. As soon as the discussion had started to die down, she said, "I'd better go now and face whatever is waiting for me at home."

Ordinarily, there would have been banter in response to this, but nothing seemed appropriate after the terrible turn the evening's events had taken. The group all bade her farewell, several of the girls giving her a hug and wishing her good luck for when she got home. She moved away and started to ascend the steps back up to the road.

"Anna, wait there," came a voice from behind her when she was halfway up the steps. It was Timmy, who had joined her to say goodbye.

"Anna," he said, "you were really brave tonight. And you saved me back there, at the mansion – again! I thought it was men who were supposed to protect women, not the other way around, but all you seem to do is protect me. I'm not sure my pride is ever going to get over it!"

"But Timmy, you too were so brave tonight, and you didn't hesitate when you needed to act, whatever danger we were in. I don't think your pride has anything to worry about. I think you're going to make the best man there ever was. And that's why you're simply going to have to get used to it. I plan to continue protecting you for as long as I'm alive!"

Timmy suddenly looked bashfully down at his shoes, as was his habit, his long fringe flopping over his face in the pale light from the street lamp above them. Anna gulped silently, slightly stunned at the boldness of her own words. What was it that came over her at times like these? Then Timmy looked up again, leaned forward and then kissed her on the lips, slowly and gently, before beating a retreat back down the steps and around the corner to re-join their friends, without another word.

Watching him go, Anna stood motionless for a moment, looking at the spot where he had been standing and absorbing every last detail of what had just happened. It had been a terrifying night, ultimately filled with tragedy and sadness, but Anna had reached the point where she could no longer take it all in. Right at that moment her heart was full, and only big enough to contain the feelings for Timmy which had just filled it to the brim.

Finally, feeling faint, Anna turned slowly around, ascended the remaining steps and headed for home.

Uncle James Lawrence

The commotion awaiting Anna when she arrived home was worse than she had expected. There was a police constable inside the house consoling her distraught mother. At first, her mother flung her arms around Anna when she arrived, and Anna was genuinely moved almost to tears by the extent of the emotion that poured out of her.

The policeman had been called by her mother; he had been searching the neighbourhood for any sign of her. Anna felt ashamed for having caused so much trouble, and she was upset for the worry, not to mention embarrassment, she had clearly caused her mother. The policeman asked her a few questions to confirm that she was all right, and quickly satisfied himself that this was nothing more than a case of a child having run a little wild. He would leave it to the child's mother to dish out the appropriate discipline to bring said child back into line. The scolding, when it began, was comprehensive, involving a great deal of 'worry', and no little 'shame'. Anna was certain the others in the house were able to hear her being reprimanded, and she could imagine the satisfaction on Lizzy's face at hearing all this, if she happened to still be there. Anna knew she had to wait for the initial fury to run its course before she would be able to explain herself, and once it had, she did her best.

She started by explaining that she was genuinely very sorry for having caused so much trouble and distress. This was true, she absolutely was. Her mother was aware that Anna had some friends in the neighbourhood, although she had never approved, so Anna kept the story as simple as possible, telling her that she had met up with them and had just lost track of the time. She knew it was weak, but it was better than the full story, and she was just too tired to think of anything more. A certain amount of interrogation followed, eliciting mostly monosyllabic responses and very little eye contact from Anna, at the end of which Anna was not sure who was more emotionally exhausted, her or her mother. Finally, she was allowed to return to her room and to bed, where she slept the deepest sleep she could remember.

Anna slept late into the following morning, finally rousing to utter confusion as to how much of yesterday's adventure had actually been real. As the picture began to clear, she still found much of it hard to believe, both the good and the appalling. But it was the memories involving Timmy that she kept close to her as she went downstairs. Upon reaching the drawing room, her heart sank to see her mother waiting for her. 'More scolding,' she thought to herself, and began to apologise once more.

"Enough, Anna! I do not wish to discuss yesterday's events any further at present. My nerves are still far too fragile for that. And it no longer matters anyway, for things are about to change." Anna did not like the sound of that.

"Our old friend Edmund Warwick came to visit me first thing this morning." Anna looked up with new hope at the mention of Mr Warwick's name. "He has decided it is time for you to begin some new instruction. I was against the idea at first, but reflecting on yesterday's little episode has convinced me that he is right. Something must be done, and you must be taught discipline and certain... truths about the world that you will need to know. I didn't want you to begin so young... but I can see now that it will be for your own good, and indeed it is perhaps not before time. So I gave Mr Warwick my blessing this morning. Your instruction will be led by Edmund and your Uncle James. It will commence this evening at Mr Warwick's shop, and your uncle will take you there. That is all."

With that, her mother rose and left the room, refusing to answer any of Anna's questions, or even to look at her daughter. Anna tried one more time, calling out, "Mother, I really am deeply sorry for yesterday," but her mother waved her words away with a gesture of her hand, without a backward glance.

At first she was distraught at the depth of her mother's disappointment in her. Would she ever regain her love and trust? Anna was very upset to see her mother like this, but there was little she could do except to vow to be a better daughter and one day to regain her mother's faith.

Anna's thoughts drifted to what her mother had told her, and her mood lifted slightly. She was about to start the instruction that Mr Warwick had hinted at when they had last met. Of course she had no real idea what this meant, but it had sounded as though it might involve explanations about auras and other deep secrets of the world. Above all though, it sounded to her like the possibility of freedom from the house, which she had feared might have been taken from her forever after last night. She hoped she would get to find out more about that man, Faulkner.

Anna was surprised that her Uncle James, of all people, would be involved in this instruction. She found it difficult to believe that her uncle could have much to do with the kindly Mr Warwick at all, for the two of them could not have been more different, or inhabited more different worlds. It was not that she did not like her uncle. She did, very much. He was the one breath of fresh air ever to freshen the oppressive atmosphere of the old house on his occasional visits, in between the events in his life that sounded infinitely more interesting. It was just that he could not have been more different from Mr Warwick, or indeed from her mother, his sister-in-law, if he tried.

Anna's mother was always ill at ease with the world outside, and was always intent on controlling it, or better still, blocking it out altogether if she could, preferring her own confined but safe version that she had created behind the closed doors of their home. To the contrary, Anna's uncle wholeheartedly embraced the world and all it had to offer, seeming to live every moment of life absolutely to the full. From the various accounts she had heard, he was always attending or participating in one high profile event or another, be that playing or watching sport, attending concerts or the theatre, or socialising at some high society function, usually well into the night. And all that was when he was not adventuring overseas.

Anna always looked forward to her uncle's visits, but that was not to say she entirely approved of him. Perhaps it was her mother's influence, but even at her young age she had the impression of slight flaws in his character. It could not be denied that he cut a dashing figure whenever he swept into their home, adding colour and a sense of adventure from the great wide world, before usually sweeping out again as suddenly he had come. That he was supremely confident was also beyond question; confidence sometimes bordering on recklessness. But it was perhaps his supreme confidence that appealed least to Anna, as it sometimes appeared to contain a streak of arrogance, an air of superiority, which Anna instinctively reacted against. But he was also more intriguing than that. Somewhere behind all that met the eye there were greater depths, depths which contained contradictions to that confident and sometimes insensitive outward appearance. She did not know her uncle well enough to understand properly, and besides she was still a little too young to fully comprehend such things, but from the things he occasionally said and the way he reacted to certain events, it did seem to her that there were other, deeper layers to his character, that he was possibly more troubled than he let on, though beyond this observation she could tell no more.

The day dragged by slowly. Anna was still plagued with guilt and deeply worried by her mother's change of attitude toward her. She managed to catch her again once that afternoon as she returned to the house from an errand.

"Mother, please believe me, I am truly sorry about yesterday. It won't happen again."

"Anna, I do not wish to speak of it any further," her mother replied tersely.

Giving up on that tack, but desperate somehow to thaw the ice, Anna asked her about the plan for that evening.

"Your uncle will come to collect you at the appointed time."

"Do you know what time that is?" Anna asked softly, trying desperately not to sound impertinent.

"No Anna, I do not know. I never know where your uncle is concerned. No doubt he will come when he is good and ready, as he always does. After supper, you are to wait for him in the drawing room until he arrives. That is all I know. I shall not be here. The staff will see him in."

Anna simply nodded and said no more. However, before her mother left, she placed her hand gently on Anna's shoulder, and without looking at her said, "Please do be careful, my darling. I don't mean with your uncle and Mr Warwick, but in the world out there. There are dangers out there beyond your imagination. Please promise you will be careful."

"Yes, mama, I promise, I will," said Anna immediately, reaching up to embrace her mother. But her mother simply moved away, her head turned from Anna so that Anna could not see her face, and she was gone.

Supper-time came and went. Anna gulped it down to be sure to be ready in case her uncle arrived early. He did not. After supper Anna waited patiently as instructed in the drawing room. The clock chimed eight o'clock and her uncle did not appear. Anna continued to wait.

The clock rang for the half hour, and still there was no sign. Anna found herself nodding off. The exertions of the last two days had taken their toll, and try as she might she could not keep her eyes open. She stirred briefly when nine chimes rang in the next hour, before returning to a deeper slumber.

Anna was still soundly asleep when the sound of a man's voice gently woke her.

"Anna, Anna, it's time to wake up now. You've had a good nap but it is approaching ten o'clock and our evening's work must begin."

Anna felt deeply disorientated, but she was keen not to reveal this to the person who stood before her. The speaker was a handsome man in his mid-thirties, with dark swept-back hair, clear brown eyes that shone brightly, and a smile that had won the hearts of more than its fair share of young ladies in its time, if half the stories that Anna had heard were true.

"Uncle James, so you've decided to come after all?" was the best she could manage as she wrestled her way out from under a cloak that she found herself beneath.

"Good to see you have lost none of your impertinence then, my little niece!" he responded with a wry smile.

"Is this yours, Uncle?" she asked, sitting up and holding up the cloak.

"Yes," he replied taking it back from her. "I arrived shortly before nine, but you were already asleep. The weather is turning and there's an autumn chill in the air, I didn't want you to get cold." Anna waited for some form of sarcasm to follow as usual, but there came none.

"Thank you," she replied simply, taken slightly aback by his thoughtfulness. It was not one of the characteristics she would normally have associated with him.

Donning the cloak and fastening the sliver clasp at the front, her uncle grabbed his hat, gloves and cane from the drawing room table and set off for the door without further ado. There was a speed and determination about his movements which told Anna he was now focused on their mission, so she quickly gathered herself to follow. Her uncle glanced over his shoulder as he left the drawing room and said, "It is good to see you, Anna".

"And you too, uncle," Anna replied, inexplicably pleased. They descended the stairs with great haste and left the house unattended, Anna snatching up her own coat as they swept past the cloak stand. Her mother wasn't there to see them off.

The carriage pulled away from the house, but upon reaching the first road junction turned left instead of carrying straight on, which would have been the most obvious and direct route to Mr Warwick's shop. Anna wondered but said nothing, keen not to give her uncle any further reason to refer to her 'impertinence'. She peered out of the carriage window at the night scenes of London which now began to slide past.

They had passed several more crossings when she saw the lights of a tavern on the left hand side of the street ahead, where a number of patrons were standing outside. As they passed, Anna glanced down the alleyway which led along the side of the establishment and glimpsed the familiar face of a young man who, with a companion, seemed to be trying to take two bundles of books from an older, more smartly dressed, but slightly inebriated man, who appeared to be resisting them. Just as the scene was slipping out of view, Anna saw the young man push the older one, who was clearly frightened, up against the wall and successfully wrestle the books off him. In an instant they were out of sight, and Anna racked her brains before she remembered who the young man was. "Archie Knowles!" she said to herself, although in a voice that was apparently audible to her uncle.

He immediately turned to her with a serious expression and said, "Where?"

Anna was taken aback by her uncle's sudden response. She was surprised that her uncle knew of this ruffian who had been threatening her friends' family. "In that alleyway we just passed. He was taking some books from another man." Books, again! Her uncle did not reply, but looked immediately out of the window behind them to see for himself before sitting back again.

"How do you know Knowles?" Anna and her uncle asked at exactly the same moment. Her uncle smiled and let Anna respond first.

"Well, I don't know him. I mean, that is to say that I have never met him or spoken to him, but I have seen him before and I know of him. He's a rough one, and we all try to keep clear of him and his friends." In the split second available she decided not to tell her uncle about Knowles's threats to Alice and Robert's brother, and their plan to bring him and Kenny Gillespie to justice.

"Hmm, yes, well you're right and that's probably a good policy for the time being. He's one of a few in the area who have gone bad, and have started to get themselves unwittingly involved in matters far more dangerous than they understand. And they may just come to pay a very heavy price for it."

Anna could not have been more surprised to learn of this overlap between her own little world and that of her high-flying uncle. She already knew that Knowles was no good, but the idea that there were things far more dangerous than even Knowles knew about worried her all the more.

"You say he was taking books from the other man? Very interesting. On another evening I would be tempted to return to intervene, but not this evening. My priority tonight is to get you safely to Mr Warwick's."

'What can all this interest in books mean?' wondered Anna, again recalling Faulkner's visit to Mr Warwick's shop. She looked out of the window for more signs of danger, but saw nothing untoward. As she sat back in the carriage, the frightened look on the face of the man from whom Knowles had been taking the books stuck in her mind. Naturally she had no idea what had been taking place, but she could only assume that the older man had been frightened by Knowles and his accomplice. She fervently hoped he would come to no harm. Her uncle had suggested that Knowles and his friend were also headed for some sort of big trouble themselves as a result of their actions... so who gained from all this? Apparently no-one. This was a theme Anna had come across time and again.

They passed a couple more streets, then Uncle James knocked on the carriage ceiling with his cane, indicating that he wanted to stop. Almost before they had come to a halt he opened the door, told Anna to stay where she was, and then left the carriage. Anna watched as he circled the vehicle looking in all directions, then gave the driver instructions. He returned inside the carriage with a flamboyant sweep of his cape and they moved off again. Anna could resist no longer.

"Uncle, I hope you don't mind my asking, but what is happening? I thought we were supposed to be going to Mr Warwick's shop but we don't seem to be going the right way. And why did you stop just then? Is something the matter?"

"Anna, as you will soon come to learn, dangerous

times are approaching. Suffice to say that we can't afford to take risks, and we must make sure that certain enemies are not tracking our movements. That is why I took us via this circuitous route, and why I made sure that we were not being followed. That is all I can say for now."

Anna was startled. Who were these enemies who might be following them? Maybe Archie Knowles was amongst them. She guessed it must also involve that sinister man, Faulkner. Was there a connection with that hideous old man they had seen in Highgate as well? The fact that even her uncle, usually so blasé and carefree, was being so earnest and cautious, now brought the full seriousness of the situation home to her. Could he have been referring to the Beast? She shuddered as she recalled that monster, and the tragic fate of Davy Green's brother. Surely he didn't mean the Beast might be following them now...? Anna swallowed hard, trying her best not to show her uncle how tense she was feeling. She looked out of the window again, her eyes wider and more attentive now.

Her uncle gave her a nudge on her shoulder and he smiled. "I know you want to know more – you do have Lawrence blood in you after all – and a lot more will be revealed very soon, when your instruction begins. So chin up!"

Anna appreciated his encouragement, but she couldn't wait to get out of that carriage to somewhere safer. She also could not wait for this 'instruction' to begin, which might finally answer some of her questions. The carriage soon took a right turn, and then began to travel back in the direction of Mr Warwick's shop. Before too long the driver was reining in the horses, and they drew up on the side of the road opposite the familiar old building with its weather-beaten green sign. Anna peered out of the window at the shop, and she noticed how clear the night was, lit by the silvery light of a moon which was almost full. At last the waiting was over, and she wondered with anticipation what it was that she was about to learn.

The bookshop was lit faintly, both by the nearest gas street lamp and by the moon which was riding high in the sky. However, from inside the shop itself emanated nothing but inky blackness.

Before Anna could alight from the coach, her uncle told her to sit back where she could not be seen, then with another sweep of his cloak he left the carriage. She sat back, deep inside the carriage as instructed, but through the window she could still see her uncle whisper orders to the driver, take a lantern from him, look both ways, then walk around the entire carriage and horses again, looking intently all around him, especially in the direction of the neighbouring canal. Clearly, he was ensuring that all was safe, and no doubt that Faulkner and his henchmen were not lurking in the darkness.

The idea that someone, or something, could really be lying in wait to attack them pushed Anna's nerves right back onto their edges again, but at the same time the presence of her uncle reassured her immensely. He was such a confident and dominating character that she found it hard to imagine anyone taking him by surprise and getting the better of him. However, she did hope he would not do or say anything too rash which might upset the kindly old bookseller.

When her uncle had finally reassured himself that no-one was lying in wait, he opened the door and beckoned for Anna to follow him quickly. She needed no second bidding and clambered out of the coach in pursuit of her uncle, who was already striding across the road with his metal-tipped cane raised at the ready as he looked up and down the street. The large moon cast an eerie sheen over his top-hatted figure, and on the whole street around them.

Anna followed her uncle's glances as best she could whilst struggling to keep up with him. Maybe it was the hour or her state of mind, but this area, which she knew so well, looked more mysterious and ghostly than she had ever known it. The gas lamps cast long, twisted shadows on the road and buildings and the bright moon lent its haunting glow to the whole scene, while the breeze stirred the branches of the tall trees which lined the canal. Other than the coach driver and horses behind them, no other movement could be seen or heard. The street appeared to be deserted.

After several long seconds they reached the bookshop door, and Anna's uncle rapped lightly on it with his cane. They waited in silence for a few moments, listening for any signs of life within the darkened shop, whilst continuing to look up and down the street. The tension increased. What if Faulkner and his gang, rather than waiting for them outside, had already somehow managed to get inside the shop and were now waiting for them somewhere in the darkness? It certainly seemed to her strange, when Mr Warwick was supposed to be inside waiting for them, that no light whatever came from the shop window.

Anna felt fear rising inside her. Her new-found confidence of two days earlier had entirely deserted her now. Despite her bravery when confronting the likes of the Marylebone Street Gang, in reality they were all people that she could understand, and whom she now had some confidence to deal with. She had seen new things in the last few days which had been utterly beyond her comprehension, let alone her ability to confront – the world of adults, and far worse... Again she looked timorously behind her but could see nothing but the carriage and horses with the driver sat aloft, he too on alert looking up and down the street.

She was on the point of voicing her concerns to her uncle about what might lie inside the shop when a faint glimmer of light appeared in the window. The door at the back of the shop had opened, letting in light from the room beyond. Moving to peer through the dusty window, Anna could make out what looked like a slightly stooped figure, making his way towards them from the back of the shop. After what seemed like an eternity, the sound of a bolt on the door being drawn back was followed by that of a latch being unlocked, and then the door opened a crack. Anna took a deep breath and braced herself for whatever might happen next.

"It is us," whispered Anna's uncle, and with that the door was opened further until, to Anna's immense relief, Mr Warwick's familiar features could be recognised. Anna's uncle gave a signal to the driver, who returned a gesture in acknowledgment. Without further hesitation her uncle reached out to usher Anna into the shop.

At first Anna could make out almost nothing in the darkness until, gradually, vague shapes started to reveal themselves as her eyes became accustomed to the dim light of Mr Warwick's lantern. Remembering her previous fear about what might be waiting for them inside, her eyes began to dart all around the dark outlines of shelves and boxes in the cluttered shop. She couldn't see any sign that someone might be lurking there, but then again it was impossible to tell, the place was in such a state of chaos. Anna reminded herself to one day ask Mr Warwick just why he didn't make more effort to tidy the place – not that she minded the dust and mess, but because that way he might actually sell something, which was something she had never actually seen him do. However, neither the time nor the frayed state of her nerves was appropriate for such talk right then. She simply shadowed the old man towards the back of the shop, looking around her all the time.

After one of the more unsettling walks of her young life, Anna and her companions finally reached the back of the shop floor, and Anna followed the old shop keeper into that same room she had visited two days earlier. Having taken the fine upholstered leather chair offered to her, facing the fire and slightly to its right, she cast her eyes around the room and was struck again by how much the atmosphere in here differed from that of the main shop. Everything spoke of a different level of attention, and indeed a different state of mind, than did the shop at the front. Anna started to wonder how the two could be owned by the same person, and what it might mean about that person.

Then something happened, something which left her utterly speechless. Her uncle had turned to face the old man, who suddenly seemed to be standing up much taller and straighter than he had but moments before, and who now had that same air of a younger man that Anna had briefly sensed during her last visit. This time though it was far more evident. Then her uncle, usually so confident and superior, went down on one knee before him, lowered his head and said, "Master, your servant is here."

"Thank you. Arise," was the shopkeeper's simple reply, accompanied by a solemn nod of the head. With that, Anna's uncle rose to his feet before removing his gloves and cloak and taking to another large, heavily upholstered chair to Anna's right, next to the now roaring fire. From the way he flung himself casually into it, Anna would never have guessed he had been down on his knees mere moments earlier. She could not have been more surprised by this turn of events than if Faulkner himself had walked straight out of the roaring fire dressed as a circus clown. Had that really happened? Had her dashing, indomitable uncle really bowed down at the feet of the portly old shopkeeper and called him 'Master'? Although now that she came to look again, it was indeed the kindly old bookseller who had the greater air of quiet confidence about him, and who actually now appeared the more powerful of the two. It was not that her uncle had changed his bearing in any way. At least, not now that he was back up off his knees! Sat in the chair waiting for the discussion to begin, his bright eyes dancing in the flickering light of the fire, he still looked every inch the bold adventurer he had always been. Rather it was the kindly old shopkeeper, who had appeared slightly frail and unsteady just moments earlier, who now looked nothing of the sort. His face looked essentially the same apart from his eyes in which the youthful look had returned, but his posture was no longer stooped and he was possessed of a certain gravitas that had been absent before. His presence was altogether more magisterial and, well, masterful now. Re-focussing her attention momentarily, Anna then saw the most surprising transformation of all. Whilst Mr Warwick's aura remained pure blue, smooth, unspoiled and perfectly spherical in shape as always, it was now significantly larger – in fact it was almost twice the size it had been! It was considerably larger even that her uncle's aura, which itself had always been a considerable size. Anna looked in amazement as she realised she was now looking at the largest aura she had ever seen, bar the single exception of Faulkner's.

This transformation was something she had never come across before, and she had no idea that it was possible for a person's aura to alter so drastically in such a short space of time. She wondered what could have happened to him in the last few days to bring about such a change. Her deep sense of wonder at this old man, whom she had thought she had known so well for years but who now seemed to have qualities and depths she had never imagined, was growing by the moment.

A volcano of questions began to erupt in her mind, but before she could put a voice to any of them the old man himself began to speak.

The Decision

"Anna, I expect you are wondering why we have asked you to come here to talk to us, why we are being so careful, and what we are going to tell you," began the old man.

"Well, um, yes," replied Anna simply, doing her real feelings no justice whatsoever.

"I imagine there will be some things you have already guessed, and others you have long wondered about. However, some of the things I am going to explain will probably be completely new to you, and may seem difficult to believe. But everything I am going to tell you this evening will be the truth, at least to the best of our understanding, and I hope you will be able to listen with an open mind.

"In addition to myself, your uncle here will play an important role in your instruction, should you choose to proceed with it, and as representative of your family, he will also be your guardian. I am sure he already has your trust, and I hope that, in time, I will come to earn your trust too.

"So, let us begin. As we sit here today, there is a major struggle fast approaching in which we are all going to be involved, whether we wish to be or not." Mr Warwick momentarily looked Anna directly in the eye with that piercing look of his. "In fact, you could more accurately call it a war, and unfortunately it is a war that has the potential to affect the entire world.

"It is unusual for these discussions to begin with one so young as you, since the gravity of what you will learn is ordinarily too much of a burden for a child to carry, and with the knowledge that we are going to share comes immense responsibilities. Additionally, most people cannot use this knowledge until they reach adulthood. Your uncle, for example, was twenty years old when I began his instruction, and any younger than that is unusual. However, we have reason to believe that you specifically may have a part to play in the approaching struggle despite your young age, and although it would have been better were you older, the time is now upon us whether we like it or not, and we must prepare you now for the events that are to come."

Then Anna's uncle spoke. "Anna, as Mr Warwick has said, many things that you will hear tonight will seem strange to you. Certainly they sounded strange to me when I first began my instruction. But I have subsequently found everything that I was taught by Mr Warwick and my other Masters to be true and consistent with my experiences since then. So I would ask that you trust Mr Warwick completely, listen carefully to what he says, understand as much as you can and be as honest as possible in your responses."

Turning from her uncle to the old man, Anna replied, "Mr Warwick, I do trust you. I trust you because... I can see it." Although she hesitated slightly in saying this, she believed he would understand what she meant.

"Thank you Anna, and yes, actually that is exactly where I would like to start, with that ability you possess which sets you apart from most other people: your ability to see essences.

"As you know already, 'essence' is the word we use

to describe a manifestation of a person's fundamental qualities. Their personality, their nature, their predispositions – the *essence* of who they are.

"Most people cannot see essences, and even those who can usually only develop the ability as they reach adulthood or later. Whether this faculty is present in all people and merely lies dormant in most of them has been the subject of great debate for many centuries. My own view is that everyone has this 'sixth sense' as one might call it, but that in most people it is never discovered. Also I believe it is sometimes the case that ordinary people can sense a great essence even though they cannot actually see it, for example when they describe someone having a great presence. However in your case, Anna, I know that you have been able to see something of other people's essences from a very young age, and unless I am mistaken I believe that you can now see them very clearly indeed."

As Anna listened to Mr Warwick, the palms of her clenched hands began to perspire. She was finally about to put aside the years of caution and discomfort in discussing this subject, and she was sure that at last she was going to learn the answers to some of the questions which had long filled her head. But, she also remembered the promise she had made to her mother several years before.

"Uncle," Anna turned to him, "my mother told me never to discuss auras – sorry, I mean essences – with anyone, unless she gave me permission. Is it all right for me to talk about them now?"

"Anna, it is good that you ask, but yes that time has come," he replied. "We have your mother's full consent."

"In that case, yes, Mr Warwick," Anna continued,

"yes, I can see essences. I have been able to for as long as I can remember. What I can see appears as a coloured image which gives me an impression of what the person is like, whether they are generally good, kind, strong-willed, weak, modest, arrogant..." At this word she tried, just too late, to stop herself glancing momentarily at her uncle, for that slight strain of arrogance was one of the flaws that she had always made out in his aura. It had only been momentary, but it had been enough for Mr Warwick to notice and a knowing, amused expression began to cross his face.

"You're not going to be able to hide much from this one, James!" he said in a jovial tone, which could not have been in greater contrast to the mood until then.

"Very amusing," her uncle replied, at first looking anything but amused, before allowing himself a rueful smile.

Anna moved on quickly. Looking up from the floor to which her gaze had fallen, she continued, "I have always been able to see, uh, essences, but if anything, in the last few years the impressions have become stronger, and I can see them more clearly now than ever."

"Can you tell me exactly what you see when you look at someone's essence? I mean beyond its general size and colouring," said the old man. His tone was still light and friendly, but Anna could sense that he was now very alert and focused on what she had to say.

"Well, there is the surface texture of the essence. In some cases, those I think of as the best, it is completely smooth. In most cases the surface has at least some parts to it which are not smooth. Sometimes there is a slight rippled effect on part or all of it." This time she resisted the urge to look at her uncle; she could see something of that effect in his aura. "In much worse cases they have cracks and crevices. People with essences like that usually also have red in them, and they are usually the type who do harm to others in one way or another. Also essences are usually not perfectly round and often have slight, deformities, but occasionally you see some really misshapen ones." She had never tried to explain these things to anyone else before, and she was finding the words surprisingly difficult to come by.

Mr Warwick remained silent for a moment, his eyes sparkling in the firelight as he exchanged glances with her uncle. Anna was now desperate to ask a question of her own. "Are there many other people who are able to see essences in the same way that I can? I know you can see them Mr Warwick, but when I mentioned them to others in the past they have treated me as though I were mad. Uncle, can you see essences?"

Her uncle merely gave a brief nod and semi-smile in response and did not speak. Nonetheless Anna's heart skipped a beat at this confirmation.

"Anna, please rest assured that you have certainly never been mad, but for the time being I would ask you to speak of them only to me or your uncle. The reason for caution is that it is in the nature of too many people to find fault with, and to make trouble for, others who are different from themselves, especially if there are things about them that they do not understand. I would go so far as to say that it is one of the major flaws in the natures of people in the world today. It is not how things should be, and hopefully they will not always be this way, but unfortunately it is still all too common at the present time. Moreover, we are now entering a very dangerous period, and we have more than people's common ignorance to worry about. We have an altogether more dangerous enemy to fight. So for now, the fewer the people who know about what we can see, the better.

"But in answer to your question, yes, your uncle and I can both see essences, although neither I nor your uncle can see them with the same clarity that it would appear you can. I can sense the overall colour of a person's essence, and I can distinguish between the different individual colours it might contain, provided they are clearly demarcated. However, I cannot see those colours in detail. Similarly, I can make out the shape of the essence, and can see if there are any fundamental markings on its surface, but I cannot make out the more minute detail of the surface that you described. I cannot, for example, see small cracks or ripples, only significant ones. And yet I believe I am able to see a person's essence with greater clarity than almost anyone, including your uncle. Would that be fair James?"

"Alas yes, that is correct," he replied. "With my Master's help I have become better able to view essences, but I have never been able to attain his level. I can see a rough impression, enough to give me the basic insights into a person's overall character, and I can also see the shape sufficiently to engage with it effectively during mental combat, which is an essential skill you will need to learn soon. But nothing close to what you are describing. Anna, I marvel at what you have told us, even if some of your insights do not make for pleasant listening! Another time when my Master is not around, I will have words with you about that!" Then he laughed, much to Anna's relief.

Smiling, Mr Warwick continued, "And there are others too who also have the ability to see essences, together with other associated powers, and we belong to a group which has existed for thousands of years, and which in English is called The Order of the Knights of the True Path. The greeting your uncle gave me earlier is one of its little traditions. You will come to learn a lot more about this group in the future.

"However, no-one that I know of today can see essences with the extreme clarity that you have just described. In former times, there have been tales of a very small number of people through history who, we are told, could see essences in great detail, amongst them some very great men and women. But these have been very few and far between across the centuries. You will learn much about the great Knights of our Order who have preceded us through history, and the battles that they fought for our cause in their own times – that will form part of your instruction. Before then though, the one thing I must ask of you is that you never mention anything about the Order to anyone unless we give you permission to do so. Is that clear, Anna?"

"Yes Mr Warwick, I will never mention it," she replied earnestly.

"Very good," the old man continued. "What is entirely unprecedented to my knowledge, is the age from which you have been able to see essences. As I mentioned, this ability usually develops only upon reaching adulthood, which makes your case all the more intriguing, indeed exciting, for the development of your own powers may yet be far from complete. Even in the cases of the very youngest students I know of from the Histories of the Struggle, even they only first became able to see essences at around the age you are now. This is why we had no idea you would reveal such an ability to the world at the age you did. Had we known, I promise you we would have managed things very differently, and you would never have had that terrible experience with Dr Evin when you were ten. Of course you were not to know that others could not see essences as you could see them. It would have been most natural to believe that everyone could see them, as no-one had explained otherwise."

"Mr Warwick," Anna suddenly interjected, a nerve having been touched, "My mother has known about my ability to see essences for a very long time because I talked to her about it when I was very young, perhaps four or five. But she didn't really explain anything to me, she just told me that this was something people never spoke of, and that I should not either. Do you know why she didn't tell me that other people cannot see essences?"

"Anna, I can understand your question. All I can tell you is that your mother has only ever acted out of the deepest love for you, and that she has only ever tried to protect you. The reality is that the Powers of which we speak have brought her much suffering in one way or another, even though she herself does not possess the Powers. Your mother cannot see essences, but your father could. What she wanted was to shield you from the harm that can come with involvement in the struggle. Whether or not things might have been better dealt with another way is not for me to say. She did what she felt was best for you, and that was her decision to make.

"When your mother fell ill it was perfectly justified and right for you to speak to the doctor, given what you did and did not know at that time. Even though we were not aware that your powers were already well developed, we knew enough of your potential to have protected you better against the dangers of the likes of that *Thrall*, Evin..."

Seeing Anna's enquiring look at that point, Mr Warwick quickly added, "My apologies, Anna. Thralls are a particular kind of person within the enemy's ranks, or perhaps more accurately put, they are a weapon that the enemy uses against us. You will learn all about such things soon in your instruction.

"However, the fact is that I only found out about your incarceration in that awful asylum a few days after it had occurred. Although I intervened swiftly enough to get you out of there before Evin executed his full, despicable plan, and crucially, before he could make your presence known to... well, others whom we did not wish to know of your existence, the fact that you had to experience that terrible place at all is a source of enormous regret. For that I can only beg your forgiveness." He bowed his head and whole upper body in a gesture of remorse.

"Mr Warwick, it wasn't your fault!" replied Anna. So Mr Warwick had helped to save her from the asylum! But what had he meant by 'others whom we did not wish to know of your existence?' Anna began to comprehend that this kindly old man had been taking on some kind of guardianship role over her. Seeing the contrition still on Mr Warwick's face, Anna continued, "the asylum was a truly ghastly place, one that I am certain actually causes madness rather than cures it, and I am grateful for whatever you did to help get me away from there. I owe you my life, so it is I who should be giving you my eternal thanks, not you offering me your apologies!"

From the corner of her eye she thought she caught an approving nod from her uncle before the old man replied, "Thank you, Anna. Your kind words mean a great deal to me. It does not lessen my own feeling of guilt, but it means a considerable amount to me to know how well you have dealt with it."

The old bookseller paused, deep in thought for a moment. "Now," he continued, "time is drawing on and we must talk of more pressing matters."

Anna sat back in her chair, sure she was to learn more about Faulkner, or possibly even the Beast of Highgate. Instead, she was stunned by the next question.

"Tell me Anna, one night about eight years ago, can you remember if you had a particular dream, a dream that was different from normal dreams, one which stayed with you vividly even after you had awoken?"

Anna knew instantly to what he was referring. She needed no help to recall that particular memory. That dream had felt so real and so true that it almost did not feel like it had been a dream at all, and she could still remember it as though it had been the night before.

"Mr Warwick, how did you know about that? Have you had a similar dream? Though if you had, I doubt you would have asked me if I could remember it, for that was something I will never forget as long as I live. Much as I wish I could."

"Yes Anna, a number of us in the Order also had a dream, all of us on the same night. But what the others and I saw was not altogether clear, and although more vivid than other dreams it was still somewhat difficult to recall in detail. We all understood that the dream had been significant and that something had occurred, something had changed in our world, and we had an idea what it must mean, but it was difficult to interpret exactly. From your reply, I sense that you were able to see rather more than we did, Anna. I understand that it may be unpleasant to recall, but do you think you could tell us what you saw? This could be extremely important."

Anna took a deep breath. This was something she had not been prepared for, and recalling that nightmare began to bring her out in a cold sweat. "Mr Warwick, you are lucky if you didn't see what I saw. Or rather, felt what I felt – the way I felt. My mother said that I cried the whole of the next day, and that is not at all like me. To be honest, the feelings of that dream haven't completely left me even now. It was the most terrible nightmare I have ever had, except it did not feel like a dream. It felt absolutely real, as though what I saw was really there. And the worst part was not the seeing, but being seen."

She stopped with a shudder, and noticed a look of momentary surprise and concern cross the kindly old man's face. Though he recovered instantly, and recognising Anna's distress he said, "Please Anna, take your time. I really would not ask you if it were not so desperately important. Please try to go on if you can, but take as much time as you need."

Anna took another deep breath then continued, "Well there was a terrible storm in my dream, with dreadful thunder and constant lightning. The wind was wild and the rain was much harder than I have ever seen it for real. And in the lightning flashes, what I could see was a big hill, and on top of the hill was what looked like a huge, rectangular stone. Then the stone was struck by a savage bolt of lightning, followed by a strange, horizontal sheet of lightning, which actually didn't look like lightning at all. It looked more like a huge tear in the sky.

"Then suddenly I was much closer to the hill, and around the base of the stone I could see a number of dark figures. I couldn't make them out clearly, but there were five of them – four roughly the same height, but one much bigger than the others. I couldn't distinguish any more about them so I have no idea why, but from that moment on I became filled with panic. Awful, uncontrollable panic. It felt as though there was enormous danger there, and that I was very much in danger myself."

Anna stopped to gather her breath. Tears had begun to run down her cheeks as she recalled what she had seen with unwanted sharpness. Forcing herself to remember was bringing those feelings back again, and she found herself wanting to burst into tears. But rather than suffer the embarrassment of crying in front of her uncle and his Master, she fought hard to regain control. At the same time, her uncle put his arm around her with a concern and genuine affection that she had never seen from him before. Knowing that he was there and ready to protect her helped a great deal. A degree of composure returned.

She looked at Mr Warwick who was leaning forward in his chair, motionless. He had been absorbing every word as though it were the last he would ever hear, and now he appeared to be examining those words, searching for a great secret they contained. Finally he spoke again.

"Anna, you are being most brave. I would like you to continue if at all possible, but please only do so when you feel completely ready," he said softly.

Encouraged by their understanding, and by the hope that they might be able to help interpret what she had seen and somehow reduce the terror that it had always induced in her, she steeled herself to relate the final, most terrible part.

"The last thing I remember is seeing the face of one of the figures. And I know that it was the face of the largest figure of the five. Although I have no idea how, I know that's who it was as surely as I know my own face in the mirror.

All I really saw were his eyes. They were utterly unlike any I have ever seen, and I hope I will never see anything like them again. The whites of his eyes were not white at all – they were blood red. Inside that, where we have colour, it was completely black, like darkness itself. Then right in the middle where we have black, I could see a faint, dark red glow, like a dim light coming from deep inside. They were horrible, but in the end it wasn't how the eyes looked that scared me most. It was that it was not just me looking at him. He was looking at me too. I mean directly into me, inside me, into my very heart – seeing and understanding everything there is to know about me. I suppose he was looking at my essence, but seeing it in extreme detail – in much more detail than I have ever been able to see anything.

"But the thing was..." and at this point she could no longer hold back and began to sob uncontrollably, in spite of her uncle's comforting, "...he was evil. I mean really evil. I don't know how I know, because I couldn't see his essence and I can't explain it myself, but in this man was evil beyond anything I could imagine. It is terrifying enough to know that such a man even exists, but it's worse still to know that he knows everything about you. And he could see everything in me, I know it. I could feel it..." The flow of tears had now turned into a torrent. Mr Warwick broke from his almost trance-like state of focus and joined her uncle at her side to console her. "Don't ask me how I know it, because I don't know myself," Anna forced out the words through her tears, "but in this man was the purest evil I have ever seen or felt, and I can still feel it even now, all these years later."

With that Anna broke down into uncontrollable floods of tears, the like of which she had not cried since the night of the dream, even in the toughest of times she had known since then. It took her two companions some considerable time to bring her back to something like her old self again, but finally her embarrassment caught up with her. She hated the idea of crying like a small child in front of these two men, whatever the justification, and it was this thought that eventually enabled her to regain control.

"I am so sorry, I don't normally cry... I'm well known for not crying. It's, it's just...," she sobbed again, "it's just that dream. It was so horrible, and it still is to me. And the most terrible thing is, I know it wasn't a dream. I know that he is out there somewhere. And something tells me that one day, whatever I do, I am going to meet him."

Uncle James put his arms around her again and told her that she did not need to say any more, and how proud he was of her courage. There was a long silence broken only by Anna's subsiding sobs, before Mr Warwick spoke again, slowly and with immense gravity.

"Anna, do not feel embarrassed by your tears. I think I know better than you might imagine how terrifying an experience that dream must have been, and how difficult it was to re-live it. Most adults would not have been able to face such a thing without great distress, let alone a six year-old girl. It is remarkable that you were able to withstand it as you did. The more I learn about you, the more I find to wonder at. There is no shame in crying at that memory, and indeed it would have been most unnatural had you not done so. You will come to understand better what I mean by that presently.

"But first I will address some of the specific points that you described. You may not like everything I am about to tell you, but in the long-run I believe it will help you to start to come to terms with what you have seen, and to prepare you for the future.

"You are right in what you said. This was not a dream in the normal sense, and what you saw in your mind's eye was real and was happening as you saw it, albeit a great distance away. I also believe you may be right that one day you will meet the one you saw. It may be that ultimately this encounter cannot be avoided. However, please take heart, for we will do whatever we can to delay that meeting for as long as possible, and we will do all in our power to ready you for it should it indeed turn out to be unavoidable."

Anna gathered from this that understanding these things would be to her advantage in the end. But having her instincts confirmed, and by someone who would ordinarily never want to scare her, in many ways made things worse. 'I might as well seek out that man now and get things over and done with,' she thought, although even the idea sent another shudder through to her core.

"Anna," the old man spoke again after another pause, "your dream is of immense significance, and in fact offers us deeper insights than I had dared to hope for. However, the content of what you saw also presents us with some worrying revelations. Indeed I would go further and say that they are profoundly shocking. I cannot be sure I have interpreted your vision absolutely correctly, but this evening I will share my insights with you, if you would like to hear them. It is the least I can do after what we have put you through..

"Some of things I am going to share are of huge importance, to the very world as we know it. If we are to proceed, I will need you to promise me, with the deepest and most sincere promise a person can make, that you will never discuss any of these subjects with anyone other than myself, your uncle and anyone we specifically tell you may be trusted. And we will not force you to embark on this journey. This is your choice to make freely, and you may take as much time as you need to think about it. But if you do decide to proceed with this instruction then you must always keep the promise I am asking you to make. If you do not, the consequences will be very serious –

indeed they could be fatal for us all."

Uncle James, who had by now returned to his seat and resumed staring into the fire, spoke again.

"Anna, you are under no obligation to us, and no-one on our side is going to take away your free will. That is one of the things that distinguishes us from our enemies. The conversations that we have begun this evening are setting you on a course which may lead you to incredible adventures and experiences, and reveal to you some of the deepest secrets of this world. However, in all likelihood it may also lead you into some of the gravest dangers imaginable. From what I understand though, I believe it more than likely that those dangers are going to find you anyway, whatever decision you make now. So the choice you are making is whether or not to accept this journey, so that you can be prepared for and influence the timing of when you encounter these dangers. I promised your mother, as representative of our family and the brother of your father, that you would not feel pressured. Whatever else you may think of me – arrogant for example," another quick smile, "I hope you know that family is of great importance to me, and I will always do whatever I can to take care of you.

"I was six years older than you are now when I was asked to make the decision to start my training, and, well, you know me – daring and fearless as I like to think, or reckless and foolhardy as others have been known to suggest – but for me it was an easy decision to make and I did not hesitate. The promise of adventure and the discovery of unknown secrets was enough for me to commit. But you are different from the person I was, certainly more cautious and analytical, though I can see you lack nothing in bravery. As Mr Warwick says, please take however long you need to decide. If that means coming back another day with your answer, then that is entirely acceptable."

It was now Anna's turn to gaze into the depths of the fire. The decision being asked of her was evidently one of great significance, even if she did not yet fully understand its consequences. She had always felt herself to be something of an outsider, but now it seemed that being different had a reason, and that there were other people like her, important and powerful people, and she was being invited to join their number. The two men asking her the question were people she respected and trusted too, people she might learn much from and even aspire to be like one day. And she could not deny the appeal, not only of being treated more like a grown up at last, but of seemingly in some small way having their respect. It also seemed that this path might answer many questions that had filled her head for so long. And there was the idea of adventure, and above all freedom, which when compared with the sheltered, oppressed life she had been forced to lead up to then, attracted her enormously. She presumed that this must be her uncle's side of the family showing itself!

However, there was one obstacle in Anna's mind, and that obstacle was immense. It was that, somewhere, ahead of her on this path, lay evil in its purest form, in the shape of that man from her dream. Such was the unspeakable, irrational terror that this idea held for her that it was almost enough to make her choose any other direction, and to run in that direction for all she was worth. But deep inside she understood that no matter how far she ran, unless she died first he would pursue her and ultimately find her. She had known this since the night of the dream itself.

The truth was that deep down she knew, and really had known from long before the question was ever put into words, that she would accept this path she was being offered, that she must accept it, wherever it would lead and whatever it would bring, good or ill. Those things about her that were unusual, and the things that had not even made sense to her so far, were now somehow just beginning to fall into place, and all the important experiences that had affected her until then had all been directing her to this very point, and to this decision.

The brief conversation she had already had that evening confirmed that she was no longer alone, and that there were people here who would understand her, guide her and support her as she became whoever it was that she was meant to become. She understood clearly at that moment, more clearly than she had ever understood anything before, that for better or for worse, this was the course she must take.

"I have made my decision," Anna replied. "I agree."

The Alpha-Omega Wars

"Very well," said the old man slowly after a long pause. "Then the time has come to explain some things about the world in which we live, as well as we can understand them, which will provide the background to all that we go on to discuss in the future. I will begin with some fundamental matters which lie at the heart of everything. And our starting point is this: it turns out that the world in which we live today, and the entire universe within which it exists, are not quite as they were... meant to be.

"Now before I go on, I want to stress that it is not my intention or desire to influence you one way or another in matters of religious faith. Acceptance of what I am about to share does not depend on any one, individual set of religious beliefs, or indeed on having any beliefs at all, neither does it need to conflict with any religious beliefs you may have. You may consider what I am about to tell you as additional, supplementary information, possibly allowing a deeper interpretation of what you already believe, in much the same way that our advancing understanding of the sciences also enables us to do.

"So, what we understand is that there was a form of fundamental, 'elemental' energy as we shall call it, that existed before the universe began, and that it was this Elemental Energy which brought the universe into being. It was this energy that set the direction of the development of the universe from its moment of inception onwards.

"However, at the time of the inception of the universe there was more than one fundamental energy in existence.

There was another energy, which had a direction that opposed that of the Elemental Energy. Or put another way, this Opposing Energy sought to create its own universe, but one according to its own, very different direction; a universe which would have been utterly different from the one in which we now live.

"As a consequence of this opposition between the Energies at the moment of the universe's inception, there is an anomaly in our universe which has existed ever since that time. Certain shadows, or echoes, of the universe which the Opposing Energy sought to create, came to be present. When speaking of this anomaly, we sometimes refer to our universe as having been 'contaminated' by the Opposing Energy, and why we use such a word will become evident. This contamination has become more apparent in the era of mankind, and even more so as civilization and societies have grown more advanced.

"The Elemental Energy's original direction would have led to a world with a great deal more harmony and mutual understanding and respect between individuals, groups, and indeed nations. A world without the unnecessary and ultimately self-defeating aggression, cruelty, jealousy, greed and so forth that we see all around us today. Also, in our world there are sometimes days when we feel inexplicably irritable and prone to anger, or we feel deeply unhappy or anxious, even though we have no real reason to feel such things. Often, these feelings are another result of the contamination of the Opposing Energy, disrupting our condition and preventing us from feeling as we should according to the Elemental Energy's direction. So in various ways, our world today is not, in fact, the 'World that was Meant to Be'. However, as natural and inevitable as these things I have mentioned may seem to us, we must not simply accept them. Much of the unnecessary pain and suffering which is created needlessly by other people is not actually logical for the stage of development which human beings have reached. These sufferings are preventing an optimal existence for us all, and they absolutely do not form part of the World that was Meant to Be.

"The opposition between the two Energies did not occur only at the start of the universe. The influences of the Energies are still at work in the world today, even right now as we speak. A war has been raging between them for all eternity, and it is a battle which continues. We have little conception of the full extent of their theatre of war, and in how many other realms beyond the world of our knowledge they are engaged in this struggle, but it is very much ongoing in this world of ours."

Mr Warwick went on to explain that people cannot see or feel the Energies in any conventional way, but that their existence was known because their effects could be observed. For ease of visualisation, these influences were sometimes described as eternal winds, attempting to push and drive people in one direction or another. Mr Warwick said that everyone in the world was subject to these winds of influence of the two Energies, and there was no place completely sheltered from them, although there were certain places where the influence of one is stronger at certain times than other places. People sometimes referred to these places as being 'magical' or having mystical qualities. He gave the example of Stonehenge, which had experienced the influences of the Energies particularly powerfully at various times throughout history, something that he said the ancients understood when they built their huge temple there. And there were many other such places around the world apparently, not always so well known, for which the same was true.

"No-one is completely immune to the influences of these invisible 'winds' from both the Energies," he continued, "but at the same time the winds do not have the power to solely determine what actions we take. No matter how strong the winds of influence, we still have free will, and we can withstand them if we choose to with sufficient determination. We are able to make our own decision to move in a different direction, though this can sometimes feel incredibly difficult."

As the light from the fire sent shadows dancing around the edges of the room which was otherwise wrapped in darkness, Anna was now listening transfixed, focussing every ounce of her attention on what Mr Warwick was saying. She was desperately scrambling to follow and understand, at a literal level, some of the strange ideas which were now flying thick and fast. They would have seemed fantastical, and probably unbelievable, under any ordinary circumstances. Yet at the same time, she felt a growing sense of excitement deep within her, like a long-awaited realisation which was starting to stir. She felt as someone who had been struggling all their life to see something that was just beyond the edge of their vision, like an object whose outline had been tantalisingly visible, but whose details had been obscured by a veil of mist. Now, that veil was just starting to be drawn aside as

Mr Warwick's story unfolded. She felt that she was about to start understanding the world as it truly was, at last.

These Energies, or winds, apparently exerted their influence by interacting with people's auras, or essences. Mr Warwick described the essence, as being like the sales of a great sailing ship, and that the purer the essence, the more open the sails were to the 'push' of influence of the Elemental Energy, and the less unfurled they were to the winds of the Opposing Energy. However the exact opposite was apparently true for flawed and discoloured essences. When someone 'acted on a whim', or an idea came to them 'out of the blue', unbeknown to them the individual was often apparently responding to the influence of one or other of the Energies.

At this point Mr Warwick had paused briefly, picked up a poker and stoked the orange and yellow blaze in the hearth, sending further, larger black shapes to join the shadowy dance on the walls and ceiling. He rubbed his hands together as though now approaching a point of great importance.

"Now, we have reason to believe that no matter how disfigured or damaged a person's essence is, the essence of a person of this world is never completely immune to the influence of the Elemental Energy. This is because every individual is born into the world that was brought into existence at the direction of the Elemental Energy, and no matter how far their behaviour strays from that direction and how far their essences become 'contaminated', their connection with the design of the world as it is meant to be can never be entirely broken. This should always remain as a crucial source of hope, no matter how bleak times may become."

Mr Warwick paused again briefly, as though to emphasise the full importance of what he had just said. He pulled out two large logs from the basket nearby and tossed them into the centre of the blaze, sending tiny orange sparks flying into the air momentarily and causing the flames to dance higher once again.

"Certain men and women have been aware of this eternal war between the Energies for thousands of years. A small number of ancient Greeks knew of the existence of the Energies, and they participated in the Struggle in their time. Since those times, in Europe we have used Greek script to describe some of the concepts we are discussing. For 'the World that was Meant to Be' according to the original Elemental direction, we use the term 'the Alpha World'. For 'the World that Should Not Be', which the Opposing Energy sought to create, we use 'Omega World'. The world that we actually inhabit today exists in a precarious state somewhere between the two."

Anna learned that the current world was in fact a highly unstable and unsustainable state. One day either the Alpha or the Omega World would prevail and become the reality. Once reached, that would then be a constant state from which there would be no return. However that final fate of the universe was not fixed or predetermined, and it was the attainment of that final state that was the subject of the ongoing wars between the Energies.

"The outcome of the Struggle could not be of greater significance for all men, women, children and all other creatures that live on this earth," continued Mr Warwick, "and for all our future descendants who are to succeed us in this world. The pure Alpha World would be, as per the original Elemental Direction, a state in which harmony exists. It would be an existence in which we would each constantly experience the kinds of stimulation and exhilaration that we sometimes glimpse today, but which we can never quite manage to sustain – those moments in which we feel uplifted and inspired. And it would be a world in which the needless suffering and cruelty caused by other people that are so often a feature of our world today would not be there. However, the Omega World would be one in which neither humans nor any other of the creatures of this world could exist at all. And worse still, the transition from our existence today into that state would be the most terrible imaginable. It would involve the step-by-step annihilation of every person and every other living creature that exists today, together with everything that we have achieved over the centuries and all that we might have gone on to achieve in the future.

"Your uncle and I, along with others like us, are champions of the Alpha World, fighters in the Struggle whose mission it is to help bring about the Alpha state and to prevent our descent into the Omega World. We have an immeasurable responsibility to all who exist today and to all future generations to achieve that Alpha state, or at least to move our world closer towards it and to do everything within our power to prevent the Omega World from coming to pass. As I'm sure you can readily appreciate, the stakes simply could not be higher."

Mr Warwick paused once more to allow time for what he had said to sink in. Anna had remained silent, leaning slightly forward in her chair almost motionless, her eyes following the old man's every expression and gesture, her mind focused on every word. Now she ventured to speak.

"Mr Warwick, may I ask you a question?"

"Of course Anna, please go ahead."

"I was wondering just how all this that you have been describing relates to my dream, and to those people that I saw. They are somehow connected with what you have just been telling me, aren't they?"

Mr Warwick looked at Anna momentarily, then replied, "You are right Anna, they are. All this background was necessary to provide the context and grounding, but you are right, it is now time to get to the heart of the matters that are most pressing to us – if you still have the energy for it that is!"

Anna could only guess at the hour, but for the first time in her life she was out of the house this late with permission, and she had never felt more awake. "Yes Mr Warwick, please do go on."

"Very well then," said the old man. "As I have just described, the world in which we live today is in fact balanced on a knife edge. The Elemental and the Opposing Energies are, right now, engaged in the most titanic struggle, like a deadly, all-transcending game of chess dating back to the beginning of time, finally to bring about the universe that each originally conceived. It is this ongoing Struggle," he continued, now turning back to face Anna, "this eternal war to bring about the Alpha or the Omega state, which lies at the heart of your dream."

Mr Warwick's eyes were now blazing in the reflected light from the fire. They had reached the point about which Anna had been most eager to learn, but the one about which she was most fearful. She leant slowly back into her chair, tightened her grip on its arms, and held her breath.

A New Threat

"Intermittently, over the centuries, as far back in history as we have records, the contamination of the Omega World has appeared in our world in a more direct, physical way than merely in people's flawed essences and in the hurtful and destructive acts that some people commit. It occasionally appears in the form of living, sentient beings. These are more than mere echoes of the Omega World. They are actual creations of the Opposing Energy, physical manifestations of its direction, conscious beings with their own will.

"They do not take the form that a creature from the true Omega World would take. These creatures emerge from a twilight dimension we refer to as the Beta World as I will explain another time, but in our world they are transitional beings which exist in a form that is able to survive amongst us. When they are here, they exist in order to achieve one aim and one aim alone: to bring about the final transition of the Omega World." Mr Warwick's tone began to harden with each word he spoke, as though he were fighting to control immense passions that were stirring within him. "These beings are not of this world, they were not part of the Elemental Energy's design, and they do not belong here. They exist purely to oppose the Alpha World, and they have been the sworn enemy of every knight for thousands of years, since the founding of our order. We call these creatures *Satals*.

"Satal appearances do not occur often. Sometimes long periods may pass without a visitation, though their appearances do seem to have grown more frequent in recent times. When they do appear, they always cause terrible suffering and destruction – for that is precisely their purpose. Satals are physical agents of the Omega World in the same way that we are agents of the Alpha World. Their objective whilst here is to intervene directly in the affairs of our world, to move it towards the Omega state. Without exception, their means of doing so involves causing disruption to harmony and peaceful existence, be that in the form of hatred between individuals or wars between nations, the creation of conditions in which disease may more readily spread or any other means by which they may wreak their misery. The bleaker aspects of the world in which we live that are the result of the contamination by the Omega design, these are the things on which they thrive, and which they seek to exacerbate – and the more they succeed, the further we move away from the Alpha World.

"A significant number of the most terrible events in human history have been brought about by the direct intervention of Satals in our world. The stories of the events themselves are known to all, but the population at large does not know their true, hidden causes. We will come to teach you about the history of the Struggle in the future. But what I want to get back to now is your dream. You see Anna, I am certain that what you saw in your mind's eye in that dream were in fact Satals. I say this because a number of our Order felt a disruption on the same night. It felt to us as though the course of the future had changed direction, and that a shift towards the Omega state had occurred. From its strength we could guess it was significant. We feared that not one, but possibly two or three Satals might have entered our world simultaneously, which has not happened for centuries. That would have been terrible enough, since defeating even one Satal is an extremely formidable challenge, and one that is usually achieved only after a lot of pain, misery and death has been inflicted on our world.

"However, from what you have told us, it seems that even our worst fears had underestimated the true magnitude of what happened that night. It would appear that not two or three, but five agents of the Omega World materialised at the same time."

"Five Satals? Here at the *same time*?" Uncle James suddenly interjected, jumping to his feet. "Surely not, Edmund. Can you be sure?"

"Well, it would certainly explain the unprecedented strength of what we felt," Mr Warwick responded.

"Anna, I know this is all new information to you and you cannot possibly comprehend its full implications, but your uncle and I can. Despite all my studies and all that I know about the history of our great Struggle and the fearsome battles that have taken place in the past, I am not aware of any time when we have faced five Satals in our world at one time. If I had time to recount to you now some of the battles that have taken place in the past to rid the world of Satals, you would understand just how terrible, and indeed terrifying, this revelation is. The slight shift in direction towards the Omega state that we felt that night will become an enormous leap if these Satals are allowed to execute their evil work. Indeed with so many, I wonder if this isn't a more fundamental move from the

Opposing Energy than we have ever seen before – some kind of major offensive to bring about the Omega World once and for all, in our own time."

"However can we defeat *five* Satals, master?" asked Uncle James, his usual calm, self-assured demeanour suddenly gone. "However will we muster the forces needed to take on such an enemy?"

"You are right, James, it will truly take a mighty, combined effort to bring about the defeat of such a number. And if only that was all we had to deal with here... But there was something else that you said, Anna, something which, believe it or not, may be the worst revelation of all.

"Anna, you mentioned that one of the five figures was considerably larger than the others. And you said that it was this larger one to whom you were drawn, and who looked at you. Is that correct?"

"That's right," said Anna, her voice now barely audible. She could feel the weight of Mr Warwick's words bearing down on her chest. A feeling of dread was starting to crawl slowly over her.

"Well," continued the old man, his own voice too now reduced to little more than a whisper, "my interpretation, unless I have been mistaken, and oh how deeply I hope that I have been, is that this largest of the Satals was in fact not a Satal at all. It was something far, far worse. This was something that I myself had already come to believe had happened that night for various reasons, or rather I had feared it had with all my soul. I now believe that your dream has confirmed it. I believe that the creature you saw was a being known as a Gorgal."

Silence engulfed the room. Anna's uncle stood

motionless, unblinking, and Anna did not dare to speak. She was about to find out the identity of the image which had haunted her all these years. But it was her uncle who spoke first. "Can this really be true, master? A Gorgal? Surely the Gorgal is nothing more than a legend? Are you saying that you already suspected this...?" His voice tailed off. He seemed to be wrestling with disbelief.

"It is the thing I most feared, James. Like you, most people believe that the Gorgal is nothing more than a legendary, mythical monster, but after so many of us felt the disruption that night, an occurrence that has never been documented before with a Satal's appearance, I began to study the ancient stories again. And sure enough, according to the Histories, prior to the last Gorgal's appearance in the West there were also reports of seers feeling a disruption immediately before its appearance.

"Mr Warwick, what's a Gorgal?" asked Anna, who could hold herself back no more.

"A Gorgal, Anna, has not been seen in this world for a very long time, in fact for over a thousand years in the West. And very grateful we should be for that too." By now the old man too was out of his chair and had begun pacing the floor in front of Anna and her uncle, his hands clasped behind his back. "Indeed, so long ago was the last appearance that among our own Order, most people do not believe Gorgals ever existed, although having now studied the evidence I think it points rather strongly in the other direction. But certainly there has been no evidence of Gorgal presence in our world for many hundreds of years – and we would surely know if there had been one.

"Like a Satal, a Gorgal is also an agent of the Omega

World. It too is a creation of the Opposing Energy, and is not born of our world. But the histories teach us that the Gorgal represents the Omega World in a far purer and more powerful form. Satals are powerful in their own right as I have said, and are able to bring a considerable direct influence on the course of important events through the manipulation of situations and of people by various means. Sometimes they have seemed to be aware of the winds of influence of the Opposing Energy and have worked in conjunction with those winds. However, a Gorgal's power is of a far greater order of magnitude. It has the power to influence the course of history more profoundly, by actually channelling and driving those winds of the Opposing Energy – if we are to believe the ancient histories that is. This gives them the ability to influence people's behaviour en masse, on a scale far greater than any Satal ever could. The Histories lead us to believe that the introduction of a Gorgal is the most direct intervention that the Opposing Energy can make to help it bring about the Omega World. To return to the analogy of the Struggle being like a mighty, all-transcending game of chess, through the appearance of Satals, the Opposing Energy introduces new and deadly pieces into the game to tip the balance in its favour. However, in introducing a Gorgal, it is playing a piece so powerful that it can profoundly alter the course of the entire game, and the course of history, not only by a step but by an enormous leap towards final victory.

"The last visitation by a Gorgal that we know of is believed to have taken place in the East of Asia, in the first half of this millennium. We know of its appearance, and the enormously disruptive effect it unleashed in that part of the world from the Orders of East Asian knights, with whom we have come into increasing contact over recent centuries, and whom we understand to have been engaged in the Struggle for as long as we have in the West. The effects of that Gorgal's large-scale intervention are still being felt there, as can be seen in the temporary relative demise in strength and influence of the civilisations of East Asia in the last five hundred years. Countries in that region have led the world in terms of civilisation and technological advancement for long periods, and I have no doubt that they will do so again in the future. But their advancement was set back by centuries as a result of events instigated by that Gorgal.

"The last Gorgal to have been seen in Europe was even longer ago, in the early centuries AD. Before its final defeat, it was able to set in place an irreversible chain of events that led to the decline of the whole of European civilisation, into what are now known as the Dark Ages. That period of relative lawlessness and anarchy lasted for almost a thousand years until the Renaissance. Prior to the appearance of that Gorgal, Europe had reached a relatively ordered state, albeit sometimes still brutal, but with a considerable level of sophistication, knowledge of the sciences, well-developed cultural lives, and so on. This relative civilisation had been spread far and wide by the might of the Romans, albeit sometimes brutally as I say, and they themselves were building on the foundations of civilisation and advancement laid by the Greeks, and of other even more ancient civilisations of the Middle Eastern lands that had developed and prospered before them. Although there were still many practices that we consider barbaric today, we have strong reason to believe that the organised society and civilisation of Europe before the last Gorgal would have developed on the path away from brutality, towards harmony. European civilisation would then have come together with those of the Asian world and the other continents, and a great advancement of humanity could have taken place. Our world would by now not only be a place far more advanced and sophisticated, but also one more harmonious, idyllic and essentially happier for all, than it is today. In other words, it would be a world much closer to the Alpha state than it is.

"As it is, the devastating effects of the last European Gorgal lasted for many centuries, during which time much of the European world descended into anarchy, bloodshed, disease and misery – a world that was worse than the old Roman civilisation by almost any measure. It was not until the Renaissance that we in the West began to relearn those things that we had known many centuries before. In the intervening period, it was the Muslim world of the Middle East and North Africa that had carried, retained and developed the knowledge that had largely been lost in Europe. Their world had been less impacted by the presence of that Gorgal.

"The Histories tell us that it has always required an enormous, almost superhuman effort on the part of armies of knights to defeat a Gorgal. And the consequences of the time that the Gorgal spends here before it is finally vanquished, have been disastrous for the world. Disastrous, verging on the catastrophic."

Anna was still absorbing these revelations about the supposed identity of the man from her dream as Mr Warwick explained how legends told of the appearance of Gorgals in other great continents in the last two thousand years, such as in Africa and in the Americas before the arrival of the Europeans. Horrific damage and suffering was apparently inflicted on the civilisations there too, with some even being wiped out entirely due to the malevolent work of a Gorgal in those regions. "The essential point, Anna, is this, the Gorgal is by far the most powerful and destructive weapon that the Opposing Energy has available to unleash on our world. And unfortunately for all of us who strive to realise the Alpha World state, it seems that it is now, in our own time, that the next appearance of a Gorgal is upon us.

"However, this time the Gorgal is not alone. It would appear that it has been accompanied by four Satals. Even I had not expected this. To the best of my knowledge, throughout the whole of history there has never been such a presence from the Omega World in this world at one time. I do not believe our world, and the prospects for the Alpha World, have ever before faced a threat of this magnitude. It would seem that the Opposing Energy has now played a potentially devastating hand..."

Awakening

With that, the room fell almost silent, as though the true gravity of the discovery were now bearing down and squeezing the very sound from it. Anna felt it, like a physical weight upon her. The implications of the things she had just heard were beyond her capacity to fully comprehend, but no more information was needed to understand the clear and extreme danger that threatened her and all those she knew and cared about. The silence lasted for what seemed like an age as Anna's two older companions looked into their own space, each absorbing the implications of what had just been discussed, and neither willing to add to it. The only sound was the quiet crackling of the fire, and a muffled curse, or was it an oath, accompanied by fist pounding into palm of hand, from the direction of Anna's uncle, sounds that she took to represent defiance.

Finally it was the old man who spoke up, in a slightly lighter tone which contrasted starkly with the atmosphere that had enveloped the room. "You know though, there is something else that I find very interesting about your dream, Anna. You said that the large figure was looking right at you. 'Directly into you' were the words you used, I think. That must have been a truly terrifying experience, and indeed, one that in itself might have spelt the end for most people. Unquestionably, I'm afraid it means that the Gorgal knows of your existence. That is both frightening for you, and gravely worrying for us all.

"However, I am interested that the creature appears

to have singled you out. Of all the people it could have chosen, including the great and powerful members of our Order, it chose you at the moment of its entry into our world. Additionally, at the tender age of just six, you were able to withstand its focus, albeit a brief one and probably at a great distance. Make no mistake Anna, I feel certain that it really did look into you momentarily in a way that no other being could have. I believe this alone would have been enough to render permanent and potentially fatal damage to a normal person's essence. And I mean the essence of a full-grown adult trained in the Powers.

"That it should have sought you out specifically, and that you survived the encounter essentially unscathed, confirms something I have long suspected. You are no ordinary person, Anna, not ordinary even amongst our Order, and it may just be that you have the potential to become a mighty force for the side of the Alpha World. My belief is that this is why the Gorgal's focus was drawn specifically to you. A strange thing to take hope from you might think, but it sought you out for a reason, and it may just be that it did so because somehow you represent a threat.

"I do not know the full potential of the power that you may come to develop, Anna, but if there is something in you that even the mightiest of our enemies ever to walk the planet considers to be a danger, then that is a cause for hope. And at a time like this, we should accept any of that particular commodity we can find."

Anna had started to stir uncomfortably in her chair. The things she was hearing about the power of this mythical monster might have sounded absurd, even compared to the other things she had heard, were it not for her dream. But the man from her dream, and the raw terror that he had instilled, perfectly matched the description put to them. Again she was filled with fear at the idea that she might somehow have been singled out by that man as a threat. It was nice to be thought of as someone special, but she had no idea in what way she could be, except perhaps that she could see auras more clearly than others. She had no conception of how she was actually supposed to pose a threat to something so clearly, overwhelmingly powerful as this Gorgal. She did, however, have every idea that a creature like that could probably wipe her out at any time in the blink of any eye.

The room had fallen silent once more, and had now become very dark. The fire was on the wane, and the dancing shadows seemed to be stooping lower and moving less frenetically, as though even they felt the burden of what had been shared that evening. Mr Warwick sat in his chair in the gloom, entirely consumed in his own thoughts. 'I'm not the only one who has had a lot to take in during this conversation,' Anna reminded herself. Finally looking up, his face eerily lit by the red glow of what remained of the fire, which made the lines in his face look even deeper, he spoke again.

"If the stories from ancient times are to be believed, then it is going to take a truly enormous effort unprecedented in history, to counter the enemy successfully. As part of your training, we must teach you all that we can find out about Gorgals, and how they have been fought. We also face a slight complication in that respect but we shall come to that all in good time."

He paused, and Anna thought she saw a look of sadness in his face. "If only I were a younger man, still in my prime. But even then..." His voice tailed off again, and in the red half-light Anna saw a look of regret as well as concern, etched onto his kind features.

It was Anna's turn to search for something to change the atmosphere, and for a reason to believe that she might be able one day to support Mr Warwick and her uncle, and to share this new burden with them. A question returned to her, which had actually been the one that she had pondered most during her life.

"Mr Warwick, this might sound like a silly question, but can you tell me what my essence looks like? Because I have never been able to see my own, and I have often wondered." Her heart began to race, because she immediately realised that in posing this question, in effect, she was asking him what kind of a person she was at the most fundamental level.

"Anna that is not a silly question, far from it. In fact, it is a most natural one to ask, since none of us are able to see our own essences. So I will tell you."

Anna watched as Mr Warwick changed his focus subtly to observe her essence, just as she herself had done on so many occasions.

"Although I cannot see with the same clarity that you can," he began, "I can tell you that your essence appears to me as a beautiful sphere, coloured in the brightest shade of sky blue. And its surface does not contain a single blemish that I can make out. Which means, Anna, as I assume you will already understand, that you are a very good person with a very pure heart, and that your essence is close to the way all would be in the World that was Meant to Be. It is not the largest essence, but there is plenty of time for that to develop as you mature, your instruction progresses and your own powers and your ability to influence the outside world grow.

"The power that you go on to develop in the future is in your own hands Anna, although surely we will try to help you in every way we can. Ultimately it will depend on how much you want to develop it and how hard you are prepared to work. What I want you to know is that your essence is, and always has been since you were very young, the purest I have ever seen, and a joy to behold for all those of us who can see these things. What it, and you, may become in the future, only time will reveal."

Anna was relieved. She was not quite sure what she would have done if there had turned out to be any red in there! The old man continued, "Whatever potential you may possess in the Powers still remains untapped, other than your unusual ability to see essences with such clarity. The rest will come, first through awareness, then with training, and finally with lengthy and continuous practice. This, Anna, if you are willing, is the journey that you will now undertake. It will be a hard one, particularly for one so young, possibly tougher than you can yet imagine, but nevertheless one for which I judge you are ready.

"We have covered enough for one evening. Looking at the quantity of wood we have consumed it must be very late indeed. The final point I want to make is this: it is vital that we do nothing to make the agents of the Opposing Energy, including the Gorgal, wherever it may be at this time, aware of your location. The Gorgal may already know more than we would like, but it is my belief that it does not know where you are now, so let's take every possible precaution in order that things may remain that way."

"Mr Warwick, believe me there is no-one keener than me to stop him... it, finding me! I will tell no-one about any of this."

"Very good," responded the old man. "Just as a precaution, James, I recommend that you stay at your sister-in-law's house whenever possible, starting tonight when you may need to explain to her why we are so late, to save young Anna here from the interrogation I fear she might otherwise receive!" He gave Anna a wink, and Anna smiled in return.

"There is strong reason to believe that events are coming to a head, at least in terms of the next battle of this war, so I would like to have you close at hand when possible from now on, to protect Anna whenever needed, and also to support me. It is even clearer that we need to start Anna's training apace. For the time being, the sessions will take place here in my shop. That is not without risk, but until various matters are completed and until I have safely relocated certain items from the shop, I am not prepared to spend long periods away from it. However, we should run the instruction at night as far as possible so as to minimise the risk of detection and interruption by any unwanted visitors. Provided we take all necessary precautions, remain extra vigilant and never leave Anna unaccompanied, I believe we will be safe for now."

Anna expected her headstrong uncle to resist anything that might impact his much-loved freedom, especially in the evenings, but she was pleasantly surprised by his immediate response. "Of course, Edmund, I will do exactly as you say." Evidently this situation was different. It was a call to duty in the struggle of their lives, and Uncle James could not have sounded more determined.

"Thank you, James. I know you had another trip to the continent planned from tomorrow, and I believe you should still make that trip, but now with an additional purpose. You must make our colleagues in the centres of the Order aware of the new discoveries we have made this evening, and I shall do the same with our Order within these shores. I will not be gone long, and I shall have someone guard this shop while I am away from it. I must now try to galvanise the Order into action. Come and see me tomorrow morning, by which time I will have some letters for you to take to our friends in Europe, and I will share with you what I believe the most important points of your discussions need to be. But more on that tomorrow." Mr Warwick lit a lantern and then turned back to Anna, apparently fully restored to his affable old self.

"Then I shall bid you both farewell. Anna, your training will commence as soon as your uncle and I return from our travels – assuming, of course, that you are still willing to proceed after this evening. Mark my words, the study will be extremely hard!" He shot her a questioning glance, in response to which she nodded her confirmation immediately. "Your uncle will accompany you to your home tonight, and he will inform your mother as to what we have agreed. I will also speak with her when there is an opportunity, but she has already accepted that the time for this has come. Mind you, that doesn't necessarily mean she's about to slacken your bonds for the rest of the time!" He laughed, then added, "Now, let us be on our way."

As Anna prepared to leave, she reflected on the full implication of her mother having given permission for this instruction, and that she too knew about these Alpha and Omega Worlds, and Satals and all the rest of it. That thought stunned her. Clearly her mother's overbearing strictness had been partly to protect her from these things. She resolved that, when the time was right, she would have a heart-to-heart with her mother, however awkward it might feel, to rebuild the damaged bridges and create a new understanding between them.

Mr Warwick led Anna and her uncle back across the shadowy, but thankfully empty, shop floor. He was about to unlock the door when something seemed to prompt him to turn back and address Anna one more time. Looking directly into her eyes in that piercing way which she knew by now meant he was going to say something of great significance, Mr Warwick added, "Anna, please do take heart. The journey you are beginning is a truly exciting one, it will take you to the centre of some of the greatest secrets of our world. It is a journey that only a select few have taken, but one that is of the greatest importance to all of human kind. It is an exciting moment for any young person, and in all history exceptionally few have been able to begin the journey so young. In your case, I have a sense that your journey could turn out to be truly spectacular. If you remain brave, if you always remain true to those things that you know to be right, and if you never give up no matter how hopeless things may seem, I think it might just become one of the greatest we have ever known."

It did not seem possible that Mr Warwick's gaze could become more intense, but somehow it did, almost as though, just momentarily, he was looking directly at her soul. Anna was able to see his aura without having to make any effort to focus her attention – at that moment it was the most vivid, pure and bright blue colour that she had ever seen. "I say this because in you I am starting to see certain things that I have never seen before. Anna, if we can complete your instruction successfully and in time before the immense events ahead are upon us, you may indeed be in store for the most unimaginably exciting of times before your days are done. So take heart!"

With that, the old man opened the door and let her uncle out first to talk to their driver who had been waiting for them, and to check once again that the coast was clear. On receipt of his signal, Anna joined him on the other side of the door. Mr Warwick bade farewell, locked the door, and retreated back inside his shop, his lantern slowly disappearing from view through the window. While her uncle completed a brief discussion with the driver, Anna stood absolutely still, absorbing what had just been said, and the feelings that began to stir inside her. She looked across at her uncle to see if he was ready for her to begin the journey home. Lit by his own lantern, he crossed the road to join her, and at first his look was as impenetrable as his thoughts were unfathomable. It was clear that he too was in the midst of the deepest contemplation of something, but then he suddenly broke into a grin and shook his head disbelievingly at her.

"You know Anna, I have known the Master since I

was a very young man, and I believe I have become lucky enough to know him now better than most. You would not believe the high esteem in which he is held amongst the Order. Of all the many great people I have had the pleasure of meeting on my travels, there is no-one for whom I hold a greater respect than Mr Warwick. And yet I have never heard him speak in such a way as he did just then. Anna, you should not underestimate the significance of those words – they were not spoken lightly. And for my part, I could not be prouder of you, my little niece!"

He shot Anna another grin, which this time she returned somewhat sheepishly. Without another word, Uncle James ushered Anna through the darkness across the deserted road, opened the carriage door, held it and gestured for Anna to pass through. It was strange, indeed faintly ridiculous, but there was almost a slight air of deference in his demeanour as he did so. She had no idea how to react, she simply followed his guidance and passed through the open door, then waited inside for him to join her and give the driver the signal to leave.

On the ride back to her house, Anna continued to digest the evening's events. An insatiable appetite to know more had grown inside her, and very late though it was, she had not wanted the discussion to end. There had been talk of hard study, but that did not concern her. For Anna, this instruction would be a welcome relief and escape from her normal life locked up in the house. But it was more than that – she was fascinated by the things she had begun to learn. Some of it had also been shocking to her, but at the same time Mr Warwick's final parting words had left her feeling inspired. For the first time in her life, she allowed herself to believe that she might one day actually achieve something important.

In recent years, Anna's interest in history had grown, in the stories of the great events and deeds of heroes and heroines from times gone by, and in the whole story of how human kind had come to be where it was. Now she had learned that there were deeper truths that lay behind some of those stories, and this fired her imagination. She could not wait for the instruction to start. But there was something more significant to her than that. There was a feeling that an understanding of elemental truths which had always been known to her, but which had lain dormant, were finally awakening. An awakening, not only of her understanding of the world, but of her *powers*. She still really had no idea what abilities she might possess, but she had felt something new, an assured confidence that she could deal with those things which life had continually thrown at her and which had scared her until now. That new-found confidence brought with it a feeling of exhilaration. Her awareness and her senses, including her ability to see auras, were growing sharper by the day, and although she could not yet understand it all, she felt that her own ability to influence events and the world outside was starting to grow. And now Mr Warwick and her uncle were going to explain to her what these changes were, and they would guide her in how she could harness them, and teach her about the grand sweep of history within which all this fitted. Those things about her which marked her out as different, which had been the cause of so much pain until now, were transforming into the source of her greatest strength. Yes, there were plenty of dangers and challenges that needed to be overcome, but as long as she was together with her two guardians, she felt as though there was nothing that the three of them together could not conquer. Even, dare she believe it, that dreaded man from her dream. Banishing him from her life once and for all was certainly a goal worth pursuing!

Then an idea flashed across her mind. Had the influence of the Elemental Energy which Mr Warwick had spoken about, been at work in that room at the back of Mr Warwick's shop that very evening? Had that same Energy been interacting Mr Warwick's aura which had been so dazzling when he turned back to her as she left the shop, *as if on a whim*, to speak those words of encouragement? She had never seen an aura shine so brightly as Mr Warwick's had at that moment. She recalled how unusually brightly Rebecca and Timmy's auras had also shone when they decided to enter the mansion to help the two Marylebone Street boys. Had the same thing been happening then? The idea that this 'Elemental Energy', which had existed since the beginning of time and which had brought the entire universe into being, might now be taking a direct hand in the events in which she was involved, not determining their outcome but applying some influence, maybe that very evening, and perhaps even at that very moment, boggled her mind but filled her with awe.

There were to be many times in the future when Anna would look back and wish she could recapture the feelings of that moment – those early feelings of assurance, confidence and excitement. As she watched the gas-lit night scenes filter by her carriage window one by one, scenes of London, that immense city in which she had grown up, she now saw it all afresh, as though seeing it for the first time. This greatest of cities, which had at times scared and hurt her, now suddenly seemed a different place, one which filled her with sheer exhilaration at the possibilities that it, and the wider world which stretched out beyond it, might now hold for her. Whatever the opportunities would turn out to be, and whatever role it might become her destiny to play in the eternal Struggle that raged between the Energies, she knew with certainty which on side she would fight until the last breath left her body. She knew her time had come.

She was ready.

Lord's

After the tumultuous events leading up to the revelations from Mr Warwick, Anna started to view her life differently. True, in most regards her life appeared little different from the outside. Mr Warwick had excited her with all his talk then promptly left town, and her uncle had left for Europe that very next evening, although thankfully not before explaining to her mother why she had returned so late. More than two weeks had passed and nothing else had happened. It was as though a hidden door to a fantastic and beautiful garden had briefly been opened sufficiently to spark her imagination and make her yearn to enter, only then to have been slammed shut again.

However despite all that, something inside Anna had changed. What she had heard from Mr Warwick and her uncle were truths that felt fundamental and eternal, and they would return to resume the story soon enough. She kicked herself that she had still not asked them about Faulkner, but there had been so much information to take on board that there had really been no opportunity. She longed for the day to come soon when they could resume the conversation and she might ask such questions. Luckily, she was well practiced in waiting.

As significant as anything that Mr Warwick had told her though had been her encounters with Timmy. These had been enough to fill her mind, and her heart, with other new hopes and dreams of what the future might hold. She yearned to see him now more than ever, but with a sense of excitement and hope that had been absent before. This time, after the trip to Highgate and the precious moments they had shared, Anna allowed herself to believe that Timmy too shared some of her feelings. For the time-being that was enough to sustain her through the long days. Anna remained true to her vow to try not to worry and upset her mother again by slipping out of the house, even though she could not entirely prevent the idea from popping into her head. She was sure the opportunity would arise to see Timmy again before too long, and she just had to hope that his feelings would not change with the passing of time.

Finally, after further time had passed, Anna's mother paid a rare visit to Anna's room to solemnly inform her that Mr Warwick and her uncle had returned, and that her full instruction was to resume the following day. Her mother may have been beset with concerns, but Anna was overjoyed – at last the wait was over. She was less excited at the meeting place her uncle had chosen. Jim, the junior butler of their household for the last couple of years, was to take Anna to meet with her uncle at Lord's cricket ground. 'Lord's'. The name loomed large in her psyche.

Lord's had been a venerable sporting venue of some repute ever since Napoleonic times. It was also the hub of social activity in Anna's neighbourhood, and turned its tranquil environment into a writhing mass of unwanted humanity when thousands of people descended on their little world for a match. She could not deny that Lord's must hold some great significance to attract such numbers of people from so many different parts, and such a diversity of people too. Young and old, the very rich and the seemingly not so rich, the sober and the far less so, and people with accents from all corners of England and from far beyond its shores – they all came.

But on the whole she did not approve of the place. It seemed like some kind of sporting temple, whose worshippers unfortunately created too much disruption, too close to her home. As far as she was concerned it belonged further away, in the heart of the City or the West End where the streets were already hectic and where a little more madness would not be so out of place. However, whether she liked it or not, Lord's was within walking distance of her house, and now she was to go there to meet with her uncle.

When her mother had passed on the message, it had contained the explanation as to why they were to meet there, although her mother had clearly barely understood it herself. The message was that there was no better place to start Anna's instruction than at Lord's, as all of human life was on display there. She was to observe and study the auras of those around her, and watch how they subtly altered as the match progressed. She was also to observe how the cricketers themselves behaved and conducted themselves and responded to the different situations they found themselves in during the game, as apparently 'cricket was an activity which reveals every aspect of a player's character'. There were lessons to be learned from this which would be directly applicable to her studies, she was told. Finally, this was also to be an opportunity for her to meet certain people who would become important companions to her in the future as her studies progressed. There was one player in particular who she was to look out for, a young fellow named Gregory Matthews, an acquaintance of her uncle, from whom she could apparently learn much. Having delivered the message, Anna's mother looked just as nonplussed by it all as Anna did!

Jim's reaction to the news that he was to go to Lord's could not have been in greater contrast to Anna's. Not only would he have the day off work, but Anna's uncle had also paid for his entry ticket. Jim apparently liked cricket and all that went with it, and he was in extremely high spirits when the morning arrived. Anna liked Jim, who was a burly man in his mid-twenties, with light brown hair and blue-grey eyes. Whenever they met in the house he was always very pleasant and, unlike with some of the others, she never sensed resentment or suspicion from him. For the most part, he left Anna alone unless they had reason to speak, and this suited her perfectly. Perhaps most importantly of all though, his aura was a lovely shade of sky blue. The season was reaching the very end of summer, but it was a beautifully sunlit morning as Anna and Jim left the house. The sunshine, coupled with Jim's irrepressibly good mood, made Anna feel slightly better about having to make the short trip to their famous neighbourhood landmark, which Jim enthusiastically informed her was the 'Home of Cricket'.

Cricket? What was the attraction, she wondered, and why did it need a home? Regardless of what her uncle had said about it revealing people's characters and so on, she really had no idea what it was all about or why people were so interested. All she had was a vague perception that to watch it must surely be the dullest way imaginable to spend a day. Or indeed a number of days for a single match apparently. The idea that she was to be forced to endure a whole day of it before she could finally resume her instruction just seemed like cruel and unnecessary torture.

Despite all this though, there was no denying it was a fine day for it. Anna tried not to think of what other more exciting activities might have occupied her rare freedom on such a day, and who else she might have spent that freedom with. They were lucky that the air had once again been borne in from the west and Anna decided to make the best of the time and whatever it might bring. The sun filtered through the leaves of the trees that lined her street, catching the first yellow and orange ones that had started to flutter to the ground in a way that gave the place a slightly magical feel. The colours were almost as bright as they had been on the way to Highgate a number of weeks earlier, and even more varied now that the season was beginning to change. Anna began to feel exhilaration again in the presence of such breath-taking beauty. There was something that could almost be called 'spiritual' about the feeling – something fundamental about what it meant to be alive.

However there was no time to ponder such things too deeply today, for cricket awaited, and Jim appeared intent on making that wait as short as possible. Anna wondered if Timmy liked cricket. Unsurprisingly it was not a topic which had ever come up, but she thought it might help if she imagined he did.

"It should be a good match today, Anna," said Jim eagerly, hastening their already brisk pace still further as they crossed the road. "The final game of the season, perfect conditions and two good teams."

"Who are the teams?" Anna asked.

"You mean to say you don't know who's playing?" Jim seemed genuinely surprised. "Why, it's Middlesex versus Surrey, a county match and a proper local derby. Surrey are our nearest rivals from south of the river, and nothing's better than beating them. They're a good team though, mind."

"Are you supporting Middlesex then?" asked Anna, thinking that this might be a worthwhile thing to know. Her question was met with a look of slight exasperation from Jim.

"Yes, Anna, I most certainly am. And so should you be too, being that it's your local team and all."

"Jim, I'm afraid I really don't know anything about cricket. I don't want to trouble you, but could you explain it a little, so that I might have some idea?"

"Why yes Anna, I'd be more than happy to. I love cricket," added Jim, unnecessarily.

As the pair turned a corner onto a busier street and they joined a steady stream of people making their way to the ground, Jim launched into a detailed explanation of the rules of the game which lasted until they were almost at the ground itself. It was clear that he could have talked a lot longer about the sport, indeed quite possibly for ever, but he was forced to draw to a close with the promise of further explanations once they were inside.

"Thank you Jim," replied Anna, to whom it had all made some basic sense, whilst at the same time of course sounding completely pointless. As they drew close to the ground, there were hundreds, if not thousands of people approaching from all directions, and Anna fought to quell a slight feeling of panic as she concentrated on ensuring that she didn't become separated from Jim. As they neared the entry gate, the crowd grew still denser. Anna was struck by the array of people who surrounded her, from affluent gentlemen in their top hats, long coats and waistcoats with shiny golden watch chains, to altogether scruffier looking folk with shorter, flatter hats. What they all did have in common, however, was that they were all considerably taller than she was, making her feel increasingly enclosed as the crowd began to funnel towards the gate.

"Mind out for the young lady!" Jim said on a number of occasions when people got too near, and each time the members of the crowd did as they were told. Through the throng Anna noticed a particularly tall man ahead of them, with very dark hair visible under his top hat and wearing a very fine coat. 'Faulkner!' she gasped inwardly and instinctively shrank back, only to be relieved when the man turned his head to reveal a clean-shaven face and much friendlier eyes than those owned by the man she had seen in Mr Warwick's shop.

By now there was a palpable feeling of excitement and anticipation amongst the crowd all around them, each group engrossed in deep discussions about the game ahead. Almost in spite of herself, Anna felt her own sense of anticipation start to grow too. There was still some time before play was due to begin, and as they emerged and Anna was able to see the playing area itself for the first time, she took a sharp intake of breath. For all the hubbub of people moving this way and that around her, she could not help but be struck by the splendour of the scene. They were facing westwards with the sun still only midway through its upward journey behind them, and in that morning light the grass of the playing surface appeared like the great lawn of a grand country house. And beyond that, directly in front of them at the far side of the ground stood the splendid country house itself, or 'the pavilion' as Jim informed her it was called, where the players and the other most important people could be found. "That is where your uncle will be. He's a member of the MCC," said Jim with an air of reverence that suggested this was something of immense significance, whatever it might be. The building was a suitably elaborate and impressive one and looked quite magnificent as it reflected the morning sunlight. Anna could easily picture her uncle atop one of its balconies, where he would undoubtedly be in his element. The edifice dominated the other spectator areas.

As the space around them filled, Anna noted that she was younger than nearly all of the other spectators, but was pleased to find that no-one was paying her any particular attention. Suddenly this seemed like the ideal observation point. And there was such a variety of characters present! Anna shifted her focus to the auras of those nearest to her. There was the usual mix of the pure and the somewhat less pure, but in general they did not seem to be a bad crowd.

As time passed, Jim started to become more and more agitated, looking all around him. At first Anna thought he was simply excited by the event and trying to take it all in, but it soon became obvious he was looking for someone. Anna wanted to ask, but her usual reticence stopped her. Then, suddenly, all became clear. An attractive young lady who looked to be in her early twenties approached. On catching Jim's eye her face lit up and she came over to them immediately and embraced him! Jim could not have looked happier. He turned to Anna and said, "Anna, allow me to introduce Miss Emily Barmby. Emily, this is my mistress's daughter, Anna."

Emily bowed her head politely in Anna's direction, greeted her and offered a slight curtsy, and Anna returned the gesture. Anna noted that Emily spoke in a very proper way, suggesting that she too might have been 'born to expect only the finest things in life' and other such nonsense, but had successfully ignored those artificial constraints to find a good heart, which she had surely found in Jim.

"Very pleased to meet you," Anna responded, and they both smiled. Emily seemed to relax slightly, and Anna couldn't help but notice the beauty of this young lady. The light brown curls of her hair on either side perfectly framed the pale skin of her face. Her lips were full and curled upwards into a delightful smile, a sight which Anna imagined must have set many a young man's heart racing. However, it was her twinkling light brown eyes that somehow shone in the light which did most to highlight the prettiness of her face, especially when she smiled. Anna shifted her focus for a moment and, just as she had hoped, Emily's aura was every bit as pure and as blue as Jim's, though it was actually considerably larger.

Jim lent towards Anna and said in a quiet voice, "Anna, I would appreciate it if you wouldn't mention Miss Emily to anyone in the household. I am very fond of Emily, but our parents don't yet know of it, and I'd very much like for us to tell people ourselves when we're both ready to do so. I feel sure I can trust you Anna, which is why I agreed with your uncle that Emily could meet with us here. Your uncle knows Emily's here. But you won't say a word to anyone else about her, will you?"

"No, Jim, I promise," replied Anna, smiling again as she realised that Jim's excitement had not been entirely due to the cricket match after all! Anna had been taken by surprise, but now she felt strangely happy. Happy for Jim and Emily because they looked so content together, and happy also because she had some inkling as to how he must feel. She silently wished them every good fortune for the future.

Emily was delightful, not to mention amusing, company once they had both overcome their initial natural shyness. She had an easy air, and Anna warmed to the young woman immediately. She soon learned that Emily had not originally been at all interested in cricket either but that she had gradually become so, first through her father's influence, and then through that of Jim. Anna laughed as Emily explained that although the concept of grown men using up so much of their precious and scarce energy on throwing and hitting a lump of red leather with sticks was nothing short of bizarre, as it was clearly something that meant so much to the men in her life, she had determined to suspend all common sense and attempt to find some form of enjoyment in it. And to her genuine surprise, she had found herself increasingly engrossed – so much so that when Jim had told her of the opportunity to meet with him at this match, she couldn't be quite sure what she was looking forward to more, seeing her beloved again or watching the contest! Jim pretended momentarily to be crestfallen before joining in the laughter.

Emily then leant across in front of Jim and whispered in Anna's ear, deliberately loud enough for Jim to hear, "And some of the players are extremely handsome too!" Emily grinned at Jim, who returned the smile with mock sarcasm, before she continued, "So beware Anna, and take my advice as an older and more experienced woman. Cricket can become a dangerously attractive proposition. You have received fair warning!"

A distant bell rang from somewhere within the pavilion, and the fielding team, followed by the two opening batsmen, took the field, all dressed from head to foot in cream-white. The murmur of conversation quietened, as Jim, Emily and everyone around them turned their attention to the men in white and this strange ritual on the pristine lawn in front of them. Finally play got underway.

The morning drew on towards lunchtime, and Anna gradually became more and more absorbed by what was going on around her. Some of the people, specifically the men, had already started to drink various liquids that she assumed to be alcohol. Some were doing so subtly from concealed hip flasks, while others were altogether more obvious, pouring various red and brown liquids openly into glasses before sipping from them. As they did so, they seemed to be engaging in ever more lively and animated discussions, making jokes and laughing uproariously. Anna had never drunk more than the occasional glass of wine on specific occasions in her house, but she had sometimes seen what it could do to others, and wondered what state some of these spectators would be in come the end of the day, given that it was not yet even lunchtime! Anyway, at least she wasn't bored as she had thought she might have been, and she was also treated to a delicious picnic lunch brought by Emily.

Then something happened on the field of play which focused everyone's attention in that direction. At the end of one over, as Anna learned was the term used for each set of six bowls by the bowler, a murmur spread around the crowd that someone called Higgins was coming on to bowl for the Surrey side. Higgins was a very large, bulky man, with a huge handlebar moustache and enormous shoulders and arms. He was clearly well known to the crowd, though not in a good way, judging by the boos, jibes and hisses that began to fill the air.

"You're nothing but a bully, Higgins!" shouted one.

"Get back to the Oval, you animal!" shouted another.

"Yeah, get back south of the river, you're not welcome here!" cried another. And there was plenty more.

Anna was fascinated and looked to Jim for an explanation. "Ronald Higgins is the Surrey captain, and there's history between him and Middlesex," he explained to her. "To be honest, there's history between Higgins and most teams, but particularly with us. He's considered quite a ruffian you see. Last year when Surrey played here, he broke the hand of our captain, Walter Smythe, who's now batting at the other end, with a high-bouncing ball. Then, in the return match at the Oval in Kennington, which is the home of Surrey, two more of our players had to retire with injuries caused by his aggressive bowling. The umpire had warned him, and then suspended him from bowling for the remainder of the match following those incidents. I've heard that it got so heated down there that some of the crowd turned ugly, which never normally happens during cricket, and there was nearly a riot at the end of the game. You needn't worry though," he quickly added, probably noticing a concerned expression crossing Anna's face, "people would never get so carried away here at Lord's!"

Anna watched with intrigue as Higgins came in from a long run-up to release his first ball at the Middlesex batsman. It kept low and darted through to the player behind the batsman, referred to as the 'wicket-keeper', without damaging anyone. The second and third balls kept similarly low as they bounced towards the batsman, one of them passing in front of him as he stood side-on to its direction of travel, and the other changing direction as it bounced, eluding his swing entirely. The batsman this time had attempted to drive the ball off the field but had missed it completely, leaving him looking rather stupid. None of these balls had seemed to place the batsman in any great physical danger though, and Anna started to wonder if all the fuss had really been justified. However, when Higgins had thundered in for his fourth ball of the over, she suddenly understood. The big bowler seemed to bounce the ball on the wicket closer to himself than he had with the previous deliveries, causing the ball to rear right up towards the head of the batsman, who only realised what was happening in the nick of time. He jerked his head out of the way of the onrushing ball but a split second before it cut through the air, precisely where his head had been, missing him by an inch at the most.

Anna was briefly horrified at the thought of what

might have happened had the batsman's reaction been any slower, and she imagined the bowler would be similarly concerned and apologetic. To her shock, however, and no little disgust, she could just make out the oversized Higgins taunting the poor batsman, as though telling him what the next ball would do to his head, before he turned back for his next run up with a smirk. Derisive shouts rose from the crowd around her.

"Ban him umpire, before he injures anyone else," shouted one young man now standing not far from Anna. He was one of those who had been sipping from his hip-flask all morning, and Anna could see the ruddy shade of his cheeks as he took another slug of whatever its fiery contents might be.

Then it was time for the next ball, and seeing Higgins thundering in again, Anna began to fear that he might indeed embed this one exactly where he had said he would. It was another short ball, but to her relief, this time Anna could see it moving in the air clearly away from the batsman. The latter took a swipe at it with a horizontal bat, but the movement of the ball in the air had deceived him and he was only able to make the slightest of contacts with the upper edge of his bat before it flew into the waiting hands of the wicket-keeper. There was joy from the fielders, and also the many Surrey supporters who suddenly became noisily evident amongst them, having travelled north of the Thames for the event. The rather forlorn-looking batsman trudged disconsolately back to the pavilion. Well, that's all right. At least he didn't get injured, or end up with the ball between his eyes," said Anna.

"That is not the point, Anna!" responded Jim, who was now becoming quite animated, though still much more controlled than most of the people around them. "He let Higgins bully him into making a ridiculous shot, and now he's out. The ball before ruffled him completely, it scared him I think, and then he lost his head and swung wildly at the next one. Higgins did him all right, and not just physically either – he out-thought him."

Anna had not expected this reply. It made it sound as though the aggressive bowling and threats of injury to the batsmen were all part of the game, and that winning was more important than the players' health. And what was more, the players themselves seemed to take this view too, judging by the demeanour of the departing batsman who appeared distraught rather than looking relieved to have escaped with his life. 'Oh well', thought Anna, 'I suppose no-one is forcing them to play this game, and they know the dangers they will face.' She was still far from understanding why anyone would choose to risk such danger simply for a game, but she had a feeling it had something to do with them being male!

The next Middlesex batsman took to the field, assumed his position at the crease and awaited the final delivery of the over. Higgins, having soaked up the adulation of his team like a huge, smug walrus, now roared in again at the newcomer. It was the first ball faced by the new batsman, but no quarter was given as the ball once again pitched short and bounced in the direction of his head. With no time to spare, the batsman brought up his hands which held his bat to protect his ducking head, and the ball careered into the fingers of his left hand. The batsman's cry was audible to them all as he let his bat drop to the ground and clutched his hand to his chest, clearly in great pain. Howls filled the air all around Anna as the batsman sank to his knees, cradling his injured hand. Higgins merely fired him a disdainful, dismissive glare, before smirking again and turning to begin the journey back to the start of his run up. As he did so, Walter Smythe, the Middlesex captain whose own hand Higgins had apparently broken in the same match the previous year and who was standing at the opposite end, stepped into the path of the larger man and began to speak angrily. Higgins did not slow down however. Instead he continued until his moustached face was inches from Smythe's and fired a torrent of abuse back at the home captain. For a moment, Anna feared the two might come to blows, but the umpire intervened, shooed Smythe away and ushered Higgins back towards the start of his run-up.

Curses and boos continued to fill the air, and Anna noticed that even Emily now looked serious and angry. Jim, however, remained surprisingly balanced and unsympathetic about the plight of his own team's batsmen.

"It was his own fault. He took his eye completely off the ball. With a bowler like Higgins you simply can't do that – you deserve to be hit. We're in danger of throwing this away if we don't raise our game!"

"But Jim," said Anna, "surely Higgins isn't playing fair. He's trying to injure them to prevent them playing. That can't be right, can it?"

"That's as maybe Anna, but that's what you get with Higgins. We already knew that. He might be trying to injure them, but he's also trying to intimidate them, and he's succeeding. All the Middlesex players knew of his tactics before play began – that's why they needed to be extra careful and keep their heads, but he's already got them rattled, you can see it.

"You are right though, Anna, the way that Higgins plays is not in the spirit of the game. I only wish one of our players would stand up to him, hold his nerve and see him off. That's the best way to teach him. Look – the batsman's going off!"

Sure enough, having faced only one ball, the new batsman was already on his way back to the pavilion, retired hurt. This time the Surrey supporters remained quiet, knowing that removing a batsman in such a way was not to be celebrated.

"What makes it worse is that we still have one more ball to face from Higgins in this over, and the new batsman is going to have to face it. I hope we don't lose another one now."

'This is becoming serious,' thought Anna, 'people are being injured. How long will they allow it to continue before someone has the sense to stop it?' She reflected on the behaviour she had seen so far from the players, and wondered what her uncle thought she might be able to learn from this.

Then a sudden roar rose up from the Middlesex support. Looking up, Anna could see a very young looking man coming out from the pavilion, evidently the next Middlesex batsman. Very young looking, and also extremely handsome unless Anna was much mistaken! The supporters rose to their feet to welcome the new batsman as though he were a gladiator of old entering the arena of battle. Jim also gave a cheer and Emily leaned forward and grinned at Anna, clapping her hands vigorously. The young man's looks clearly hadn't escaped her notice either!

"It's Greg Matthews," explained Jim. "He's only twenty and still at Oxford, but he's a fine young prospect. He grew up locally, and he has recently made the county side during the university summer holiday. He's already had a marvellous debut season. There's still much he has to learn, but he's got the heart of a lion, this one." It was the player that his uncle had told her to look out for in his message.

Anna watched as the young man took his place at the crease. Unlike most of the players he was not wearing a cap, and his dark brown, swept-back hair which was fairly long on top, ruffled slightly in the breeze. Now he was a little closer, Anna could see that he was even more pleasing on the eye than she had first thought. 'And he has the heart of a lion too!' she mused.

"I'm not too sure he's ready for Higgins though," added Jim, as Higgins began to walk towards the start of his run-up for his last ball of the over. "I'm not sure he's got the experience to deal with this."

With those words, the gravity of the situation returned to Anna, and she was gripped by the drama that was now unfolding. She felt slightly embarrassed as she found herself hoping desperately for the safety of this young man, who she had only seen for the first time but moments earlier. Dark clouds had started to drift menacingly across the previously unblemished sky, almost as though conjured up by the events taking place on the pitch before them. They obscured the sun and lent an altogether more threatening feel to the atmosphere. An eerie silence fell upon the supporters of both teams as Higgins reached his bowling mark, then he turned and began his run. He was moving very fast now, seeming to be reaching his full pace. As the ball left his hand, Anna clearly heard the aggressive bowler grunt loudly, possibly a result of the effort he had put into bowling the ball, but Anna felt sure that it was designed more to distract the new batsman from his first ball.

Once again the ball pitched very short on the wicket, before rearing up wickedly towards the head of Gregory Matthews. It seemed to Anna that the noise Higgins had made had indeed momentarily distracted Matthews, or perhaps it was the light which had now started to deteriorate, or maybe he simply needed some time to settle in, but whatever the reason, Matthews hesitated, and at the speed the ball was travelling it could quite literally have been fatal. Anna gasped as the ball careered towards the young man's head. Matthews had not taken his eye from the ball though, he had not panicked, and though his reaction was late he had managed to move his head partially out of the line of the ball. However he was not quite fast enough to avoid it completely, and the ball made grazing contact with his cheekbone. Not enough to break the bone, but sufficient to cut the skin, causing it to bleed.

Anna was shocked and felt momentarily sick. It was true that Matthews had chosen to face this monstrous bully, nobody had forced him, but surely Higgins should not be allowed to continue to attack the opposition players in such a way. She simply could not believe that such behaviour could be within the rules of any sport. The vast majority of the crowd around her were clearly in agreement, though they expressed themselves in a slightly different manner which Anna would never have been capable of! Indeed some of their shouts made Anna wonder if they weren't even crazier than Higgins himself!

Smythe directed more angry words at Higgins, to which the latter responded merely by spitting on the ground not far from the Middlesex captain, before the umpire, having seen the damage inflicted by another short ball from Higgins, entered into a lengthy discussion with the big bowler, gesturing more than once in the direction of the pavilion as he did so. This time Higgins maintained a straight face, but Anna could tell even from where she was sitting that there was not an ounce of remorse in his large body.

"Ban him!" shouted a voice from behind them. "Lock him up and throw away the key!" shouted another man just in front, and to Anna's surprise, this one could not have been a day under seventy years old! However to the dismay and in some quarters derision of the crowd, the umpire took no further action, and that eventful over was at an end.

Anna wasn't sure who scared her more now, Higgins or the crowd of which she was a part. However nobody was angry with her, and with Jim there for protection she felt safe enough, and also strangely exhilarated again. She felt alive.

The next over was a complete and very welcome contrast to the aggression of the previous one. A shorter and rounder, bearded Surrey player bowled a series of much slower, spinning deliveries to Smythe from the other end. They might have been slower, but they were clearly no easier to hit as one after another pitched in a different place, and bounced and turned to varying extents. The Middlesex captain tried and failed to make contact time and again. The craft of the rather rotund Surrey bowler was plain for all to see, as the ball sometimes reached a fair height, sometimes stayed low, and on one occasion Anna could have sworn that it actually bounced in the opposite direction to all the others. There was a great deal of art and finesse involved in this over, thought Anna, surprised at how absorbed she had become.

On the last ball of the spinner's over, Smythe was finally able to connect with the ball, sending it most of the way towards the pavilion before it was picked up by a running Surrey fielder. Smythe ran one run and then stopped, which meant that it would be Smythe and not Matthews who would face the first ball of the next over from Higgins, much to Anna's relief. However, although Smythe gestured to Matthews to stay where he was after that run, Matthews shouted "Again!", and effectively forced his captain to return for a second run. Both batsmen reached their respective ends moments before the ball reached the wicket-keeper, and they were safely in. 'Safely in', thought Anna, but Matthews obviously knew that in taking the second run he would now have to face Higgins again for the next ball. 'How brave,' she thought, but oh how she hoped he would not come to regret it.

The fielders took their positions on the opposite end of the pitch for the next over to begin, and once again boos filled the air as the Surrey captain beckoned for the ball to be thrown to him. Anna's feeling of sickness returned as she looked at the handsome young face of the batsman, scarred and bleeding from his cheek, as he faced the raging bull now charging towards him. She was struck by the look on the young man's face. Etched onto it was an expression of concentrated determination, without a trace of fear for what was to come.

Higgins released the ball, another short one, and once again it reared up dangerously towards the batsman. This time its flight was absolutely straight, and Matthews followed it clearly from the moment it left the bowler's hand. With perfect timing and poise, the young man took one step back swung his bat horizontally towards the onrushing ball, and with the face of the bat angled downwards and his eyes focused on the ball right up to the point of contact, he made a perfect connection with the middle of his bat. The crack of heavy wood on hard leather echoed across the ground like a rifle shot, as the angle of the bat sent the ball safely to the ground, beyond the nearest diving fielder and away to the boundary rope for what Anna now understood would be four runs. She realised that she had not breathed for quite some time, and she took a deep one before joining Jim and the other spectators who were on their feet applauding. She searched Matthews's expression for signs of jubilation or relief, but found neither. Instead, he had maintained the same look of steely concentration, which had not a hint of self-congratulation. Anna was starting to understand what her uncle's message had meant about this young man.

"You beauty, Matthews! That'll show you Higgins, you bullyboy!" was one of the more repeatable cries that could be heard all around Anna.

"That's more like it," said Jim, to everyone and no-one in particular, "he's using his head and he's not allowing the occasion to get the better of him. A few more like that and we'll soon see Higgins off!"

Then Higgins turned to begin the long walk back to the start of his run-up, receiving a barrage of abuse from all four corners of the ground. The last ball had been his fastest delivery yet, albeit a dead straight one, and to see it dispatched with such apparent ease by this young upstart he had intended to intimidate, and to such joy and ridicule from the enemy crowd, had clearly not gone down well with him. He was visibly snarling and seemed all the more fired up, as though the only thought in his mind was revenge.

Concentrated silence once again swept across the entire crowd, everyone wondering what would unfold. Anna's brief euphoria evaporated as quickly as it had come. The look on Higgins's face as he approached the start of his run up was one of pure murder now, as though his sole intent was to run right down and tear the batsman limb from limb. "Oh dear, I have a bad feeling about this," muttered Anna in a small voice.

"Yes, Anna, I know what you mean," replied Jim, the tone of his voice quite changed. "Did you see the look on Higgins's face? Matthews is a brave one all right, and he's got the makings of a fine batsman, but he might be too inexperienced for this. There's not many around, even amongst the most experienced players I've seen, who could survive the kind of bowling Higgins dishes out when he's in this mood. It's not even legal, most of it.

And I must say, I don't think I've ever seen him look quite so riled as he does now."

Anna's heart was in her mouth. Her own fears were made ten times worse knowing that even Jim now shared her sense of danger. Time seemed to stop as Higgins reached the start of his run-up and slowly began to turn. Anna's senses felt sharp as a razor. She gripped the seat in front, her knuckles whitened, as Higgins began to thunder in again.

Gallantry and Villainy

Higgins reached the wicket, and then it happened again – a very loud grunt as the ball left his hand. It was as though he had shouted something at the batsman at the moment he released the ball. Whatever it had been, it had the same distracting effect as before. The young batsman seemed momentarily to lose concentration, and he failed to react in time to the short pitching of the ball. This time, although it was pitched short, it did not rise as high as the previous deliveries, instead darting up off the pitch at a slight angle like a bullet, straight towards Matthews's chest! Matthews brought his bat up belatedly to meet the ball, but due to his hesitation and the lateral movement of the ball in the air he failed to find its line. A sickening thud was clearly audible even from where Anna was sitting, as the ball made contact with the young man's ribcage. There was a momentary silence, crowd and players alike stunned by the ferocity of what had just occurred.

Matthews slumped down onto one knee. He dropped his bat, put his left hand onto the grass to keep himself from falling over and somehow managed to remain upright. The grimace on his face was visible even from Anna's distance and she could see that he was in enormous pain. Such was the speed at which the ball had been travelling she could not be quite certain precisely where it had struck, but to escape with no broken bones would have been very lucky, and the consequences would be even worse if the impact was anywhere near his heart. The silence suddenly fractured as the crowd all around them erupted in outrage, and this time Anna was on her feet with them.

"You brute! You monster! How could he do such a thing? This shouldn't be allowed!" she shouted at the top of her voice, though still barely audible amid the general uproar. The crowd was extremely agitated, most were on their feet screaming blue murder at Higgins. Looking across from Jim, Anna could see that Emily too was on her feet, shouting things which were presumably equally unladylike, although there was no way of telling above the din. Despite the crowd's noisy discontent, Anna noted that no-one from the crowd ever crossed the playing-field boundary rope. It was as if some invisible magic prevented anyone from encroaching on the hallowed turf. "Well, this is Lord's!" Jim was to offer later by way of explanation.

"Surely he can't be allowed to get away with that?" asked Anna, calming down just a little and turning to Jim.

"Well no, he shouldn't be allowed to," replied Jim, and this time even he could find nowhere else to direct the blame but at the big moustachioed brute. "Aside from the written laws of the game, there are gentlemen's rules in cricket, which is one of the great things about the sport. Not only has Higgins broken the gentlemen's rules, and he ain't no gent, no doubt about that, he has probably broken the written laws too and even the legal laws of the land by now. That was nothing short of assault and battery, that was. Anna, I do promise you that cricket isn't normally played this way – at least, not when Higgins isn't playing – it's usually a very gentlemanly pursuit. The problem is, he hasn't got a captain to take him to one side and have a word with him, or better still take him off bowling altogether, because he is the captain! He can bowl for as long likes, in whatever way he likes. But this simply isn't cricket. It's a disgrace." The look of intense, concentrated fascination on Jim's face waited to see what would happen next, however, hardly suggested he was about to storm out in disgust!

By now, members of the Middlesex staff and officials had come onto the pitch to see if Matthews was all right, and several of them seemed to be urging him to leave the field. However Matthews, who had forced himself back onto his feet, was making it clear that he intended to continue, and no amount of coercion was going to persuade him otherwise. Smythe had also been talking to him in a concerned manner, but he finally seemed convinced that Matthews was in a fit state to continue his innings, and the captain returned to his end of the pitch.

"Matthews is a brave one all right. Told you he had the heart of a lion, didn't I, eh?" said Jim, his voice filled with admiration.

"Yes, he is brave," agreed Anna, in a much softer tone, but no less impressed. He was a lesson in bravery in fact. And then in a lower tone still she added, "I only hope he lives to see the day out."

Finally, the Middlesex staff gave up their attempts to encourage the injured batsman to leave the field, and the fielders took up their positions once more. Anna looked on in grim and fearful fascination as the brave young batsman took his guard again and prepared himself for the next ball. Higgins walked back to his bowling mark, catching the ball in his right hand from one of the fielders as he did so. Though the hail of abuse continued all around him, he now looked the calmest man in the ground. So calm in fact, that as he got closer to them, Anna could see he was smiling again! What did this man have to smile about? Anna had not thought it possible for Higgins to slip any lower in her estimation, but plumb new depths he had.

"Surely he won't bowl any more of those high bouncers, will he? Not after that?" Anna asked, turning again to Jim and Emily.

"I'm sure you're right, Anna. Surely even Higgins knows when enough's enough. He's had his revenge and left his mark – now let's hope he starts playing some proper cricket."

As Higgins finally approached the start of his run up, silence gripped the crowd once more. It was as though everyone was wondering the same thing. Would he dare do it again?

As Higgins reached his mark and turned to begin his run up, it would have been possible to hear a pin drop. The contrast with the uproarious din moments earlier could not have been more dramatic. Once again time seemed to have slowed and it took an eternity for Higgins to get into his stride. Anna looked at the plucky young batsman, whose marked face had returned to its former expression of resolute determination, but whose stance had altered slightly, evidently due to the pain in his side – the same side that faced the onrushing bowler now. And here he came roaring in, letting the ball rip from his hand. No grunt this time, but sure enough he had pitched it short yet again! The ball tore off the pitch and reared up like a spitting cobra, this time directly at the young man's head! However for all his pain, the batsman kept his eyes fixed on the ball, and this time it was met not with more venomous derision from the crowd but a roar of triumph, as the gallant young man had stepped backwards and slightly to the left, moved his body outside the line of the ball and glanced it downwards, sending it through a gap in the fielders waiting behind the wicket and rocketing towards the boundary rope, skilfully using the bowler's aggressive speed and power against him.

The noise of the crowd was deafening, and Anna joined them on their feet. However she was no longer shouting or even talking, for she was fully engrossed in the confrontation between the two men centre stage. Initially unnoticed by most, Higgins had continued down the pitch towards Matthews, gesticulating aggressively in a way which was clearly indicating to Matthews what the next ball would do to his head. However Matthews was unmoved, showing signs neither of fear nor aggression; he was the embodiment of controlled calm. He simply maintained his gaze, staring straight back into the eyes of his aggressor. This time the brute came within inches of the younger man's face, still shouting and gesturing at him in a way that made Anna briefly think he was actually about to strike him, before several of the Surrey players themselves intervened, and pushed their captain back in the direction he was bowling from.

"Not smirking now, is he? Doesn't like it when he doesn't get his own way. A classic bully!" shouted Jim above the cacophony, which had finally turned from ecstasy to wrath when everyone had realised what was happening. Anna nodded but did not speak. The duel between these two men, one so apparently gallant and one so clearly malevolent, held her entire attention. Oh how she wished she could have seen their respective auras at that moment. She could not, for the distance between her and them was too great, but she felt sure she already knew what their appearances would have revealed about their owners. How interesting this cricket had turned out to be, that it brought out the characters of its participants so clearly on the field of play! Anna was more deeply impressed by the young batsman than she could possibly have expressed, and it was no longer due to anything to do with his looks. It was the way in which he handled himself, the way he faced down the aggressive bully and refused to bow to his underhand methods, and above all the way he had maintained his calm, composure and control. Her uncle had been right – there was a huge amount to be learned here about the right and wrong way to conduct yourself, not only on the field of play but also in life and, she imagined, in the Struggle.

Anna contrasted Matthews's demeanour with the bedlam all about her, and indeed her own anger that she had felt only moments previously – the same anger she always felt in the face of injustice. Though she thought her outrage had been justified, she wondered about the effect that it might have on her own aura if it were sustained. The young man in the middle was teaching her the best way to deal with and channel such outrage, rather than allowing it to grow into uncontrolled aggression which would surely become self-damaging.

Back in the middle of the field, Matthews had not backed down an inch, nor had he broken eye contact with the bowler. The two of them stood face-to-face for several of the longest seconds Anna could remember, before the umpire finally seemed to remember his job and intervened to usher Higgins back on his way again. Anna could only imagine what Higgins had promised to do to Matthews, but the gallant batsman had not been intimidated, nor had he responded with any abuse of his own. Instead he had retained his air of pure calm and concentration as he stared down his opponent.

Anna looked up at the pavilion and wondered where her uncle might be. Of course she could not make him out, but she was certain that he would be up there somewhere, looking on and holding court over what was unfolding with the great and the good up there. She was also sure he would be sharing her sense of indignation, though knowing her uncle she had her suspicions that he would also secretly be revelling in the theatre of it all!

The sky had now been covered by a layer of even darker and more threatening clouds. It was almost as though the weather was following the match and changing according to its mood. Higgins had continued to roar in for ball after ball under that dark sky, and had unleashed one assault after another at his young opponent. The battle was even at first, Matthews striking some balls powerfully, whilst hanging on for dear life against others which threatened to see him off the field, and off this earth, for good. But he steadfastly refused to be cowed by the onslaught, or to show any outward signs of being intimidated, and as the overs passed the injurious blows from Higgins had become interspersed with more and more scoring shots from Matthews.

When it appeared that Higgins had done his worst

and that he would end this duel the beaten man, on the penultimate ball of what Jim had predicted would be his last over of this spell, the burly aggressor managed to summon from somewhere what looked to be not only his fastest ball of the day but also his deadliest of all. The venomous delivery reared fiercely off the pitch and darted treacherously from left to right through the air in the direction of Matthews' chest again, ultimately striking Matthews hard on the fingers of his right hand as he desperately brought his bat round to protect his inured ribs. The ball hit Matthews with a ferocity at least as great as that which had caused the previous batsman to retire hurt, and everyone thought his game was up and he would surely not be able to continue.

When Matthews again refused to leave the field, an enormous roar of approval swept across the entire ground, causing the hairs on Anna's neck to stand on end. The final ball of that over, another violent ball which had bounced up dangerously, was greeted with an almighty 'crack' as the bat sent it shooting straight back over the flailing hands of the big bowler and right over the boundary rope in front of Anna, having bounced only once. Anna had looked back to Matthews, who was now completing his dead-straight stroke, his front arm and uninjured left hand raised high in the air with his bat moving forward and upwards in a beautiful vertical arc. Not only had he managed to survive one of the most aggressive bowling spells ever seen at the venerable home of cricket, he had somehow come out of it on top.

For the first time since he had taken centre stage, Higgins suddenly took on the look of a beaten man.

The mighty crack of that last shot had been like a fatal wound to his own heart. He had thrown his worst into his underhand play, only to learn at the last that it had not been enough. He picked up his large cap from the umpire and looked at his team for some kind of support and encouragement, but none came. Finally he turned to take his place in the middle of the outfield on the left hand side, cutting a suddenly forlorn and downcast figure as the standing ovation for the young batsman continued unabated all around him.

Higgins had indeed taken himself out of the bowling after that over, and although he was to return later for three more overs, he was never again able to generate the same pace, line or aggression that he had achieved in that first session. Despite his various injuries, and several more short, high-bouncing balls delivered in his direction, Matthews had continued to gain in strength and had hit the burly bully all over the ground with strokes of ever increasing elegance and timing. Smythe had also started to inflict similar damage from the other end, taking his revenge for the harm that had been done to him in their last encounter here. Having had his bowling hammered to all sides of the ground, the brutish bowler had finally withdrawn himself from the attack for good, a defeated man.

Both Matthews and Smythe went on to make fine hundreds that day in a victory that would be spoken about at the home of cricket for many a long year, and the tearful standing ovation which greeted Matthews's century, during which the new Surrey bowler ignored the instructions of his captain and indeed the umpire and waited until the applause was finished before continuing, became the stuff of folklore. It transpired later that Matthews had suffered two broken fingers in his right hand and severe bruising to his ribs, with one or two suspected to have been cracked, and many of those who were there would maintain to their dying days that it was the bravest innings they ever saw.

The Long Room

When the day's play was finally over and the jubilant crowd had begun to disperse, Jim's attention returned to his mission, which was to get Anna safely to her uncle. Jim led Emily and Anna gently against the tide of people, and headed towards the pavilion. The entrances facing the pitch were strictly for players and members, they were informed, and they would need to approach the edifice from the back if they wished to inquire further.

Upon rounding the building, Jim paused, looked a little sheepishly at Emily and said, "Darling, there's something I need to tell you. The pavilion is for members only, and members are only men, so I don't think you'll be allowed in. I'm so sorry, my dear."

"Don't worry Jim, I already knew that. You know I don't approve of that kind of thing, but I understand the rules and conventions, especially in places such as this, and today is not the day to fight that battle. There are more and more of us who believe that these old rules which govern society are going to change one of these days – and I believe the time will come when even this place will accept women, you mark my words!" Anna noted the sudden sparkle in Emily's eyes as she spoke.

Jim responded, "Well you know I have great sympathy for your cause darling, and I hope you're right. But I don't think even you can bring about that change in the next twenty minutes, so if you could wait outside where there are plenty of stewards to keep you safe..."

Emily laughed, "Yes, of course I will Jim, don't worry.

I'll wait for you here. But you're not a member either, and as attractive and well-mannered a young person as Anna is, I don't think she is going to qualify as a gentleman either," she grinned at Anna, "so how are you going to get in?"

"To be quite honest I don't rightly know myself. I suppose we're relying on Anna's uncle to sort all that out. It was his idea to meet Anna in here after all."

Anna gave Emily a last look, received the encouragement she sought, took a deep breath and began to follow Jim's ascent up the stone steps in front of them. They led to the door of the large building, at once both majestic and imposing, and with each step Anna grew more nervous. The appearance of those around them and the overall atmosphere told her that they were now entering a place of some importance, and from what she had heard and the looks she was receiving, she was far from sure that they were going to be welcomed. Anna disliked having attention drawn to her at the best of times, and doubly so in a place of such apparent significance as this. Whatever happened, she did not want to be the cause of a scene here.

As they approached the double doors at the top of the stairs, a formally dressed man in a top hat, long coat and brightly-coloured red and gold striped cravat prevented any further progress inside. "No ladies or girls allowed, and you are not dressed appropriately to enter yourself sir, either." There was no mistaking the slight disdain in the man's voice as he leant slightly forward and continued, looking down his nose, "Are you a member sir?" The look in the man's beady eyes and the angle of his raised left eyebrow indicated that he already knew the answer to that question.

"No sir, I'm sorry, I am not a member. But this young lady's uncle is, and he asked that she be brought here to meet him."

"Oh yes? And who might her uncle be?" asked the steward, his eyes narrowing, his voice steeped in suspicion.

"His name is James Lawrence," replied Jim simply. Anna was not sure if Jim had known the transformative effect that these words might have, but at their very mention their inquisitor's demeanour changed entirely.

"Mr Lawrence? Oh I see. Why, you should have mentioned that sooner!" was the steward's response, suddenly almost standing to attention. All hint of suspicion had vanished as though it had been a mere figment of their imaginations. "Please wait here – I shall ask him if he's ready to see you." With that he made off briskly inside the building.

In the couple of minutes it took for him to reappear, several formally dressed men entered and left the pavilion. Much to Anna's relief, none seemed to pay them much attention, perhaps not considering it could possibly be their intention to enter the hallowed sanctuary. Of course there was not a woman amongst them. For his part, Jim stood motionless, looking down to avoid the gaze of any of those who passed them. It was as though they really were standing on the steps of some holy temple, being passed by priests in whose presence they were not worthy.

Anna's musings were soon brought to an end by the return of the steward, whose transformation into a polite and respectful human being was now complete. Addressing Jim, he said, "The young lady may enter to meet her uncle. You may accompany her until she is safely with him." Jim and Anna both offered their grateful thanks and followed the man through the doors.

Once inside, Anna could make little out as her eyes took time to grow accustomed to the relative darkness. The first thing that struck her was the thick smell of tobacco smoke that lay heavily on the air. As they followed the steward, she gradually began to make out the room they were in more clearly. It was a long room, with paintings of cricketers, presumably famous ones from times past, filling much of the wall space, separated only by the odd tall bookcase – no doubt filled with books about cricket.

The furniture and décor all looked rather fine and expensive, and altogether this seemed to be a far more refined place than anything which lay outside. The conversations that could be heard all around them were about the match just finished – the underhand deeds, the epic struggle and the heroic conclusion to the day. Important-looking men with grave faces in one group were discussing some fine details of the laws of the game in the light of the day's events, whilst several other groups were busily dissecting every aspect of the performances. There was one thing which was common to all – a deep and profound knowledge of cricket. 'It's still only a game,' thought Anna, 'and yet clearly it's a good deal more than that. It's part of an entire way of life for these people, and it sounds from their talk as though they try to apply the codes of conduct from this sport to life in general.' Anna had to concede that cricket had turned out to be a far more interesting phenomenon than she had thought.

As they were gradually led into the heart of the room, Anna was better able to make out the individual faces of the men they were being ushered past, and the further they progressed the more those faces began to express their surprise. Surprise, and some disapproval it had to be said. Anna searched desperately amongst the faces for that of her uncle, but without success.

As they approached the far side of the room, led by the steward, one senior gentleman with ruddy round cheeks, bulging eyes and a silver-grey waistcoat stretched so tightly across his ample belly that Anna feared the buttons might fire off in all directions at any moment, finally voiced what all the other looks had been expressing. "Excuse me steward, but what do you mean by allowing a girl into the pavilion? Not to mention her inappropriately dressed companion?"

There were one or two grunts of support for this line of questioning, if not for its manner. As always in such situations, Anna switched her focus to the portly man's aura, and was surprised to find it an essentially blue specimen, indicating the character of a fundamentally good man, albeit with some tell-tale roughness and markings near its surface which Anna took to indicate a certain arrogance, and the intransigence which his words had already suggested. On hearing the man's challenge, Anna started to brace herself for that scene she had been so keen to avoid when another, more familiar voice spoke up from behind them.

"Sir Cuthbert, I do beg your pardon, but this young lady is my niece and it was I that asked the steward to bring her in here to meet me. I do understand that it goes against our code for females of any kind to be allowed in here – indeed, I don't ever recall seeing one in here before – but I needed to meet with my niece on some urgent family business that could not wait. I intend to hold our meeting in one of the committee rooms at the back, so we will not disturb you. I trust that we may be permitted to make a brief exception to the rules in this case?"

What Sir Cuthbert had made of Uncle James's proposition was never to be known, however. For just at that moment, from the other direction, a small group of men wearing cricketers' whites were making their way through the room towards them, and generating even more attention as they did so than Jim and Anna had. They were Surrey players, and in their midst was the hulking figure of their captain, Higgins. He was carrying a large tankard of frothy liquid, some of which had already applied itself to his long, drooping moustache, somehow making him look even more like a walrus than before. The ruddiness of the big man's cheeks suggested that this was not his first such tankard of the evening either. Though the language of the finely-dressed gentlemen who were now crowding around the players was more restrained than it had been outside, as everything in this place was, they left no doubt as to their opinions regarding the spectacle they had seen earlier that day.

One particularly tall, stick-like man with a long, protruding nose, who was clutching a small glass of dark red-brown liquid, poked a bony finger in the direction of the burly cricketer and said, "You, sir, are nothing but a cad and a blaggard. You should never again be allowed to set foot on a field of play and stain the honourable name of our great game with your barbaric behaviour." Murmurs of support and 'hear hear' sounded from all around. Higgins had been ultimately humiliated on the field, and in the process had evolved from a hated enemy to a figure of mockery in the minds of the massed ranks of Middlesex supporters outside. However, the men of this pavilion had longer memories and deeper sensibilities regarding the sanctity of the game, and the transgressions of this burly ruffian had gone far beyond the point of jest and merry-making. A line of acceptability had been crossed – or rather, decimated – and for that there could be no forgiveness.

Higgins might have been humbled in the match, and his team might have fallen to a heavy defeat, but there was something in the barbs directed at him from this cricketing establishment which seemed to make his hackles rise again. A defiant look crossed his broad face once more, and as he jutted out his chin, his long, be-frothed, walrus-like moustache drooped into even more of a frown than before.

"Get out of my way," he grunted, shoving his way past the long, thin, finger-poking man, causing the latter to lose his balance and topple clean over. Higgins continued to march forward, chin first, without so much as a backward glance at the sprawling figure behind him, who was finally helped back to his feet by various outraged companions. As the protests grew more vociferous, Higgins came to a stop again and suddenly let out a huge guffaw. He had clapped eyes on Anna.

"And what's all this then?" he barked with sudden

glee at this opportunity presented to him. "So you allow womenfolk in your club now, do you? And not even a woman come to that, but a little girl? In the 'Home of Cricket'? I knew you'd let your standards drop, but I had no idea of the depths to which you had plunged, allowing little girls to run around freely in here. Mind you, it may be no bad thing, given what a bunch of old women the rest of you all are – needed some younger females in here to even out the ages a little!" Higgins laughed heartily, clearly very pleased with his own joke, and looked around at his Surrey team mates for approval. The latter, however, turned out to be much more aware than Higgins of their surroundings, and they refrained from joining in his merriment. They looked as though they would rather be anywhere other than there, or more precisely, anywhere other than with Higgins, and several began to apologise to those around them for their captain's behaviour.

In the meantime, Anna's blood had started to rise again. The sight alone, close-up, of this big bully who had behaved in such an abominable way earlier had already set her off, and his words, especially his dismissive reference to her being a 'little girl' in front of all these presumably important people, was the final straw. Anna had focused momentarily on his aura, and she had seen exactly what she was expecting. It was the horribly discoloured and disfigured specimen of a man whose arrogance overrode all other qualities, and whose consideration for the feelings of others had over the years become almost non-existent. Trying to channel her anger in the way she had seen Matthews do in dealing with this same man, Anna's outrage overcame her customary shyness. Before anyone else was able to respond, Anna replied to the large man in a tone which, on later reflection, was to remind her of her own mother.

"Higgins, you are nothing but a bully and a coward. You should be thoroughly ashamed of yourself for what you did today, and even more so for what you tried to do. I was told that cricket was a game played by gentlemen, but I don't believe you have a gentlemanly bone or an ounce of decency in your entire body. I'm so glad that Matthews put you in your place. He is everything you're not. A noble hero and a true gentleman. Those are qualities that you will never possess, and he showed us all that bullies and ruffians like you will always lose in the end!" Even Anna herself wasn't quite sure where this little speech had come from, but she supposed it had been building up inside her the entire afternoon.

Higgins's face started to redden and he appeared genuinely stunned that this meek little object of his ridicule should take it upon itself to answer him back in such a way. He grappled for a response, but his predicament was compounded by the sudden, uproarious laughter and support for Anna's outburst from all around them. It seemed that in the face of a common foe as despicable as Higgins, any disapproval of Anna's gender and age could be set to one side. Well, for the time being.

Finding his day's humiliation in danger of being completed by a mere child, a girl, here in the very heartland of his enemy, Higgins now seemed to lose all self-control. He threw his tankard to the ground, sending its frothy contents in all directions, and lunged forward threateningly towards Anna. Anna braced herself, and she felt Jim make a move from her side to protect her, but the moustachioed bully coming towards them was able to take no more than two steps before a tall, strong, elegantly-dressed figure stepped directly in front of him and stopped him dead in his tracks.

"Lay one finger on her, and know that it will be the last movement you ever make," said Anna's uncle in a voice more commanding than any Anna had ever heard, as he looked directly into the bulkier man's eyes. Higgins stopped suddenly at this intervention. Triggered by a recent memory, her heart now beating fast, Anna instinctively shifted her focus to the two men's auras. She could see that her uncle's pure blue aura already had a grip upon the other man's, and it appeared that through this contact he had rendered the burly ruffian immediately helpless. So her uncle really did have the same power she had! All laughter and other sounds around them had now ceased as everyone trained their eyes on the confrontation, ready no doubt to intervene if needed. However, it was all over in an instant. Anna's uncle slightly loosened his grip on his opponent's aura, and spoke in the same clear and commanding tone. "Now leave this place where you are not welcome, and never return!"

Higgins hesitated a moment more, his expression a combination of surprise and confusion, and then he did as he was told. With a gentle, final push from Uncle James's aura on his, Higgins turned on his heel, and muttering under his breath he lumbered his way back through the parting crowd and out of the room, head down, looking only at the ground.

Applause broke out all around them, interspersed with

the occasional 'Bravo!' and 'Well done, James!'

"And well said young lady!" added Sir Cuthbert, turning to Anna and giving her an approving wink of one bulbous eye before turning away to discuss these latest events with his companions. No-one had any more to say about Anna's gender in their hallowed meeting place, and Uncle James was able to lead her and Jim to a door at the back of the room, hindered now only by hearty handshakes, slaps on the back and congratulatory comments from all those they passed.

"All in all, Higgins has had a very bad day," remarked Anna's uncle with a large grin after passing through the door and closing it behind them, "and one I don't believe he will forget for a long time. I do hope he has learned his lesson. I do not believe he will disrespect this great game of ours again in quite such a hurry – not here at Lord's anyhow. Would that all instances of right and wrong were so easily dealt with, and that all men who would cause needless injury and humiliation were so easily dispatched. Alas that is not always so, but today has been a good day at least. Here's to justice being done and to a momentous Middlesex victory!" With that he raised the wine glass which had been handed to him on their passage through the crowd in a toast, and without letting the small detail that neither of his companions had a glass between them deter him, he drained the contents with great satisfaction. Anna suspected this was far from the first such glass he had drunk that day, and yet he appeared still to be well in control.

"By the way Anna, well done for standing up to Higgins out there. I don't mind admitting that you took me completely by surprise at how you dealt with him, so I can't begin to imagine what it did to Higgins. I've never seen you talk like that before – but I commend you. Made me proud to be your uncle!"

"I hope I didn't offend anyone by speaking so, um, directly," responded Anna, attempting hurriedly to disguise the sudden rush of inexplicable pride at his words. "I mean, I know I'm only a girl and that I'm not even supposed to be in here. I do hope you won't get into any trouble for bringing such an unladylike niece into this place!" she laughed a little nervously.

"Anna, so good of you to think of such things, but please do not concern yourself. On the contrary, I would think they might be calling you a chip off the old Lawrence block, or at least I flatter myself to hope they might. The members may have very particular ways and traditions which they protect most fiercely – and most of them are good traditions and kept for good reason, if not quite all – but most importantly they have a very acute sense of fair play. What we witnessed on the cricket field today was not a joke, it went far beyond anything that might be considered funny, and every one of the members here saw it as not only rough play, but as a personal insult to them and to the spirit of cricket. So to see the way you confronted that ruffian, and to hear you express so eloquently the things that everyone had felt – well I don't think they could have been more pleased with you. Even that pompous ass Sir Cuthbert seemed to have been won over. It means more to me than I can say to see that you have that kind of spirit in you. It is exactly that spirit which we are going to need in the Struggle ahead." And with that last remark, her uncle's face became deadly serious again. Serious and, Anna noted, suddenly rather tired-looking.

Turning to Jim, Uncle James continued, "And I would like to thank you very much for bringing Anna here today and for making sure she was safe. I am very grateful to you."

Anna was startled by what happened next, for Jim suddenly went down onto one knee, bowed his head and said, "Master, it was my pleasure to carry out the bidding of the Order." It was just how her uncle had behaved with Mr Warwick. Anna's uncle however showed not a glimmer of surprise as he gave a brief but formal nod of his head in return. And with that, Jim rose to his feet again and turned to leave the room.

"Thank you for everything, Jim," Anna called out behind him as he opened the door.

"My pleasure, Anna, my absolute pleasure. Maybe you'll come with me to the cricket again sometime?" He smiled, bade farewell and left.

Anna and her uncle ate some ham, bread and cheese that Uncle James had ordered, then they set off for Mr Warwick's shop. Their journey this time was happily uneventful. Seeing Mr Warwick again for the first time in a while upon their arrival, Anna noticed that like her uncle, he too looked more tired than the last time they had met, although he still retained his customarily jovial air.

"My dear Anna, so good to see you again," he greeted her.

"It is good to see you too, Mr Warwick," she responded, and she meant it. The excitement was starting to build inside her – the long wait to resume the dialogue with Mr

Warwick was finally over.

"The time has come for your instruction to begin," said Mr Warwick, as he brought several large books which appeared to be of great age over to his chair. Anna was about to begin the journey which would finally reveal those truths about the world of which she had been shown such tantalising glimpses of late. Her pulse quickened as she waited for Mr Warwick to begin.

Instruction

"Now," said the old man, "there exists an enormous body of thought and practice relating to the Powers and the Struggle, in fact more knowledge than any one person could learn in a lifetime. The purpose of the first stage of your instruction is to equip you with the basic elements of knowledge and practical training in the Powers, and to begin your journey in the cause of the Alpha World – a journey that will last for the rest of your days.

"It is unfortunate for us all that you are about to undertake this instruction at a point in history when we face a very grave threat from the Omega World, possibly the gravest we have ever faced. What this means is that we will conduct your training in a shorter space of time than usual, since we cannot be sure when you will need to apply the skills and knowledge you are going to learn. However, your teaching will still cover the five major elements which have formed the basis of instruction within our Order for centuries.

"The first element is 'The Theory', which covers the nature of the Alpha World that we are striving to achieve, what we know of the Omega World, the winds of influence of the Opposing Energy, the nature of the essence and how it may change or be changed over time, and other related matters. It is in The Theory that we start to lay out the philosophy of the Alpha World, and it is important, because we defeat the forces of the Omega World not only through our skills in combat, but also through our knowledge and our purity of thought.

"The second element of the instruction is 'The Histories', which cover the known human history of the Alpha-Omega Struggle and the lessons we can learn from it. We study The Histories not only for the interest of understanding the key events in the Struggle which underpinned some of the great events in the history of the general population, but because we can draw from it a set of practical lessons and strategies which may be applied to the future challenges we will face. The Histories also provide us with a tremendous source of inspiration, through the deeds of the great knights who have gone before us, and through the bravery and the determination that they displayed in their own time to persevere and never to be defeated in the cause that they believed to be right.

"The third element of your instruction will be 'The Nature of the Enemy'. This takes us from the overall Theory into the specifics of the different forms that our enemies take, of which there are many, what we know of how they operate, the kinds of individual missions they tend to run and the ways in which each may be defeated. It is by knowing our enemy and understanding who they are, what they seek to achieve, their modus operandi, in fact everything we can about them, that we may gain the upper hand and maximise our chance of defeating them when the time for combat comes.

"The fourth element is 'The Order of the Knights of the True Path', where we will explain to you more about the Order to which I keep referring. This will explain who we are, our hierarchy and how we are organised. We will also explain something of our history, the different roles and abilities of our members, for example Seers, Healers and so on, and the unbreakable Codes of Honour by which we all live and act.

"Then the fifth and final element is 'The Practice', in which the lessons from the other four elements are brought together and the key techniques in applying the Powers in the real world are practiced. This involves training in reading and interacting with essences – one topic on which you may also actually be able to teach us, Anna! It will also include Seeing, which covers reading the patterns and foreseeing certain things yet to come, although there are few who possess this skill with any real strength, so it remains theoretical for most people. Then there is Healing, which teaches how damaged essences may be healed, and for those who have this power, the fundamental rules which must be followed in doing so. And then there is the area that appears to excite most new scholars the greatest," a quick, knowing glance from Mr Warwick at her uncle, "at least that is until they fully understand it and its terrifying implications. That is mental 'Combat'. I believe your uncle here, for example, initially would happily have foregone any and all of the first four elements and probably a good deal of the fifth too, to have launched straight into his mental combat training, such was his nature. However, that training would not have been in any way effective had I allowed him to do so. James, would you agree?"

Uncle James reacted with a somewhat injured expression, which he turned first on his old Master and then on Anna, before creasing it into a crooked smile and replying, "That is, in fact, absolutely true – but indeed, what else would you have expected of me? Alas, I'm afraid that was part of my nature, for better or for worse – and indeed at different times it turned out to be for both! However, Anna, I now freely acknowledge that to be truly effective in mental combat, it is essential to understand the theory first. Without this you will be fighting blind, and you will be bound for defeat in the end." Then turning back to his master he added, "By the way Edmund, did the Order ever give you that medal you said you had earned for persevering with me and finally turning me into the fine mental combatant I am today?"

"No, as a matter of fact, I don't believe they did! What I would add though, Anna, is that since learning this lesson and taking the theoretical elements of the instruction on board, your uncle has in fact become a very fine exponent of the art of mental combat – in fact I do not flatter him, although I do run the risk of feeding his already not insubstantial self-esteem even further, by calling him one of the very finest amongst our Order at his age. If only he had listened to what he was told a bit sooner, imagine how good he could have been..." said Mr Warwick with another quick, sly grin.

"So to conclude, The Practice, including mental combat and defence, will form a critical element of your training, as soon as the theoretical groundwork has been laid. And it is in The Practice that you will learn the techniques of combating and ultimately defeating a Satal.

"Now, on this topic there is something important that I should make you aware of. To the best of my knowledge, you may be the youngest person ever to receive this instruction – certainly in modern times anyhow. We should not underestimate the toll this may take on you. For of necessity, to practice the techniques and truly prepare you for combat with a Satal, and the emotions that go with such an experience, we must replicate that combat situation. For the training to be effective we have no choice but to do this, but it can sometimes be a terrifying experience even for a grown adult. To prepare you fully there is no way around this, and I do not pretend that it will be without its dangers, but all I ask is that you trust us to conduct this combat practice as safely as we can. You have my word that we will, and that of your uncle."

"Mr Warwick," Anna spoke up, "I'm afraid I don't feel the same way my uncle did regarding mental combat. To be honest I was shocked to learn that essences can be used as a *weapon*. Until recently I had only seen essences as a reflection of a person's character and personality, and the purer it was the better. It just doesn't seem right to me that an essence should be used to fight other people!"

"Very interesting, Anna. You have been able to see these things since you were a very small child, so it is natural that you do not see the essence as something to be used actively. And in fact it is our firm belief that if the pure Alpha state were to be achieved, there would be no need for mental combat. However in the unstable, contaminated world in which we exist today, there are those who would attack us against whom we must defend ourselves, and then of course there are creatures such as Satals who are not of this world, and whom we can only defeat and banish using mental combat. So, undesirable as it may seem, I am afraid that to finally achieve the Alpha state we have no choice but to learn the art and be prepared to engage in mental combat with our enemies. However, your instincts are still valid in one sense. It is the way in which we engage in mental combat that is of crucial importance. There is a right way, one which will not lead to self-inflicted damage of our own essences through our conduct, and wrong ways, which can do extreme damage to them. All this we will explain to you."

Her uncle re-joined the conversation. "Anna, I haven't mentioned this to you, but young Gregory Matthews who you saw in action at the cricket match this afternoon is in fact a student of mine, and I am leading his instruction in the Powers at the moment, in the same way that Mr Warwick has now started to lead yours. Indeed, to see Greg in action was one of the main reasons I asked for you to attend today's match – and thankfully he did not disappoint! Hopefully you learned something from watching him."

Anna was dumbfounded. So that dashing young hero Matthews also had 'the Powers', and he was a student of her uncle!

"Now although the cricket field is clearly different from the field of mental combat, there were lessons to be taken from how Greg faced down Higgins this afternoon, such as the way to conduct yourself in a situation of confrontation, without compromising yourself and jeopardising the purity of your own essence. I could not have been prouder of Greg today, not for the century he scored but for the way in which he controlled his emotions and conducted himself. Even the fact that he resisted using his essence against Higgins on the field of play when he could easily have done so, showed that he was in full control of his emotions and temper. Greg is one of the very finest young students in the Powers of his generation, and you will have the chance to meet him in person before too long. Indeed it is a meeting I very much look forward to, as I believe you may both one day go on to play very important roles in the Struggle in your own ways, in the fullness of time."

Anna merely nodded, wide-eyed, to indicate her understanding. In recalling the gallantry and bravery she had witnessed that afternoon, the fires of excitement about her own instruction roared brighter still.

"Yes indeed," Mr Warwick added, "young Matthews is indeed one of our finest prospects, and another who brings us hope for the Alpha World. And by all accounts he is not a bad batsman either!"

"Yes his performance was amazing today, and I really did feel that I learned a lot from watching him. I look forward to meeting him." Anna's mind was racing now. She decided to seize the opportunity to change the subject slightly and raise one of her biggest questions.

"Mr Warwick, I know we are about to start my instruction, but may I ask you a question first? Because I think it may be related to the Struggle. Have you heard about the Beast of Highgate?" Anna sensed both men freeze momentarily, their full attention upon her.

"Yes Anna, I have heard the news stories," Mr Warwick was the first to respond, carefully. "May I inquire why you ask?"

This initial reaction of the two men made Anna hesitate. They were bound to know that she was not supposed to the leave the house without permission, and they would be particularly concerned if they knew how much danger she had got herself into. However, her mother already knew all about it and had scolded her thoroughly, and she was sure her two mentors would understand the course of events if she shared the whole story with them. But in particular, she felt sure that the information she now had might be important to them, and equally she was desperate to have some of her own questions answered. She might learn something useful in her mission to help her friends and their families out of their troubles.

"Well, Mr Warwick, um, you see..." she replied, "I have seen the Beast." Her statement was met with total stunned silence. She felt the level focus upon her raised yet another notch.

"You have seen the Beast? Would you mind very much if I asked you to tell us when this was and what happened?" Again it was Mr Warwick who spoke. His voice was calm and light, but it was clear he had been taken by surprise by this news. Anna's uncle's face now bore a deadly serious expression.

"No, I wouldn't mind, Mr Warwick. I want to talk about it," Anna responded. She shared all the relevant details of her adventure in Highgate and Hampstead. Both men listened with avid interest as she spoke. First she told of the stories she had heard concerning the Beast of Highgate, then of the trouble that Knowles and Kenny Gillespie were making for her friends' brothers and their intention to find information that could put them in jail. She recounted the journey to Highgate and the sighting of the odious old man in the decrepit house, then of the struggle outside the mansion, and finally of their encounter with the Beast itself. Anna spared none of the details she thought could be important, from the ugly black jewel on the old man's finger and the condition of his aura, to the physical appearance of the Beast. Neither man spoke throughout her retelling of the story, although she could sense the tension building within them both as they listened. In particular, at the description of the old man with the black ring, Anna's uncle growled audibly and even spat uncharacteristically into the roaring fire. She had seldom seen him so agitated. For his part, Mr Warwick made no sound at all as he sat motionless, listening, but his eyes blazed.

As Anna described the battle on the stairs outside the mansion, when she reached the point at which the old man had attempted to stab Timmy's aura with his own which had been transformed into that terrible spike, Anna's uncle again cursed audibly under his breath and he began to pace the room, his hands clasped behind his back, his face a picture of fury. He looked angrier than Anna had ever seen him, and it was clear that he knew the identity of this old man. Her own curiosity was roused further still, but she continued with her story. When she relayed the details of the old villain being unceremoniously thrown over the wall of the stairs into the darkness below, she heard her uncle mutter almost as though to himself, "Good girl, Anna, good girl! Well done!" Anna could tell that both men were storing a mountain of questions, and for her part she was dying to ask a number of her own, but all were held in check until her story was over. It was only when she had finished recounting how the demonic winged creature had finally carried the body away over the house rooftop and how they had all escaped that either man broke his silence. As usual, it was Mr Warwick who did so first.

"Anna, well, that was quite some adventure you had! Not to mention a tragic one in the end. And you really were in the most fearful danger yourself too, though from the way you have described it, it is clear that you already understood that at the time. In fact I believe you even knew that certain decisions you were making might literally have been fatal, and yet you made them nonetheless and you did what you believed to be the right thing. You certainly put yourself freely in harm's way without support, and I am more relieved than you may ever know that in the end harm did not come to you.

"A not insignificant part of me wants to scold you for being so reckless and for taking such chances. However I shall resist on this occasion, and I shall not criticise you for your actions. Apart from anything else, I am certain you have already received a full reprimand from your mother," Mr Warwick gave Anna a quick wink at that before continuing, "and additionally, in the final analysis you acted as the best amongst our Order – the very best – would have sought to do in that situation. Although it is my most fervent hope that you do not find yourself alone in such a position again for a very long time, I cannot fault your conduct and your bravery."

"But Mr Warwick, I wasn't alone. I was with friends who acted just as bravely as me, and they faced the same danger to try to save those two boys."

"Anna, you are right, and I stand corrected. I was so preoccupied with your situation that I did not pay due respect to your friends. However you are right, you have a remarkable group of companions there, and I am greatly encouraged to hear it. But rather, to put it more plainly, I meant to say that you faced this situation without the support of people fully trained in the Powers, and specifically in the art of mental combat.

"Anna, although you did not think of it in these terms at the time, in the events you described you took on a truly formidable foe in mental combat without any training whatsoever, and somehow you were able to emerge victorious. There are precious few within our Order with years of training who could have been confident in taking on such an enemy and achieving that outcome. I do not doubt that the element of surprise may have come to your aid somewhat, but nonetheless, the fact that you were able to gain the upper hand before your training has even begun quite takes my breath away."

Pausing for a moment to gather his thoughts, a slight look of concern crossed his face as he continued, "Anna, in saving the life of your friend, and make no mistake, the blow aimed at your companion's essence could well have killed him had you not intervened, it sounds as though you received a savage blow to your own essence. Would you permit me to view it now, so that we might confirm that no lasting damage has been done?"

"Certainly Mr Warwick," she replied quickly, and she waited to hear what he had to say with more than a little apprehension as the old man subtly shifted his focus. Mr Warwick appeared to be examining something in his mind's eye for several moments and her uncle also drew closer and joined him. Finally, having apparently completed his study, his look returned to meet Anna's nervous one and he spoke again.

"Anna, I think it must have been a truly savage blow you received, for your essence still contains visible signs of the impact it made. I can see that the wound did indeed go very deep." At that, Anna heard the sound of a fist pounding into a palm and another oath uttered from the direction of her uncle whose back was now turned again. Mr Warwick continued, "I can understand just how painful this must have been for you at the time, and you were remarkably strong and brave to be able to withstand such an attack and to fight back.

"However, most importantly of all, I do not believe any lasting harm has been done, for although the mark is still visible, the blow has done nothing to discolour your essence; there is merely an area where the blue is more transparent. I can already see that the full colour is returning to this area from the centre, and I am confident that your essence will be fully restored very soon."

"Oh, thank you Mr Warwick," said Anna, immensely relieved, and glancing up she saw a look of equal relief in the eyes of her uncle.

Mr Warwick continued, "Anna, I am as pleased as you are to find out just how tremendously resilient you are! I'm sure there are many who would not have been able to withstand such an attack, and as with so many things that we are learning about you, this bodes well for what lies ahead of us."

The old man paused again, deciding where to take the conversation next. "Anna, would you mind very much if we now asked you some questions about what happened?"

"No, of course not Mr Warwick, and I hope you may be able to explain to me some of the things that I have been wondering about as well."

"I think we may indeed be able to do that. But first, that house you described in Highgate town, where you first saw the old man with the ring. Can you remember the name of the street?" The distinctive name came back to her immediately. "Yes, it was called Eagle Street."

"Eagle Street," repeated Mr Warwick thoughtfully, as though running the name over in his mind. "I don't suppose you happen to remember the house number do you?"

"Um, sorry, no Mr Warwick, I'm afraid I don't. But you would certainly recognise it if you saw it. It looks completely different from all the other houses there. It's the same design and shape as the rest, but somehow it looks much older and in a much poorer condition than all the others."

"All right, Anna that should be good enough then. And that old man, you say he wore a ring with a black jewel on it?"

"Yes, that's right," Anna replied.

"Damn him!" Anna's uncle suddenly broke his silence. "How dare he wear it so openly, so brazenly?"

Anna half expected Mr Warwick to rebuke her uncle for speaking up in such a way, but instead he merely nodded in silence for a moment. Anna was sure she could read a slight look of sadness in his expression.

"Mr Warwick, Uncle, could you tell me who that horrible man was?" she asked, looking from one man to the other and then back again. "It's clear that you both know him. He isn't a Satal is he? From what you have told me before, I don't suppose we would have been able to fight him and survive if he had been."

Anna's uncle let out a brief snort as Anna was speaking, but it was Mr Warwick who answered the question, after first taking a deep breath.

"Anna, yes we do know who that man is. His name is Mortlock. Joseph Mortlock. And you are correct, he is not a Satal. Much might he enjoy the comparison, I fancy. But Anna, please make no mistake, although he is not a Satal and he does not possess the power of one, he is still a very dangerous man indeed."

There was a long pause now, as the kindly old man gathered himself for the story he was about to tell, exchanging meaningful glances with Anna's uncle as he did so. Then finally he began, and completely stunned Anna with his very first sentence.

Joseph Mortlock

"Many years ago, when I was but a young man of twenty-one and still in the very early stages of my own instruction, I counted Joseph Mortlock as my best friend in the world. Inseparable we were, and two of the finest students of the Powers of our generation they used to say, if you will excuse my immodesty for the sake of recounting the story. Difficult though it is to imagine, looking upon him now, Joseph Mortlock was once a fine, upstanding young man, and a very good one. Not to mention devilishly handsome. Very popular with the young ladies was Joseph, but he always handled himself in the most gentlemanly manner. Perhaps another time when I have more stomach for it, I will tell you more about his younger days, and the adventures he and I had together. But I'm afraid that will not be tonight."

Anna couldn't believe what she was hearing. That foul old man, with such an ugly sneer and evil-looking aura – he had been Mr Warwick's best friend? And a good man? And handsome? A more complete transformation in a person she could not imagine. What could possibly have happened to cause that?

"During your instruction, amongst many other things you will learn more about the nature of our enemy in the Struggle. The Opposing Energy uses a variety of foes against us, but some of the most dangerous, and some of the saddest cases, are what we call 'Turners'. Turners are people who start on the Alpha side of the struggle, but whose heads become influenced by the illusory allures of the Opposing Energy, and they turn their powers against us. Most sadly for me, not to mention for the cause that we all share, Joseph Mortlock is such a case.

"Until we were both around twenty-five, Joseph was still a good man, with a large and predominantly pure blue essence. I say predominantly; at the time everyone thought him very pure indeed. However, being better able to view people's essences than most, in truth I was aware of certain minor flaws in his essence, what appeared to be tiny blemishes on the surface of its sphere. But at that time I did not understand what they might suggest, or more precisely, what vulnerabilities they might indicate, and I did not give the matter too much thought when through all his actions Joseph had always shown himself to be the most splendid of fellows. And he was a good mental combatant too. He could hold his own with almost anyone in a battle of the essences, but he always fought in the most even-handed of ways.

"Things only started to change sometime after his twenty-fifth birthday. I had no idea at the time, but in hindsight it seems that, despite his many gifts and strengths in the Powers, Joseph also had his insecurities. And, unbelievable though it would have been to me then, I learned later that he harboured some kind of jealousy towards my achievements. Now I tell you Anna, and not through any modesty on my part, I do not believe my achievements in the Powers actually outshone Joseph's at all. Certainly we each had our own particular areas of expertise in which one excelled over the other, but in truth I believe we were very well matched, and I never thought myself the better man. And when it came to courting young ladies, well I can tell you that I lost out to Joseph by a country mile! However, whatever the reason, it seems that Joseph saw things differently. It appears that he was more desperate for approval than he let on, and with that came some degree of paranoia about his own abilities, and about what people thought of him. What I now know is that those blemishes on the surface of his essence indicated these flaws in his character, which it turns out left him fatally open to the seductive influence of the Opposing Energy.

"Who can say how the winds of malevolent influence of the Opposing Energy may have blown upon Joseph Mortlock's essence during those years of his early and mid-twenties. Who knows with what strength they bore down upon him, to what degree he attempted to resist them and what secret mental turmoil he may have gone through. Did an internal battle rage within him against their influence, or was he even conscious of them at first? We cannot know. What is certain now is that those blemishes in his essence left him vulnerable to certain aspects of the effect of those winds, like a ship's sails as I have mentioned to you previously, unfurled during a terrible storm, always vulnerable to moving in the direction that those evil winds were driving him.

"If only I had been able to read the signs at the time..." Mr Warwick was no longer looking at Anna, but into the middle distance in front of him, almost as though he were now talking to himself, "I would have dealt with Joseph entirely differently. I would have been able to help him, I am certain of it. However, to my eternal regret, I did not read the signs.

"Anna, one of the things you will learn is that the Opposing Energy plays very cleverly and subtly upon the flaws that exist within people's characters, and well it might, since those flaws are a direct result of the very contamination of the universe which the Opposing Energy itself caused. Two examples of the flaws to which I refer are jealousy and greed, which make people hunger for things they do not need, and which ultimately will not make them happy, but which they crave and yearn for nonetheless. Joseph Mortlock had such character flaws, although he did precious little outwardly to reveal them until it was too late.

"The Opposing Energy has ways of luring people to move in its direction by playing on their desires, offering its victims wealth, power, praise, fame... whatever it is that the person most craves from the world around them. But it does so in very gentle and gradual ways which often fail to arouse suspicion at first. Through the many tentacles that the Opposing Energy has, it has an almost infinite variety of ways to manipulate situations and to provide seemingly irresistible temptations to those who are vulnerable. This is how Joseph became ensnared.

"In the period when I was in my mid-twenties through to my early thirties, we experienced another visitation from a Satal in our world, here in this country. That Satal was eventually destroyed in a battle in which I took part, although not before it had wrought immense havoc and had set in motion various catastrophic events, the effects of which we are still living with today. Well, it was this Satal and its followers who finally turned my friend Joseph. From being my daily companion, Joseph began to disappear for periods, always with highly plausible reasons mind you, and on the occasions when he did reappear, each time his outward appearance seemed more... well, more affluent than the last. It was only in subtle ways to start with – a fine watch, a suit from an exclusive tailor and so on – not things which are in any way bad in themselves, or which might create too much cause for suspicion in isolation. However, over time it seemed that he was starting to make a lot of money by some means or other, and apparently he was also starting to become more arrogant with others around him, although he never was so with me in the early stages.

"As the years progressed though, even I started to notice the change. Whereas the young man I had known had been modest and reserved about his considerable gifts in the Powers, the man he started to become was more boastful, sometimes even engineering situations purely to allow him to demonstrate his ability. Worse still, he began to do so at the expense of others. I had heard people speak of his changed behaviour, but I remained loyal to my friend, believing that he was being wronged by gossip. Then one fateful day I witnessed him humiliating another of our Order, a very good man, and doing so purely for his own self-aggrandizement, and finally I understood that something was seriously wrong. Oh how long it took me to wake up and open my eyes!" The old man's face took on a look of deep sorrow and remorse now, and he stopped speaking for a time. Anna glanced towards her uncle, whose gesture indicated that she should allow time for the old man to gather himself again. Finally he resumed.

"Another of the things you will learn in the practical elements of your instruction is that with training and practice, it is possible to change the way one's essence appears to others, to a certain extent, to disguise it if you will, for example to make it appear smaller, or less blue than it really is, or indeed more blue. Now clearly this is not something that ought usually to be necessary in ordinary life, since most people cannot see essences anyway. However, this ability can be very important for us when confronting the forces of the Omega World, since it is frequently essential for our success that we only reveal our true identities when the time is right for us to face them, and that we retain the element of surprise until then."

This latest revelation brought another question back to Anna's mind. "Mr Warwick, the last time I saw you, and again tonight, your essence has appeared far larger and brighter than I have ever seen it before. I couldn't understand it at the time, but does this mean you have been disguising your true essence?"

"Yes, precisely! My years in the Struggle have taught me that it is better not to attract attention to myself, not until I am ready. This has been especially true in these latter years when I have been masquerading as Mr Barton the book seller to keep my whereabouts unknown to our enemies. In order to avoid attracting any suspicion as to my real identity I reduce the size of my essence's appearance all the time, except when in the company of my most trusted comrades from the Order. One of the first things I intend to teach you is to do the same thing.

"One curious fact though is that, to the best of my

knowledge, no-one has ever been able to increase the size of their essence through this technique, only to reduce it. Anyway, what you see today is my essence in its natural state, for better or worse."

This whole revelation hit Anna like a thunderbolt. It seemed fundamentally to undermine what she had always thought to be a completely reliable ability to read people and understand what kind of individuals they were. Until very recently she had not thought that anyone else could even see essences, let alone manipulate their appearance. Nothing was any longer as simple as it had seemed.

"To continue with the story then," said Mr Warwick, "I now believe that from his mid-twenties when Joseph Mortlock began to turn, he was already disguising the changes that must otherwise have been obvious in his essence, and I believe that is the reason I did not detect his transformation sooner. What we now know is that he had fallen for the promise of great wealth and widespread recognition from all whose opinions he most cared about, and we believe that the attainment of these things was being made possible indirectly by the actions of the Satal of that time. It is likely he was not even aware that the Satal was behind such things to start with, as the rest of us did not even know of its existence at first, but over time he became drawn in more and more deeply, and in the end he became effectively that Satal's slave. Certainly the riches promised became a reality, and I have no doubt that he received recognition from some, but at the same time the person he was becoming descended along the twisted paths of the Omega World and it was turning many more away from him.

"Joseph and I had some very heated arguments in our late twenties, concerning what I perceived to be his dangerous change of personality, once I had finally woken up to it, and he hurled all manner of abusive public accusations at me. I took these at face value at the time. I was considerably hurt by them, and did my best to argue against them. Now I know that he did not even believe them himself, and in his own increasingly twisted mind he merely invented them, probably in an attempt to lead me to turn as well. In any event, Mortlock finally showed his true colours to all when that particular Satal war came to a head... and those true colours were shown to be black and red. By the time we were both in our mid-thirties, Mortlock had committed many heinous crimes on the side of the Opposing Energy, and his duplicitous cover was finally lifted for good when we came to face one other on opposing sides in the great battle with that Satal who had become his master. By then he had no more use for, nor indeed interest in, disguising his true self, and when I first saw his essence as it had truly become, I won't deny it Anna, I was almost physically sick. Of course, you know because you have now seen it yourself, but just imagine if you had previously known that person as your closest and best friend, and you had known the blue purity and beauty of his former essence. To see his essence so completely transformed into that very thing we had both despised so deeply and had sworn jointly to fight... well I can tell you, it was almost too much for me.

"I will not go into the details of that battle now. Suffice to say that it ended up going well for our side, and it led us to the eventual destruction of that particular Satal.

However Mortlock himself escaped, and has remained a significant enemy to all those who support The World that was Meant to Be ever since. We have never been able to capture him or bring him down. He has continued to lead a desperate existence, as the best possible living example of the dangers of succumbing to the allures of the Opposing Energy. And the terrible irony is, for all that he used to crave the respect and adulation of others, amongst all in the Order he is now the most reviled and hated man alive. He has been forced to live a nomadic existence abroad in exile for much of his time since the defeat of his first Satal master, partly I suspect in search of new Satal masters to serve and to gain his twisted gratification from, but mainly I am sure because he knows that if he dwells in this country for long enough he will certainly be hunted down, captured and rendered such that he will never be able to harm anyone else again."

Mr Warwick paused again for a moment, and it was clear that recalling this tale had brought many buried emotions back to the surface. He had started pacing the room as he had recounted the final part of the story, but now he resumed his position in his chair by the fire.

"Anna, you will come to learn, although I fervently hope it will not be through first-hand experience, that anyone who spends too much time in the presence of a Satal will experience a tremendous malevolent influence, and will come under immense mental pressure as a result. The minds of all but the very strongest tend to end up twisted, even if that person does not realise it at first. However, from what we have subsequently learned, it pains me most deeply of all to say that Joseph Mortlock had apparently sunk so far by the time that the Satal finally revealed itself to him that he did not even attempt to resist it. Rather it seems that he embraced it with open arms. He welcomed it with an open heart. And in the end that heart was turned pure black.

"And so, your story tells us that Mortlock has returned to London. I suppose it should come as no great surprise that he has chosen now to return, for these are times in which we face possibly the greatest array of evil from the Omega World in history – a time such as Mortlock has dreamed of for decades I should imagine. He would not want to miss the party. There can be no doubt that he will be in their close service once again."

"Well then he has made the biggest mistake of his wretched, miserable life! We will have him for sure this time!" Anna's uncle almost shouted through gritted teeth, pounding his fist into his hand again.

Seeing Anna's observance of her uncle's mood, Mr Warwick added, "There is more to tell about Mortlock, plenty more, including things that are very personal to us all. But now is not yet the time for that," and at this point he looked directly in the direction of Anna's uncle, who hesitated briefly, then gave a short nod in return, in spite of himself and his agitation.

"There are other things in your story that I would now like to explore a little further if I may, Anna," said the old man, turning back to her.

"Yes, of course Mr Warwick," Anna replied, "but may I ask just one more question about Mortlock?"

"Very well Anna, yes, please go ahead," Mr Warwick answered in a kind tone, even as her uncle once again stiffened at the mention of the man's name.

"That ring he was wearing. For some reason I can't explain, my eye was really drawn to it. It was such a horrible, ugly thing... somehow it completely repulsed me. Then Uncle made reference to it earlier. Does it mean something in particular?"

"Yes, Anna, very observant as always, and it does indeed carry a particular meaning. It is a very rare kind of ring, containing a very rare kind of gemstone which is pure black, as you saw. To find such a stone of that size is very rare indeed, but there are a very small number of rings such as that which are known to exist. Legend has it that these rings were originally created by the last Gorgal of the West, at a time when jewellery making was not the fine craft that it is today, which goes some way to explain its somewhat ugly, vulgar appearance. They were created to be given to the greatest of turners who had served the Gorgal beyond normal measure in that era, helping it to achieve its evil ends. In more recent times, Satals have awarded these rings to their most faithful followers for the same reason. As such, from our point of view the ring is a sign that its wearer has been guilty of the greatest treachery and evil that a person can commit in this world. Mortlock received the ring you saw from that Satal of our youth which I spoke of earlier before its defeat, in recognition of the valued service that Mortlock had given to the Omega World. When he lined up against us on the side of our enemies on the day of that battle, he wore the ring openly, with such apparent pride that it shocked me and many others to our very cores. It was your mention of that ring that told us beyond any further doubt that the man you saw was indeed Mortlock. What is most significant though, is the fact that he now feels emboldened enough to wear it so brazenly once again, in public, right here in London.

Anna sat back in her chair and became aware of the beads of sweat that had spread across her brow. Only now did she realise just how rigidly she had been sitting.

"I believe his flagrant wearing of that ring goes beyond even the considerable normal arrogance of Joseph Mortlock. What it confirms is how formidable the enemy forces now present in our world really are. Otherwise I cannot believe he would dare to be so bold. To me this is yet more evidence that another Gorgal, the direct heir to the creature that forged the very ring that Mortlock now wears, has indeed appeared in the world in our own time. I should imagine that Mortlock now believes his day has come at last."

"Well I shall see to it that it has not, I swear it!" The words burst from Anna's uncle as though he were no longer able to hold them in. "I will bring downfall upon that old man if it takes the final breath in my body to do so. I have sworn it before, and it remains the most important mission of my life!"

Mr Wawrick paused, then he sighed. "James, no-one understands better than me the depth of passion that Joseph Mortlock instils in you, and the reasons why. We have both suffered immeasurable loss and hurt at that man's hands. You know that in this particular case I do not criticise you for your oath – you have made it in the name of the Alpha World, to defeat one of its most nefarious opponents. However, I urge caution nonetheless, for

Mortlock is a man who is both cunning and extremely dangerous. But most of all I urge caution because, as we have discussed many times, if the positive intention which you have to rid the world of this Omega influence turns into unfettered hatred and the lust for revenge, whilst you may succeed in reaping that revenge, in doing so you may do irreparable damage to your own essence in the process, and unwittingly begin your own descent toward the very direction Mortlock has gone. It would mean that the Omega World had triumphed again even in the very moment of Mortlock's demise, which would surely be the ultimate tragedy. I perceive that this danger is real, and one that the Omega forces will seek to exploit, as they seek to exploit every one of our potential weaknesses."

Uncle James stood for a moment longer, before taking a deep breath, nodding in acknowledgement of the point made by his Master, and resuming his seat.

All the talk of Mortlock had cast a blanket of gloom over the room. That such a foul and treacherous man should feel rewarded for his evil ways was something about which Anna already felt the injustice, and she could imagine the strength of feeling that he must induce in those that knew him and had witnessed his treachery first-hand. On hearing Mr Warwick's warning about the lust for revenge however, Anna began to perceive for the first time just how cunning and manipulative an enemy they faced, and how difficult and dangerous the Struggle really was.

"Now, Anna," Mr Warwick resumed, "I would like to ask you some questions about the Beast that you described. Would you mind talking about it in as much detail as you can?"

"Yes, I will try. Although I could not make out too many details as it was so dark. But the monster had long arms, or rather wings, with long claws at the ends of its fingers. The wings themselves looked more like pictures I've seen of a reptile's than a bird's, as though they were made of thick skin rather than covered with feathers of any kind. But I didn't get to see them closely, thankfully. On its feet, at the ends of its toes it had very long claws, large enough to hold the body of Green as it carried him off over the house. And its body appeared to be slightly shiny in the lamplight. I think it might have been covered in small black scales, again a little like pictures I have seen of lizards, but it was black all over.

"Its head was the most horrible part though. Its mouth was like a long beak, or a snout, and I am sure I saw large fangs when it opened its mouth to let out that awful scream. That was the other part. The screaming. Just as people had said, it really was the most appalling sound I have ever heard. In fact it actually sounded like something that was not meant to be heard in this world. I don't know, it's difficult to explain..." Anna shuddered as she recalled sound more vividly than she had done since the night itself.

"Don't worry, Anna, you have explained it more than well enough. And your uncle and I know the sound, for we have ourselves heard very similar sounds in the past. And your description was apt. For I think you already know what that beast was, don't you?"

"Well," Anna replied, sensing that her theory was about to be confirmed, "I guessed that what we saw was the Beast of Highgate, which has been in all the newspapers..."

"Go on," said Mr Warwick.

"... and, well, I had started to think that the Beast of Highgate might in fact be a Satal..." she continued.

"Anna, it is my belief that you are right on both counts. Your uncle and I suspected that these stories about the Beast of Highgate which have consumed the newspapers of late, if in fact true, did relate to the appearance of a Satal, coinciding as they have with a marked increase in the activities of our enemies here in London in recent times. In response, members of our Order have spent time in Highgate since the stories began to carry out our own investigations and finalise our plans to counter it, although no-one has actually been in the right place at the right time to witness the Beast until now. But yes Anna, I do believe it was a Satal that you and your friends faced that night. It would appear that you have come into close proximity with one of our deadliest enemies well before you were prepared and trained for it, and you have escaped unscathed, which is something for which we should all be very grateful."

"Mr Warwick, do we know for sure that this beast was not the Gorgal? It was very powerful, and to be honest it was utterly terrifying."

"Ah, Anna, yes, we may be almost certain of that, for two reasons. Firstly, you may be sure that had it been a Gorgal on the top of that mansion, the consequences would have been far, far more terrible. For a Gorgal is much more powerful and evil, even than the so-called Beast of Highgate, difficult though I am sure that must be to imagine. Such is a Gorgal's power, it would have destroyed you all without any chance of escape. And unfortunately, I believe that it would have singled you out first Anna, in a way that this Satal thankfully did not do. And secondly, following certain investigations I made after we met last time, I have strong reason to believe that the Gorgal is in fact a very long way away from London at this moment. So rest assured Anna, I feel certain that the Beast of Highgate is not the Gorgal."

Anna was naturally relieved to hear that Mr Warwick did not believe the Gorgal was anywhere near London, but the notion that the Gorgal could be much more powerful even than the beast they had encountered, brought home the full magnitude of the challenge and danger that lay ahead of them. She felt small and vulnerable again.

"Anna, there is one more important question I must ask you. I wanted to ask about that large mansion where you encountered the Beast. Exactly where was it? Please be as precise as you can."

Anna could not give an exact location or name any roads, but she described the route they had taken from the centre of Highgate to get there.

"Thank you Anna, this information is extremely helpful."

Then the other question which had constantly been on Anna's mind but she had never yet managed to raise, came back to her again. "Faulkner!" she exclaimed. Both men started violently in their seats, Anna's uncle bolting from his and immediately reaching for his cane.

"What? Where?" inquired Mr Warwick urgently, gripping both arms of his chair.

"No, I am sorry, I don't mean he's here! I do beg your pardon. I meant that I have been meaning to ask you about Mr Faulkner, and what his role is in all this. It's just that since I saw him in this shop I have heard a lot of rumours about him, that he could be a vampire and such like, and other stories about how he has been conducting evil ceremonies to summon up the spirits of hell, and that in fact it is he who has been summoning the Beast of Highgate. Well my friends believe that Faulkner may own that mansion in Highgate where we saw the Beast. Mr Warwick, do you think it is Faulkner who is summoning the Beast? Is it that that's made his essence look the way it does? He is somehow involved in the appearance of the Satal, isn't he?

Anna's uncle had slowly returned to his seat while Anna was talking, but he had not sat down and was still holding his cane like a weapon, looking all around him intently as though the very mention of Faulkner's name could have been enough to summon him out of thin air. Mr Warwick, however, had regained his composure.

"Well, Anna, another very perceptive question from you. And yes, it is my belief that what you say is in fact correct – Faulkner is indeed involved with the Satal's appearance. But there is much we need to explain to you about the nature of Satals, the exact mechanism by which we understand they appear in our world, the form they take and so on, all of which we will cover in your instruction. However there is a logical sequence to the teaching of these things in order for it to make the most sense, and I would ask that you bear with us until that point in your studies. All will become clear very soon, I promise!"

"Yes Mr Warwick, I understand," Anna replied. But at last the theory had been confirmed – the rumours about Faulkner summoning the Beast of Highgate had been right! Her head filled with further questions about the nature of these ceremonies that conjure up Satals, and where the Satal returned to until the time it was next summoned. And if Mortlock is the faithful servant of the Satals, she wondered exactly what the relationship could then be between Faulkner and Mortlock. She was itching to ask, but it was clear that now was not the time. The way of these discussions seemed to be that everything became clear in the end, so she would wait for now and look forward to whatever was coming next.

"So, to conclude Anna, your adventure was very dangerous, but it has also provided valuable information. I congratulate you on the way in which you and your friends handled yourselves on this occasion, but I must also most earnestly request that you take all care possible to avoid finding yourself in such a situation again, now that you understand the true nature of the dangers involved. If ever you do have to face a creature of the Omega World, it must only be after you have completed your training and you are fully prepared, and accompanied by others from the Order."

"Yes, Mr Warwick, I understand," Anna replied.

"Very well. So, with tonight's new revelations, I believe we have covered enough for one day. We will resume again tomorrow evening, if that is agreeable to you, Anna"

Anna confirmed that it certainly was. She could not wait to continue. With that, her uncle escorted her to her home. That night she fell asleep wondering about all the things she was about to learn, eager for the next session to begin.

Secret Liaison

The early days of Anna's instruction were amongst the happiest she could ever remember. A whole new world containing unbelievable revelations started to open up to her, and she felt freer than she had in living memory. Freer physically, being able actually to leave the house now, and mentally, her imagination being totally captivated by all she was learning. Having spent all her life feeling like an outsider, she found herself on the inside of something of the highest importance, and spending time with people who, although far older than her, she liked and respected very much. For the first time in her life she was able to see a future for herself, a life ahead of her that might be worth living, in which she might even be able to achieve something. All these things had represented a complete transformation, both of her life and of the way in which she viewed herself.

One of the first things that Mr Warwick insisted Anna should learn was how to disguise her aura. He had explained that her aura was developing, and although it was not yet a great size, it would grow larger in the future, and it was already a very pure shade of blue. So in order not to draw unwanted attention from their enemies, she should learn to reduce the size of the appearance of her aura, and then make a point of maintaining that disguise at all times from then on, just as Mr Warwick did. It was something she had never thought to try before, but the process was a surprisingly simple one, requiring her merely to envisage her aura contracting and become denser, like the effect of pursing your lips or clenching a fist. Anna could not see the results for herself, but Mr Warwick assured her that she had been able to decrease the aura in size greatly when she did this. Using a similar technique, Anna was also apparently able to make her aura look less pure in colour and to contain a few blemishes. Although she found these things easy to do, apparently this was something that students usually took a long time to master; both Mr Warwick and her uncle expressed their surprise at how quickly she had grasped the techniques. Anna found she could soon maintain the disguise without effort, from then on she made a point of keeping the disguise up at all times.

As the weeks went by, Anna's knowledge deepened, and one side of her imagination was nourished beyond all measure. However, the other side of her imagination was starting to grow restless again – for Timmy. At the time when she had no instruction to occupy her attention, she sometimes felt a yearning in her stomach to see him again which verged on physical pain. Was this love? She presumed it must be, because she could not imagine any feelings stronger than this. But what was this thing, love? How did it grow so strong, almost taking possession of her body and command her thoughts? There was no question it had the potential to make her feel happier than she had ever felt, but she was also starting to understand that it could be a double-edged sword. It reminded her of one of those addictions she had read about, and if she did not feed it, oh how it started to hurt! The passions that overcome her at these times were so strong, to the point that she was sometimes no longer sure she could trust her own judgement. Worse still, the yearning was increasingly followed by those more familiar feelings of self-doubt. By following her mother's and mentors' instructions, was she making Timmy wait too long? Would he grow tired of waiting? Who else might he be meeting? Might his feelings for her be superseded by those for another? Had she been letting the best, and perhaps only, chance she would ever have of happiness slip through her fingers while she did nothing about it? Then there were her other friends, and their troubles with Kenny Gillespie, Archie Knowles and the Marylebone Gang. She had promised to help them and their families, but she wasn't much use to them cooped up indoors. She felt as though she was letting them down when they needed her, and she worried that they might feel the same. But she stayed true to the promises she had made not to slip out of the house again without permission.

October came and went, however, and gradually Anna could bear it no longer. Her fifteenth birthday was approaching, and Timmy's birthday was a week before hers. Finally she decided it was time to act. Even if it was only possible for a short time, she would arrange to meet with Timmy to celebrate their birthdays together. That way she could see him, and also find out more about their efforts to get Gillespie and Knowles locked up by the police.

More than once she hesitated before attempting to set it up. She reflected heavily on Mr Warwick and her uncle's endless warnings concerning the dangers that lay outside the door, and even more deeply on the internal commitment she had made to avoid unnecessary worry to her mother. She vowed that she would be extremely careful. Was this going to be an unreasonable risk? Was she going to walk straight into unknown dangers? More than once she talked herself out of it. But each time she came face to face with the alternative, that of not seeing Timmy, the idea of not knowing when she might see him again served only to feed those evil twins, the pain of yearning to see him, and the even more painful paranoia that she might lose him. She needed to do something or she might go mad. Finally she decided to put her plan into action, vowing as she did so that she would be as careful as humanly possible and take no unnecessary risks.

But how to do it? Anna had grown increasingly wary of Lizzy, whose attitude had grown even colder towards her the last few times they had met in the house. Her instincts told her to avoid using Lizzy this time.

The problem was that she wasn't overwhelmed with other options. Lizzy was the only person working in the house who knew Rebecca and Timmy. She considered simply slipping out of the house without making any arrangements, and just waiting outside Rebecca and Timmy's house. But what if Timmy was not there, or what if other family members were with him and he could not speak? She couldn't afford to risk leaving the house more than once, so she needed certainty that she could meet him when she did slip out. No, there had to be another way to get a message to Timmy and to be sure he would be there to meet her. But how?

Of course everyone in the house knew the rules – Anna wasn't allowed to leave it unaccompanied under any circumstances. She would have been taking a big risk in asking any of them to help her, not to mention putting them in a difficult position themselves. The more she thought about it, the more convinced she became that there was only one viable alternative to Lizzy whom she might try, and that was Jim. Although she knew Jim to be a member of the Order, she also knew him to be a very straight and completely dependable type, and what was more she had reason to believe he might just understand her feelings and situation. After all, his situation with Emily was not so different, and Anna had kept that secret faithfully for him.

She was to be disappointed, however. Having managed firstly to engineer the time alone where no-one could have heard the conversation, she also managed to overcome the extreme embarrassment of telling Jim about Timmy – well, in as much detail as he needed to know anyway. It was the first time she had told anyone about Timmy, and it was one of the most difficult things she had ever made herself do, but the goal was so important that she got through it. For his Jim part seemed to understand fully, and to her eternal gratitude he did not treat it like some silly childhood infatuation, but with due and proper seriousness. He told her how incredibly sympathetic he was and how much he wished from the bottom of his heart that he could help, but unfortunately he could not. He repeated the message she had already heard on a thousand occasions that there was 'danger all around now', and told her that he was under the strictest instructions to ensure that she was safe. He told her that as much as he truly sympathised, he could not break his commitments and betray the trust that had been placed in him. Looking at his beautifully pure aura, looking purer and more unblemished than it ever had, Anna knew he was speaking from the heart. She understood that for someone with Jim's admirable character there was really no other response he could have given. By the end of the conversation she had given up and told him that she understood, and for his part he had promised that he would not tell a soul about Timmy. That at least was something for which she was hugely grateful.

But none of this helped her fend off her impending madness. After another day of trying again to follow the guidance of Jim and all the others, a day spent wrestling with her emotions in a state of complete inner turmoil, she returned finally to her plan and the only alternative left to her – Lizzy.

When she finally managed to catch Lizzy alone, Lizzy was her usual prickly self at first. She pointed out in no uncertain terms that she had already done more than enough to help Anna and her friends, that Anna shouldn't be putting her in that position any more. However, once Anna had weathered all of that, Lizzy's attitude started slowly to change. Whether it was due to the extent of Anna's pleading and her obvious desperation, or something else that was ticking over in Lizzy's mind, Anna couldn't tell, but finally and a little unexpectedly, Lizzy agreed to pass on the message, which was for Timmy to meet her in the usual place the following Tuesday to celebrate his birthday. Lizzy's expression had once again become unreadable by the time she agreed to meet Anna the next day in the drawing room, which was usually deserted at that time, to update Anna on Timmy's response.

When they met, that day had so far been going well.

Anna had successfully managed to negotiate the baking of a couple of small cakes with Maggie the cook, under the rather pathetic pretext of holding a secret solitary midnight feast. 'Well, only a white lie, and it seemed to make Maggie happy!' Anna had thought to herself. Of course in reality those cakes were to be smuggled out of the house and to be shared with Timmy as a small surprise to celebrate their turning fifteen.

But the day was about to take a turn for the worse. As soon as she had met Lizzy in the drawing room, Anna could sense that something wasn't right. Lizzy looked awkward and smiling even less than usual. "Did you manage to speak to him?" Anna asked urgently.

"Yes, I did speak to him, but we only had a short time before his parents turned up. But I asked him what you told me to."

"And?" Anna pressed impatiently, "Did he agree?"

"Well," Lizzy responded, now looking down at the carpet even more awkwardly, "actually no, he didn't."

"What?" Anna asked with a sudden sinking feeling in her stomach.

"Well that was it," Lizzy now managed to look up at Anna again, "he just said he couldn't see you."

"But..." Anna's head was now scrambling to take on board what this might mean. "Did he say why?"

"No, he didn't. Well no sooner had we started talking than his parents appeared, so obviously we had to cut the conversation short. But before I left he repeated it again. He said 'Look, just tell her I can't see her, all right?' And then he was gone. I got no more explanation than that."

"Did you tell him it was to celebrate his birthday?"

Anna asked, desperate now, her voice becoming faint.

"Yes Anna, I told him that to begin with, but he just said he couldn't see you. I can't tell you no more than that because there ain't no more to tell. It was only a very short conversation, he said what he said, and that was it." She looked again at Anna, and her stare softened and a look of genuine sympathy appeared. "Look, I'm sorry Anna. I suppose this ain't what you were hoping to hear, but I'm just telling you what he said. I did try, I promise!"

To say Anna was crestfallen would have been the understatement of the century. She thanked Lizzy as best she could, then retreated rapidly to her room to think through what this could mean.

In all her desperate planning of how she would arrange things and engineer her exit from the house, this had been the one outcome she had not planned for at all. Timmy had rejected her suggestion to meet up, and not even given so much as an explanation. At first she was desperate not to believe Lizzy, and Lizzy's behaviour had become so unusual lately that she had reason to be suspicious. But she had looked genuinely awkward at having to pass on the information, and she had not in any way appeared to be revelling in Anna's disappointment. Maybe there was a different explanation.

Running the words through her head again and again, she wondered if she was reading too much into them. Maybe there was a perfectly reasonable explanation as to why Timmy said he was unable to meet with her, and he just hadn't had enough time to explain any more to Lizzy. But there was another worry in her head that she was not able to remove. What Lizzy said had resonated just a little too strongly with the fears that Anna had already been harbouring. That she had left things too long, that Timmy had not been able to wait indefinitely for her, that it had become too much and that he had decided to move on. Behind that lurked an even worse fear, that in moving on he might actually have met someone else. In her more rational moments she knew that she was now jumping to conclusions based on very little, but at the same time she was quite able to believe that Timmy could have come across someone far more attractive and more interesting than she was, someone else who liked him and who deserved him more than she did. And apart from anything else, someone that he could probably actually meet up with from time to time! Each time, with a great deal of effort, Anna was able to slam the door shut to this path which she did not wish to travel down, for Timmy had not actually said anything about anyone else. But that door remained there in her mind, drawing her back towards it.

Later that troubled afternoon, Maggie appeared smiling in her room with the two cakes Anna had asked for, and was quite taken aback when Anna burst into a flood of tears at the sight of them!

It didn't help that this turn of events coincided with a break in her instruction, as Mr Warwick and her uncle both had to leave London for a time for an important mission to do with the Order, leaving her with nothing to distract her from her endless speculation. That night she had her most troubled night's sleep for a very long time, and when the first light of dawn filtered through her window she felt as though she hadn't really slept at all. In the cold light of that new day though, Anna steeled herself and decided enough was enough. She could speculate all she liked, but with almost no facts she would never find the answer, and she simply could not go on like that. She needed to find out one way or the other what the situation was. Putting her former caution to one side she resolved that, arranged or not, this time she would go to Timmy and Rebecca's house and wait around until she was able to speak to one of them. Rebecca might be able to help, even if Anna couldn't speak to Timmy. And if Anna could speak to Timmy... well, then she could find out once and for all where she stood.

Buoyed by the idea that she would now at least be able to find out the facts of Timmy's refusal to meet, and that she was going to do something about this for herself, she was able to eat a full meal at breakfast time, much to Maggie's relief. And it was then, on her return to her room to make final preparations for her mission, that she encountered Lizzy again.

"Morning Anna!" Lizzy said in a voice brighter than any Anna had heard from her in a long time. "Actually I was on my way up to see you. I've got a message for you from Timmy!"

No amount of iron plating with which Anna had surrounded her heart since their last conversation could have prevented it from leaping at these words. "Says he wants to meet you and explain things. It was another real quick conversation so I've got no idea what it is, but at least you can see him now, eh?" She looked genuinely encouraging as she said this.

"Did he say when to meet him and where?" Anna asked eagerly.

"Usual place, this afternoon at four o'clock. Now Anna, you know I don't really approve of you sneaking out of the house an' all, and you know I shouldn't be helping you. But I could tell you were right upset yesterday, so I hope it all works out well for you this time."

These kind words finally melted any remaining protection around Anna's heart, and she replied, "Oh thank you Lizzy!" and without thinking gave her a quick hug of gratitude. The messenger reacted stiffly at first, but then relaxed and returned the embrace more warmly. 'I knew I was overreacting and that there would be a rational explanation. How things can turn on their head in the space of a day!' Anna thought, the smile finally returned to her tired face. 'Or perhaps they're just turning back the right way up again!' And it warmed her heart still further to see her smile returned by Lizzy. Friends again at last.

What Anna did not see was the very different, venomous smirk that crossed Lizzy's face the moment her back was turned!

It was well before four o'clock when Anna reached the usual meeting place, and she sat there alone on the ledge under the bridge in a state of dreadful agitation. The minutes dragged by until four o'clock had come and gone, and the feelings of elation at hearing that Timmy had asked to see her started slowly to ebb away. The first dark clouds of self-doubt began to drift across her mind again as she re-examined Lizzy's latest message for clues.

Timmy had said that he wanted to meet her 'to explain things'. She had assumed this meant to explain why he had not been able to make Anna's previous suggested meeting time, but what if he had meant something else? What if there were other, different things that he needed to explain to her? Whatever the explanation, at least she would find out, and she would finally have something factual to build on instead of the endless spiralling speculation. Spiralling speculation that only ever seemed to spiral in one direction: downwards.

There she sat, cold and alone, waiting for fate to do to her what it would. More time passed, and she reached the point where Timmy could have said anything to her and she would have accepted it. Anything would have been better than this waiting. She looked up the canal and was struck how different the scene now looked compared to those heady days of summer. They were deep into autumn, closer to winter than summer, and a cold mist had started to descend around her. Straining her eyes, she was just able to make out the shape of a barge moored to the bank somewhere in the vicinity of Mr Warwick's shop. She wondered idly if it might be the cheerful yellow Canal Queen owned by the Rileys. Whether it was or not, it now appeared the same as everything else, just another shade of dull grey in the gathering gloom. There was nothing to brighten the darkening landscape. And still Timmy did not come.

Paranoia began to snap at Anna from all sides. Timmy wasn't going to come. What did that mean? Was this the final evidence that he no longer cared, regardless of how he might have felt when the sun had still been bright and the trees still full of leaves? Or had Lizzy lied to her? Had there been no message? How was she possibly supposed to tell? But if it was a lie, then that would mean that

Timmy had not contacted her at all, and that she was back to where she had been the day before.

Anna had not given up completely on Timmy, not yet – it was still possible there was some explanation that would clear up the confusion, and that everything might still turn out all right. But even in that increasingly unlikely event, in the meantime she would be left alone with only her speculation, and she simply couldn't face that. Where had her uncle and Mr Warwick gone? Where had all the hope gone from her life which had shone so preciously but so briefly just weeks before? There was nothing but cold, thickening fog and fast descending darkness, both outside and within her. This spot had once been such a happy place for her, but now she couldn't remember ever having felt so alone.

Anna waited for well over an hour, which felt more like a year, and Timmy never came. She took one last, long look at the cold dark waters of the canal, before steeling herself again for the longest walk home of her life. The worst part was the ascent up the stone steps to the road – those same steps on which Anna's world had exploded into the most dazzlingly beautiful colours when Timmy had kissed her. Where was he now? Her mind was torn in two as to whether to go and camp outside his house as she had originally planned, or just accept that things had changed and to make her way home again. This time her sensible side won out. There had been enough signs now, things must have moved on, well for one of them anyway, and she had been a fool even to have come out today and to have sat under that stupid damp bridge on her own for so long. She had broken all the rules laid down by those who cared about her most by coming here, and she would not rub any more salt into those wounds by staying out longer. She had taken enough risks, and she had to move on. For the time being she would focus all her mind and energy instead on her instruction and studying. When were Mr Warwick and her uncle going to come back? She needed them more than ever now, to help her fill her mind, and the gaping hole that had opened up in her life.

And with those thoughts, Anna began her long, lonely way home through the thickening mist, with heavy darkness falling all around her.

The Second Lamp

It was not yet very late as Anna made her lonely way back northwards along the streets to her home, but the nights were drawing in and darkness was rendered all the more impenetrable by the fast-deepening fog that swirled all around her, like an enormous blanket engulfing London. Anna looked up at the gas-lit street lamps and found that she could no longer clearly make them out – just fluorescent halos emanating from where the burners were presumably located.

Pulling her cloak around her she pressed on, eager now to forget the day's crushing misadventure, to get out of the threatening night and to return to the warm safety of her home. Following the searing disappointment of not being able to see Timmy after all, she regretted having been so foolish as to have ventured out at all. For the first time, her home now seemed like a safe haven, and especially on a night such as this it was preferable to being out in this haunting mist.

Then, as she passed a narrow side street, she heard her name called out. She froze to the spot, senses instantly sharpened. Her immediate reaction was to hope that maybe Timmy had turned up late and had caught up with her, but a second's reflection told her it had not been his voice. She peered into the foggy darkness in the direction from which it had come.

"Anna, over here," called out the voice again. It was familiar, a boy's voice, but she still could not place it. Then, through the dense fog that the gaslight could only penetrate for a short distance, Anna made out the form of someone a little taller than she was. She immediately braced herself, ready to fight or flee if necessary as the figure stepped forward.

"Anna it's me, Billy Gillespie. But don't worry, I don't mean no harm. I just want to talk to you. I really need to talk."

This was the first time Anna had encountered Gillespie since the incident on the bridge, and she had long wondered when their paths would cross again. Whenever it was to be, she had been certain the next meeting would not be a kind one. Anticipating some kind of trap, Anna looked immediately behind the emerging form of Gillespie, then quickly all around her, searching for other Maryleboners lurking in the gloom. She could see no-one, but of course that didn't mean they weren't there somewhere, obscured by the fog and darkness.

"Stop there," replied Anna. "Don't come any closer, Gillespie."

The figure stopped obediently. Its form was slightly slumped with drooping shoulders. Gillespie's demeanour certainly didn't appear threatening, if that meant anything.

"Anna, please, I don't mean you no harm. I want to ask for your help. If I meant you any harm, well I'd have tried to jump you, wouldn't I? Not called out to you to let you know I was here."

This may or may not have been true, but Anna was taking nothing for granted. She did not particularly believe that Gillespie had the wits to think of bluffing to create a false sense of security. Left to his own devices, subtlety was unlikely to play a leading role in his thinking. But

Gillespie could be someone else's pawn, either one of the Fletchers from the Marylebone Gang, or worse, someone altogether more cunning and dangerous. Nevertheless, Anna had developed a pretty good sense for people and their intentions, and Gillespie's manner appeared sufficiently sincere at least to suggest the possibility that he might be telling the truth. As long as he was on his own, after their last encounter Anna felt confident she could deal with him using her aura if he did try anything.

Anna shifted her focus to view Gillespie's aura. Although looking at auras used some sense other than regular sight, Anna's ability to see them still depended on her visual sense, and the extent to which she could see them at any given time was in proportion to her ability to see normal objects at that moment. In Gillespie's case, his aura was somewhat obscured by the fog, but she could still make it out sufficiently to draw a few conclusions.

Its appearance had changed considerably since their last encounter. There seemed to be more scarring on the surface. At the same time however, Anna had the overall impression that its owner was somehow less open to seeking trouble than before. There was unquestionably less red in Gillespie's aura than there had been, but it had been replaced by something else – a yellowish hue. Anna recognised this colouring as fear, and she knew that it took more than the short-term fear caused by a specific event to create this kind of effect in someone's aura. It required a long-term, deep-seated fear, one which had become almost a permanent part of that person's make-up. Something had happened to Gillespie since they had last met, and whatever that was she sensed it was somehow connected to him approaching her now. In spite of herself, Anna's curiosity grew.

"What do you want?" she asked, all the while keeping an eye all around her, taking a step neither forward nor back.

"It's my brother," replied Gillespie. "He's in real trouble, and I don't know what to do. You're the only person I can think of who might be able to help."

This statement sounded ridiculous, but it captured her interest further. What circumstances could possibly have befallen Gillespie's no-good brother that would make Anna the only person who he thought could help – even if she was minded to help that nasty ruffian? Anna wanted to hear more. And anything right then was a welcome distraction from thinking about Timmy. Anna was about to ask Gillespie how he knew where she was going to be, when he started speaking again, and his next words sent shivers straight down her spine.

"There's this man, a real evil man, and he's got his hooks into my brother. I'm certain he's going to kill him if someone doesn't help. I mean, this man is real evil. He goes by the name of Faulkner."

Anna felt an inward jolt at the mention of that name. Gillespie's voice had tailed off slightly as he completed the sentence, and Anna could hear a deep desperation and sadness in his tone. This had sounded entirely genuine – either that, or Gillespie was in a whole different league of cunning, not to mention acting ability, than Anna would have given him credit for. Then there was the change in the appearance and colouring of Gillespie's aura, which was consistent with his desperate plea for help. She now had a strong desire to hear what Gillespie had to say, and to understand what her supposed part in the story might be. There might just be some important information here that she could convey to Mr Warwick and her uncle, and which might also help her friends' families with their troubles with the gang.

Anna's slowly growing belief that Gillespie might be sincere had not reduced one bit her sense that she could still be in danger. Continuing the conversation here, in this place of Gillespie's choosing, and to where he could easily have been followed, was clearly too risky. On the other hand she did not want to lead him towards her home. Somehow she needed to manoeuvre him to a different place, one of her choosing and without being followed. One where she knew the terrain better than him or anyone else.

She looked all around her again, into the foggy gloom. There were no human forms to be seen, but that wasn't to say there was no-one there nonetheless, lying just beyond sight. She shifted her focus once again to search out any auras that might be glimpsed amidst the swirling fog, but again there was nothing. She made up her mind.

"If you want to talk, then you will have to do exactly as I say." Anna used the sternest tone she could manage.

"All right Anna, yes, anything," was his quick reply.

"Right. Walk in front of me up the street. I will be behind you and tell you where to go. But if you make any sudden movements or try to talk to anyone else, then the agreement is off, and you will have to pay the full consequences. Remember what happened the last time you crossed me!"

Gillespie uttered not a word of protest, and simply nodded and set off just as Anna instructed, walking past her and then proceeding up the street ahead of her. They walked for half a mile through the dense, swirling fog with Gillespie as far ahead of Anna as she could let him go without losing sight of him altogether. Anna continued to peer around her using both her visual senses, but saw no-one. That was one blessing of the eerie fog – even if anyone did try to follow them, they'd have the devil's own job trying to keep track. 'The devil's own job...' why did it have to be those words that had sprung to mind?

As the pair continued their peculiar procession, Anna tensed as she became aware of the muffled sound of hooves coming from somewhere in front of them. Then she made out a dim light approaching on the road ahead through the all-encompassing blanket of mist. Senses heightened again she moved right to the wall-lined edge of the pavement away from the road. Gillespie was continuing to walk ahead unchecked, and although now divided deeply into two minds, Anna decided it better not to let him leave her sight as the light approached.

'Stop there Gillespie,' she hissed, and he immediately did as instructed.

The sound of the horses' hooves on the cobblestones of the road was clearly audible, and the silhouette of a horse and carriage slowly emerged from the mist. Tense as a coiled watch spring, Anna crouched motionless against the wall, ceasing even to breathe as the carriage drew up alongside... and then continued on its way, without any change of speed or direction. The cloaked silhouette of the driver did not appear to look around or notice her at all as far as she could tell. Hunched forward, he appeared to be focusing all of his attention on peering into the fog and trying to keep his coach on the road. Whether or not the carriage had passengers, Anna simply could not tell – the interior was entirely obscured. The carriage slid once more into the all-enveloping fog, and was gone. After a further pause, a deep breath and another look around her, Anna looked forward and hissed to Gillespie to continue once more. He obliged instantly.

Anna knew exactly where she would direct Gillespie. There was a large house which had been deserted for some time, down one of the other residential roads that adjoined her own street. Its generous, though by now severely overgrown, garden was lined by a high wall, one section of which had almost all fallen into the garden at the end furthest from the house. On the occasions she had been able to escape from her own house, Anna had often sneaked in on her own to play in the large garden when she was younger. She had shown it to Rebecca and a couple of the others years ago, but no-one knew every inch of it in the way that she did, and she was sure that none of the Maryleboners would have set foot in there before. This was her territory not theirs, and it was the perfect place to continue her unexpected conversation with Gillespie.

Having turned into the road in question, Anna finally saw the opening created by the partial collapse of the wall, lit up faintly by a gas street light that stood next to it. She hissed again to Gillespie, "Stand under the lamp, and don't move until I say so."

Gillespie stopped and nodded. Taking one more look about her to make sure she was not seen, Anna climbed over the remains of the wall and the pile of fallen bricks that lay within, and moved into the garden. On the other side of the wall was an overgrown lawn, lined with large, equally overgrown, bushes. The bush nearest her was one that she could partially walk through, one in which she had played on numerous occasions, with a low branch where she could sit and still clearly make out the shape of the gap in the wall and the mound of old bricks, dimly illuminated by the street lamp. It was near the broken part of the wall, but even if it had been normal daylight Anna would only have been partially visible at best. In the current conditions Anna knew she could no more be seen there than if she were hidden behind a wall of solid granite. It struck her that she was possibly being ridiculously cautious, but ridiculous caution was the order of the day now, especially if what she was about to hear was in any way connected to Faulkner.

"All right Gillespie," said Anna again, slightly louder than before, "walk in a straight line towards me, and step just inside the wall where you can't be seen from the street. When you're inside the wall, sit on the pile of bricks, facing the direction my voice is coming from. I want you to stay in the light of the street lamp so that I can still see you."

Gillespie did exactly as he was told. Stepping over the low remnants of the wall, he sat himself atop the pile created by the bricks that had collapsed into the garden.

"Is here all right?" he asked in a low, slightly shaky voice. It was perfect. Anna could clearly see his figure silhouetted against the light of the gas lamp, and could hear his voice without him raising it. She was confident in the knowledge that she was invisible to him, and she would also be able to see if anyone else entered from the street. "It'll do," she said.

Anna allowed a feeling of excitement to rise inside her, sufficient for the first time to match her nervous apprehension. Her plan had worked like clockwork so far, and she was certain she was about to learn something new and unexpected that might prove to be of great importance. She could not help but notice the tremulous tone in Gillespie's voice, and she considered for the first time how nerve-wrenching this episode must be for him, unfolding as it was in this dense, ominous fog. Unexpectedly she began to find herself feeling slightly sorry for him, before snapping out of it and reminding herself that in these circumstances his feelings were not her first concern.

"Right, speak quietly, and tell me what it is you have to say," she instructed.

There was a pause, and Anna could see Gillespie's form hug itself in the increasing chill of the damp night. This time it was Gillespie's turn to look around him to make sure that no-one was listening. Anna felt sure she was right, both about his sincerity in wanting to talk to her without any trap, and that he was scared out of his wits. Bracing himself, Gillespie began to speak.

"You know my brother, Kenny?" he started. Of course she did, but she withheld reply, sensing that the less she spoke the more she retained the upper hand.

Gillespie continued, "Well he's been working for that man I mentioned, Faulkner, for some time now. Not just one job though – Faulkner has him doing all kinds of things, see, and he pays him a wage to keep him and a number of others available whenever he needs something doing." In other words he's a full-time, paid-up member of Faulkner's gang, thought Anna to herself. "And Faulkner pays well, too, provided you do exactly as he says.

"At first everything was all right, seemed like easy money. I even helped him with some of the errands he had to run, like delivering packages, that kind of thing. A lot of the early work seemed to be getting hold of rare books, some of them very old-looking, usually written in strange languages no-one could read. Someone reckoned they were written in that, what's it called, Latin? And old Greek and that kind of thing, but most of the gang can't hardly even read English so no-one was sure. No-one could understand what Faulkner could want with a bunch of old books, stolen or otherwise, but the talk started that the books were about devil-worshipping rituals, evil spells and such – you know, black magic and that kind of thing. But this was just talk, and the work seemed harmless enough.

"But then things started to change. Some of the work began to get a bit, well, closer to the edge of the law if you know what I mean, and, you know, a bit rougher. But my brother thought he could cope with that because he's a pretty tough type."

Yes, she understood all too well what he meant – his brother was a ruffian who didn't mind breaking the law, or hurting other people, provided there was a profit in it – exactly the kind of person who made the world worse for everyone else. Her dislike for Kenny Gillespie and her determination to do whatever she could to help stop him hardened, but she said nothing and waited for the silhouette to continue its story.

"So, he could deal fine with the work he was asked to do for a while. But, see, Faulkner, well, he ain't no normal man, and he ain't up to no normal business neither. And he has some others working for him too – not like Kenny and his mates they ain't, but right cruel, vicious types. And in particular there's this one evil old man who seems to be closest to Faulkner – old but strong, a real nasty piece of work he is. The kind of person who hurts people just for the fun of it."

'Mortlock,' Anna guessed immediately. She focused on Gillespie's words with every ounce of her attention.

"Like I say, my brother's a tough one, and he'll do a job for you if the pay's right, but him and his mates didn't like these other men of Faulkner's. Now rumours were going round amongst the gang about what Faulkner was up to, and what was in some of them parcels and boxes that he was sending and receiving. There was serious talk that Faulkner was into that occult business and doing black magic, and that objects were being gathered to use in his evil ceremonies. All manner of wild stories, even that some of the boxes might contain parts of bodies. And they reckoned that the other older man was part of it as well – some even thought it was him that had corrupted Faulkner and turned him evil. But most of the talk was about Faulkner. Who he was? Where had he come from? What was his real game? Where did he get all his money? None of their talk ever stopped them from doing his work, mind – as long as he kept paying them well, they kept doing as he asked them."

Gillespie paused and drew his shabby coat more tightly around him. As Anna sat on her low branch, she peered intently at the silhouetted figure of the storyteller. The dense fog all around him seemed, if anything, to be intensifying, almost as though it had become a living thing which was beginning to envelop its prey. In spite of her advantage in every aspect of their situation, a chill slowly began to spread through her body. Sure enough the night was growing colder by the minute, but the chill that Anna was beginning to feel inside was colder. It wasn't because of anything that had yet been said, but where this was all leading. What was more, she couldn't escape the irrational fear that by divulging Faulkner's secret business, Gillespie was somehow almost invoking his dreaded presence. But she needed to hear the whole story.

By this time, poor Gillespie was starting to suffer. Anna could see him shivering inside his coat. She just resisted the urge to go over and put her arm around him. Why was he telling her all this? Anna spoke in the most commanding tone she could still manage, "Continue."

"Well," Gillespie carried on, "then all those stories started about the 'Beast of Highgate'." Anna tensed further. "You must have heard some of them. Well there was them in the gang that reckoned they'd seen and heard this beast, always late at night, in the area around Faulkner's big old house up in Hampstead. Reckoned it looked like some kind of demon they did, huge, like one of them statues you see on them old churches. And the awful sound of it, they said it was like something only the devil himself could make." Anna recalled the terrible, inhuman noise again. Once more she looked all around as the storyteller continued. "And always there were stories of people disappearing around the same time as the Beast had been sighted. Well, you can imagine the talk about just what kind of business of Faulkner's they were involved with, and what his connection with the Beast might be. The stories grew wilder and wilder. And more and more of the gang started to believe that it was Faulkner who was summoning the Beast from the pits of hell through his occult ceremonies, although others still thought this was just drunken talk. But it made all of them more curious to know what was in them boxes they were carrying for him, which were usually nailed shut so no-one could see, and what the contents might be used for by Faulkner, in his ceremonies or otherwise."

Until just a few months before, as dictated by her nature, Anna would not have believed any such stories involving demonic monsters and the like, but that had all changed. She had seen that there were things in this world which were not of it, which should not be here but which had nonetheless appeared. Anna had yet to learn exactly how Faulkner summoned such a being in his ceremonies, and where he summoned them from, but whatever it was that drove Faulkner to conjure up their presence, it must surely be connected to the hideous state of his aura. She considered the disappearances that Gillespie had mentioned, and wondered just how many victims of this beast there had been, beyond those who had made the papers. She shivered as she continued to listen.

"Well, Kenny's best mate, Archie Knowles, him that my brother ran all his errands with, well, his curiosity started getting the better of him. He wasn't for leaving

Faulkner's employment or nothing, the pay was too good for that, but he reckoned that no-one paid the kind of money Faulkner was paying without having something serious to hide. Archie wasn't complaining about it, but he wanted to know what Faulkner's business was. Probably thought there might be even more money in it if they knew what was going on, knowing Archie...

"So, early the other morning, after Faulkner gave Kenny and Archie their next errand – more boxes to deliver with their lids nailed down – Archie said he was going to open it and take a look inside. Kenny warned Archie against it, said they shouldn't look a gift horse in the mouth and should just deliver the things as they were told to. But Archie wasn't for changing his mind. Never was one for caution, wasn't Archie.

"They were supposed to deliver the boxes to an address south of the river in Lambeth. Well, Archie decided they should make a quick detour to one of the rail warehouses by Marylebone Station on the way, where no-one would see them, and take a look inside the box. He said it couldn't do no harm, and that no-one but them would know.

"Anna, you know we know that area real well, so it was no problem for them to find an empty spot with no-one around. The box Archie was carrying was wooden and about a foot and a half long, with the lid nailed shut with small tacks – easy for someone who knew what they was doing to open up, and then re-seal again without much sign of what had gone on.

"So Archie sets about opening it. He prizes the lid partly up and peers inside. And it sounded like he was disappointed with what was in there. 'Just more stupid books!' was what he said. But before he'd had time to get the lid fixed on again, Faulkner was there! Now there's no way Faulkner could know the Marylebone warehouses like Kenny and Archie did, and there's no way he should've been able to find them without them knowing. But there he was, and his rage was terrible!"

Gillespie paused again, as though the words were now growing harder to come by. The living fog slowly tightened its grip around his form in the dim lamplight.

"Like I said, Kenny and Archie are pretty tough, two of the toughest around, and they know how to look after themselves all right. But they didn't know how to deal with what happened next. Faulkner screamed at Archie that he should never have tried to cross him, and that now he was going to pay for it. Archie tried to fight him off with his stick, but Faulkner just smashed it aside like it was made of straw."

Gillespie stopped again, by now he was starting to breathe heavily, almost as though the fog that enveloped him was crushing the very air out of his lungs with its swirling grip. Anna felt a shiver of fear at what was coming next. Impossible though she would have believed it even minutes earlier, she now started to feel for that undesirable duo, Kenny and Archie. They were the enemy, but now she was starting to see that they were really just pawns in a far more evil world that Faulkner was creating. She suddenly hoped that they would somehow get out from this tale unscathed, that their rough, underhand natures would somehow help them to find a way to escape the undoubtedly far greater evil that was Faulkner, and the Beast he could summon. "Go on," she said simply, in the calmest tone she could muster.

"Well..." Gillespie hesitated again, hugging his knees to his chest as his voice almost seemed to dry up completely. "I reckon you ain't going to believe what I'm going to tell you next. But this ain't just another story Anna, like what you may have heard before. I swear this is the truth. And I can swear it because I saw it with my own eyes. And I ain't mad Anna – at least, not yet, although I reckon that's where I may be headed.

"See, I wanted to go with them on this errand that day, same as I sometimes had on other ones. But I heard Archie explaining his plan to Kenny, and then they both turned on me and told me I couldn't join them. Archie threatened me with a hiding if I didn't leave them to it, so I left them. But I was also burning to find out myself what it was we'd been carrying for Faulkner, so I secretly followed them. And I know the warehouses around Marylebone even better than they do I reckon – maybe better than anyone. They was much too focused on that box and where they should open it to notice me tailing them, and it was no problem for me to get to a good spying spot behind some old cargo trucks. From where I was, I couldn't see the direction that Faulkner approached them from myself, but Kenny and Archie should've been able to see him. But they didn't see nothing until it was too late.

"When Faulkner appeared and started going for Archie, I thought I'd better get nearer, in case I could help them out somehow. So I made my way down the side of the trucks I was hiding behind, and I lost of sight of them all for a while. But when I got to the end of the trucks and was able to see them clearly again, it wasn't Faulkner that Archie was fighting with no more – at least, not as you'd recognise him. Faulkner the man weren't there no more. In his place was this huge creature, a demon just like the stories, but even worse! And it was closing down on Archie who'd tried to make a run for it."

Anna was momentarily dumbstruck. "You mean..." she asked, trying but failing to retain the calmness in her voice, "... that Faulkner *is* the Beast of Highgate?"

"Yes, Anna, that's what I'm saying. I didn't see him change on account of being behind them trucks, but one minute Archie was fighting with Faulkner, and the next it was the Beast!"

Anna was totally shaken by what she heard. "Gillespie, are you absolutely sure? Couldn't it just be that Faulkner summoned up the Beast and then disappeared?"

"No Anna. I know it was him. The torn remains of his clothes were on the ground where it stood, and the last strips of his shirt were still hanging off its arms! I tell you Anna, Faulkner *is* the Beast of Highgate!"

Anna gripped with both hands the branch she was sitting on. So, when Mr Warwick had bundled her into that secret room in his shop, he had actually been saving her from the Satal itself! And when they had faced the beast up at that Hampstead mansion, the creature that had swooped down at them from the rooftop had in fact been Faulkner, transformed into that unearthly monster. Did Mr Warwick know this, Anna wondered. When he had confirmed to her that Faulkner was responsible for the Satal's appearance but that there was more he needed to explain, was this what he had meant? Of course Gillespie could be lying, but the thing above all else which told

Anna that what Gillespie was saying was true was her recollection of Faulkner's aura. From its size to its shape to its colouring, it had been like nothing she had ever come across before – it had looked utterly inhuman! And utterly evil. Now she understood why. It had been the aura of a Satal.

Gillespie had stopped again, gasping for breath and beginning to sob. The freezing fog, which was drifting slowly but ever more thickly into the garden through the hole in the wall, already had Gillespie held tightly in its sinister grip, and now it was starting to envelop Anna too. Gillespie's form grew more difficult to make out. But Anna continued sitting motionless, almost unable to move, gripped with grim fascination. Somehow, with what must have been close to superhuman effort on his part, Gillespie continued with what he had to say, his voice little more than a croak, as if he believed his life depended on finishing his piece.

"Like in the stories I'd heard from those who'd claimed to have seen it, this demon creature was covered in some kind of shiny black scales. Its head was long and sharp with long horns, and it had huge fangs. Its head was the same kind of shiny black as the rest of its body. Instead of arms it had huge, black wings with long claws at the ends, and it had a long, pointed tail. I swear to you, it was just like a creature from the pits of hell. Which is the only place I reckon it could have come from! This beast, or demon, or whatever it was, well it set about Archie in a real furious frenzy. He tried to run away from it, but it was on him again in seconds. And the noise the creature was making... Anna, I tell you it was like nothing I've heard, like this terrible, shrieking sound – I can still hear it in my head, clear as day." Gillespie shuddered visibly at the recollection, and so did Anna.

"At the same time Kenny was also trying to run away in the other direction. Now you know Kenny ain't no coward, and normally I reckon he'd have done whatever he could to save his mate. But see, faced with something like that, well there was nothing he could have done – nothing anyone could have done. And I don't mind telling you, I was terrified myself an' all. I ducked back under the truck and hid. I couldn't watch no more – I hid my face, but I couldn't block out those terrible screams..."

By now, Gillespie was in floods of tears. "Poor Archie," he continued, "he could be a hard one, he could, and he gave me the odd hiding or two when he thought I'd warranted it, but I don't reckon he deserved that. No-one deserves an end like that."

Gillespie clearly didn't want to give any more detail regarding Archie's demise, and neither did Anna wish to hear any. "So what about Kenny?" she prompted, still trying to keep her tone calm.

The question helped refocus Gillespie's mind. He started again. "While Faulkner was setting about Archie, Kenny had made a run for it. Like I say, there wasn't nothing he could have done, and he knew it. So he tried to scarper. The Beast was focused on devouring Archie for a while, and it was a bit of time before it turned its attention on Kenny, and he'd almost reached the door by that time. It flung Archie's body to the ground, beat those black wings it had and began to fly. Its wings grew real long, and it went up high, up near the roof, before diving down after my brother. Kenny just made it through the metal door, and slammed and bolted it shut, just a second before the thing went crashing into it. Then it let out more of that screaming, and it started to beat at the metal door. Luckily though it was a strong old door, and it took it a while to smash it off its hinges. That gave Kenny a good head start, and like I said, he knows that area real well, and he was able to get away.

"Well I was scared out my wits. I just stayed right where I was without moving a muscle, hidden under them railway cars for hours until long after the sound of that beast had gone. When I finally decided it was safe to get out of there, I headed straight for Kenny's lodgings south of the river. Kenny wasn't there, but I managed to find him in another of his hideaways that very few apart from me know about. He was in a right state Anna, like you'd imagine. I told him I'd been there and I'd seen what had happened. He was right shocked, and yelled at me how careful I needed to be, that I'd seen what Faulkner was and what he could do, and he'd be sure to kill me if he ever knew I'd been there. He said he was sure that Faulkner had got his hooks into him somehow, and that he was sure he'd track him down one way or another wherever he was if he stayed in London. So he was going to do a runner, maybe catch a ship and go overseas, somewhere where Faulkner wouldn't be able to find him – if there was anywhere. He told me to look after myself and the family, and whatever I did I was not to follow him. And then he was gone.

"I didn't know what to do, Anna. Kenny was real clear that I wasn't to follow him this time, real clear, so this time I did what he said. My dad's in jail, my mother was away at work and I didn't feel safe, so I decided to go and find my mates up in Marylebone. It was several hours later and I was on my way to our normal meeting place, when suddenly he was there, Faulkner, back in his normal human shape, all dressed up like a proper gent again. It was like he'd known I'd be coming, and he was waiting for me.

"I turned to run, but he had hold of me before I got more than a couple of steps. He was strong Anna, real strong. I've got a good wriggle on me and I can get out of most holds even by adults, but there was no escaping his grip – I swear it was like iron, and it hurt plenty I can tell you.

"He dragged me off down a side alley. It was broad daylight and there was people about on the main street, but no-one did anything to help me. Well, I suppose the sight of a well-dressed gent like Faulkner sorting out a young ruffian like me... and I suppose I haven't got a great name amongst them shopkeepers that know me around that area... I suppose they probably thought I deserved a good hiding. They was probably pleased to see someone taking me in hand. Anyway no-one batted an eyelid and no-one followed us, in spite of me screaming for help."

Gillespie stopped again for breath. He had been talking fast as the memories had come back to him in a rush, but now that he started to recall Faulkner he began to slow down, as though the words were becoming harder to speak.

"Well, he dragged me down that alley and pinned me against the wall. He slowly lowered his head towards mine and looked at me with this terrible stare. God Anna, it was awful. He's got these eyes that go right through you. I can still see them in me head now. He was looking right into me." Anna understood all too well. This had not been a man but a Satal looking into him, looking at his aura, penetrating his heart. The dream she experienced all those years before returned to her. Gillespie struggled for words and breath. But he battled on.

"He started asking me where my brother was, and whether I'd seen him. I said I hadn't seen him for a few days, and I didn't know where he'd been or what he'd been up to. I was doing my best to lie, and I rate myself as a pretty good liar too when I need to be. But it was like he was looking right inside my head, I felt like there was no deceiving him. He started to grip my arms even tighter and he hammered me against the wall. I'd seen what he could do back in the warehouse and I thought that was it, my time was up. I was sure he was going to do for me one way or another right there and then – probably turn into the Beast again, tear me limb from limb or something worse.

"But he didn't do me no more harm – no harm to my body I mean. But he did do something to me. I can't really explain what happened next, but he kept staring into my eyes, and I started to feel the most dreadful thing, Anna. I don't understand it and I don't have no words to describe it, but all I can say is, it was like he had his hands round my soul, and he was slowly strangling the life out of it. I felt sick to my stomach, I felt terror right to my core. I felt like I was inches from death. Then I started to feel like I was on the very edge of some terrible other place, like if he pushed me one more inch I would be gone there, wherever it was – and that it would be a place much worse than death."

Anna was transfixed. She knew what Gillespie was describing must have come from Faulkner's contact with his aura, but exactly what evil act had he been performing? This time it was beyond anything she had experienced or seen before.

"Anna, I've never felt nothing like it in my life, I didn't know you could feel like that. But Faulkner was somehow inside me, and he had my whole being in his grip, ready to snuff out me life, or doom me to far worse forever if he wanted to.

"If he'd asked me again where Kenny was, I reckon I'd have told him all I knew. Not even to save myself no more, but because I was powerless – completely in his power. But he never asked me. I reckon he'd looked inside me with them damned eyes and seen all there was to know. Then I was no more use to him, so he just threw me to the ground and left. He could have killed me as easy as killing a fly, but I reckon it just made no odds to him whether I lived or not – once he'd got what he wanted, my life wasn't important to him one way or the other. And that's the only reason I'm still here, I reckon. But what he did to me Anna, what he made me feel, it was worse than anything I've ever known or imagined – worse, much worse I reckon than if he'd torn me apart like what he did with Archie."

Anna could see that Gillespie was now in a terrible state as he relived these events, and she could hold back no more. He was a broken child, shattered by the experiences he'd had and he posed no more of a threat to her now than he had when he had stood defenceless in front of her on that canal bridge – in fact far less. Mustering the considerable effort needed to free herself from the almost physical hold the freezing fog seemed to have on her, she laid her caution to one side and moved forward from her place of concealment to sit beside him. She continued to look about as she put her arm around Gillespie's shoulder to console him, then she gave him a hug. She noticed again just how dense and frozen the fog had become, especially around him. It seemed to dispel just slightly with her arrival.

Slowly, Gillespie lowered his head onto Anna's shoulder, and tears streamed down his cheeks. Anna could never have imagined feeling so sorry for this person, who until that night had been her sworn enemy. But in the face of the infinitely greater evil represented by Faulkner, their previous differences now seemed utterly trivial. Anna continued to hold Gillespie close until the sobbing began to subside. She then put a voice to the question that had been burning inside her since Gillespie had started all this.

"Billy, why did you come to find me tonight, and why have you been telling me all this? You said something about wanting me to help you – and I really wish I could help you, I honestly do – but why me? What is it you think I can do? I'd have thought you'd be looking for help from your Marylebone... uh... friends."

"After Faulkner had finished with me, I knew there was nothing any of them could do. If I told them this story they wouldn't have believed me. They'd just have mocked me and called me mad. But even if they had believed me, well what could they have done? We're a tough bunch, but not as tough as Kenny and Archie. They'd have just ended up the same way as Archie if I'd got them involved. And anyway, our gang's not as big as it was. Bobby and Davy both disappeared in the summer, along with Davy's brother, and no-one knows where they've gone."

Watson and Green had not been seen since the summer? Did that mean they had not been seen since the encounter with the Beast outside the Hampstead mansion? Anna wondered what had become of them.

"No Anna, the reason I wanted to find you and talk to you," and for the first time since she had come to sit next to him, Gillespie raised his head and looked into her eyes, his own glistening with tears in the dim light of the street-lamp, "is that I reckon you're the one person who might be able to do something about Faulkner and save Kenny... and save me. Or at least help me get over whatever Faulkner did to me. If anyone can..." With that his voice faltered, and he lowered his head once more.

Anna was stunned. What could possibly have led Gillespie to make this connection? "What do you mean, Billy? What is it that you think I can do? I'm only a child still, and not even hardened, grown men seem to be any match for Faulkner."

Gillespie was silent for a moment, then he said, "Anna, you remember that time we faced each other on the bridge over the canal? When you threw me over the side into the water?"

"Yes, of course I remember it. But Billy, I don't really think it's the same as - "

"Well I felt something that day too," continued

Gillespie, "something deep inside me – the same kind of place I felt Faulkner had a hold of me.

"Anna, I reckon I'm stronger than you, physically I mean, but when you walked towards me you had me completely helpless before you'd even laid a finger on me. You was also looking right into me, real intense like – but right pretty at the same time." This time Anna felt herself suddenly and unexpectedly blush, in spite of herself and the situation!

"But when I look back on it, you did something like what Faulkner did to me, I'm sure of it. It's like you reached right inside me and touched me, like you were touching my soul or something. But it weren't nothing like the way Faulkner did it. See Anna, when you approached me and did what you did, I felt a huge calm inside me, like all my troubles were being soothed – I felt better than I've ever felt I reckon, really blissful – but also I was completely in your power. When you reached me and pushed me over the side, I couldn't resist you any more than I could've resisted landing in the water straight after. But I didn't feel no hatred from you Anna, not like with Faulkner, and I didn't feel no hatred for you either." He was looking at her again, his eyes slightly clearer and brighter now.

"What you did was something like what Faulkner did, but the feeling was the opposite, if you know what I mean. I don't know what it is but you're both able to do something, you can reach inside people and change them, either in a good way, or the most awful way. Anna, I don't understand any of this, I swear I don't, but I'm just desperate. I've got nowhere else to go and I reckon you're my last hope of finding something that might help against

Faulkner, or at least undo whatever he's done to me, and help me save Kenny, better than any grown man armed with weapons."

Although it was crystal clear that Gillespie scarcely understood himself what he had felt and what he was attempting to articulate, there was no doubt what he was referring to. Here was confirmation of what Mr Warwick and her uncle had told her about Satals and their ability to manipulate a person's aura in the most terrible ways. And now he had given her first-hand evidence that the power she possessed also touched a person's aura in a way that was recognisably similar. Although she understood something of the theory, it was nonetheless still deeply shocking to have it confirmed through someone's real experience. Like it or not, she and Faulkner shared some of the same powers, regardless of their entirely opposite intentions. The idea that she might have anything that connected her with a monster like Faulkner – a *Satal* – was utterly abhorrent. She wanted to have nothing whatsoever in common with that monster, and with a power which had such evil potential. But at least Gillespie had explained that the effect of each of them had felt entirely different. She held onto that thought.

As they sat close to one another, Anna was able to see Gillespie's aura in detail for the first time. Although she had already noticed the increased scarring on its surface when she had looked from some distance, now she could see it more clearly, what she saw made her gasp.

The scars on the surface of the aura, though not wide, ran far deeper than she had realised. It looked almost as though this aura had undergone some kind of frenzied attack, leaving its surface deeply lacerated. Although the overall hue of the aura was still yellow as she had previously observed, the colouration in and around the scars themselves was black. This was the aura of someone who had undergone a brief but quite ferocious mental attack. The image of Faulkner's savage aura returned to her mind, with its sharp spikes. The damage was unlike anything Anna had seen before. Looking again, she felt an irresistible urge to try to mend some of the harm that had been done, to heal him and to restore his aura at least a little way back towards a pure state. Visualising her own aura, she reached out and began gently to massage Gillespie's. Little by little, she was able to smooth out the surface of the aura, and to reduce the extent of the black colouration, if only to a small degree.

Gillespie felt the effect immediately. Looking up at her as she paused, he said "Yes Anna. That's it. That's the first time I've felt anything like peace since Faulkner got to me. I knew you could help. I knew it. Thank you!"

Encouraged, Anna looked back to Gillespie's aura again, ready to try to soothe it more. But at that instant, the deep scars in its surface flashed momentarily with a terrible, bright scarlet colour, before returning to their former black! Anna looked on startled as Gillespie winced visibly with pain. Then another scarlet flash and another gasp from Gillespie. This time Anna jumped. She had never seen anything like this before, but all her instincts told her one thing – somehow it must be Faulkner causing this to happen. She was filled with a sudden chill of fear... was he somewhere near? She no longer felt safe in this place. She had the sudden and growing sense that staying in any one place too long might be a fatal mistake. They had to move, and move right now!

She told Gillespie with great urgency that they needed to get away from there. She helped him slowly to his feet. "But Anna, I don't think I can move no more," Gillespie croaked – not surprisingly, given all that he had been through and was now experiencing again.

But Anna would not take 'no' for an answer, and Gillespie continued to sob as she began to lead his stumbling form slowly away from the pile of rubble. She had to think fast. Back onto the road, where anyone might be waiting in ambush for them? Or deeper into the garden, where at least she would know the terrain better than anyone else, although from which it might be more difficult to escape? With no more time to think, she chose the latter.

As hurriedly as Gillespie's almost immobile legs would allow, they passed through the long grass of the lawn, through the swirling mist to the far side of the garden, which was also lined with tall bushes, then moved some way up the garden away from the point where they had crossed. Having put some considerable distance between themselves and the spot where they had just been, Anna led Gillespie through the low branches of a large bush, sufficiently deeply to be concealed from all but a few feet away. Anna stopped and looked urgently back through the leaves, across the lawn to the spot from which they had just come. Their leaving had coincided with a slight thinning of the fog – or had it been their movement and increased energy that had actually caused it to disperse? There was something supernatural about the fog that night that made anything seem possible.

Then, out of the corner of her eye, below the barely visible gas lamp of the street, Anna thought she glimpsed another, fainter light, moving slowly along the pavement side of the broken wall. She peered harder through the foggy darkness, and there was no mistaking it – there was definitely a second lamp! It came to a halt at the point where the lowest part of the wall was located, and Anna was gripped by absolute fear. She knew this garden almost like the back of her hand, and she also knew that all means of escape other than the way they had come were equally difficult, requiring either the scaling of high garden walls or else breaking into the old house itself. Worries began to attack her. Had this been a trap all along? Had Gillespie in fact somehow outsmarted her after all and distracted her with his stories until his accomplices could arrive? She suddenly heard his intake of breath next to her as he too noticed the second light. She felt him reach for her hand – however not in a way intended to capture her, but rather with a grip that articulated only his own, intense fear.

"Oh my God Anna, we've got to get out of here!" Anna could feel Gillespie physically trembling. She put all thoughts of his possible deception out of her mind, once and for all. He could already have given her away by now had he chosen to, and his condition showed that he was now in a state of absolute terror.

They both stared in silence across the misty abyss towards the far side of the garden. The light had slowly started to move again, slightly upwards in a motion that suggested its bearer was now climbing over something. The lamp lowered again, before once more moving gradually forward and upward, then stopping. The swirling fog cleared slightly, and just for an instant they were both able to make out the dark, silhouetted outline of a very tall man stood astride the rubble mound where they themselves had been just moments before. The figure, wearing a top hat and a long cape that reached almost to the ground, appeared to be brandishing a walking cane in his right hand whilst holding aloft a lamp in his left. The man began to take a step forward into the garden towards them, then he was enveloped once more by fog. It had been no more than a glimpse, but it had been unmistakable.

"It's him!" Gillespie breathed, almost inaudibly into Anna's ear. "Oh my God, it's him. He's here, Anna. We've got to get out of here!" Gillespie was now in the grip of complete and utter, blind panic.

"Don't worry, Billy, I have a plan – you must trust me," said Anna, lying desperately and gripping his hand, no longer worried by the possibility of his treachery so much as the danger that his fear might give them away. "Don't move or make a sound unless I say so!" Trembling from head to toe, Gillespie fell silent.

Anna fought desperately to control her own, crippling fear which was slowly creeping up her body. This had been the one situation above all others that Mr Warwick and her uncle had most feared – the very one which they had urged her at all costs to avoid. Her training had barely begun, and she was entirely unprepared. Not only did she not have anyone there from the Order to help her, she did not even have any of her own friends with her. The thought of Timmy returned to her mind. She had felt so safe in his company when they had fled from the

Hampstead mansion together; she had felt that they would always be all right as long as they were together. But what had happened since then? Where was Timmy now? He had seemingly gone from her life. Mr Warwick and her uncle were miles away and now there was no-one to help her when she needed it most desperately.

As she stared into the fog, which had become impenetrable once more, she could see nothing, but she could sense the figure they had glimpsed slowly approaching. She started to feel physically sick to the pit of her stomach. He was going to find them. How could she have let this happen? How could she have been so stupid? She had been trapped after all – and in a trap of her own making! Seven words from Mr Warwick returned to her: 'The malevolent influence of the Opposing Energy...' Had it in fact been the enemy's influence that had lured her to this point, and to her doom? Was this where her short life was to end, right here in this garden, all her supposed potential entirely unfulfilled, and despite all Mr Warwick's hopes, nothing in the end achieved for the cause of the Alpha World?

For Gillespie was right. Faulkner, Satal of the Omega World, had hunted them down and was now right there inside the garden with them!

The Hunter and the Prey

Anna fought desperately to regain control of her emotions, to resist the tide of raw fear that had already consumed her companion. She had to think clearly, and very fast.

There was no way that Faulkner could have known in advance that Anna was going to lead Gillespie here to this garden. Even Anna herself had not known that beforehand. If he had somehow managed to follow them unseen through the fog, surely he would have arrived at the garden far sooner than he had. She did not fully understand, but she felt sure it was something to do with the effect she had seen in Gillespie's aura – those red flashes in the scars on its surface. Faulkner appeared to have some kind of contact with Gillespie's aura that had enabled him to locate Gillespie, then hunt him down. If that were true, presumably he would soon be able to track them right here to their hiding spot! Their only chance was to find a way to break the connection between Faulkner and Gillespie's aura.

Trusting entirely to her intuition, Anna began to visualise her own aura moving over that of Gillespie. In her mind she pictured it gradually engulfing and finally surrounding it entirely. She could not see, but she could feel the contact with her companion's aura, and it felt as though she had managed to contain and enclose it within her own. She had no idea whether what she was attempting would have any kind of positive effect, but no sooner had she done it than she felt a strange sensation in her own aura, like a prickling feeling all over its surface. She wondered if this was somehow connected with the scarlet flashes she had seen in Gillespie's aura. It felt as though Faulkner was sending out some kind of pulse, presumably from his own aura, which was making contact with Gillespie's and identifying Gillespie's location. Anna guessed the connection had been created at the time Gillespie had received those terrible scars on his aura. Faulkner must have done something else to Gillespie's aura that had made that contact possible. But this time, although Anna had felt that prickling sensation on her own aura, the scars in Gillespie's aura had not flashed red. Was it possible she was now successfully shielding Gillespie from Faulkner's reach? She had no way to be sure, but a first glimmer of hope appeared in her heart.

Holding the trembling hand of her silent but terrified companion even more tightly, she whispered words of encouragement as she peered intently into the foggy darkness. Another wave of the prickling feeling swept over her aura, more forceful than the first, and now she braced herself for an onslaught, imagining Faulkner's snarling face suddenly emerging from the fog right in front of them – or worse still, that of the Beast. As she looked, Anna started to see images of the Beast in the fog itself, coming at her, but she fought to block them from her mind. Once again Gillespie's aura did not flash, and no-one appeared.

As the moments passed, Anna noticed the haunting mist start to part again as it swirled in the night. Straining her eyes in the direction from which they had fled, once again she glimpsed it – the cloaked figure of Faulkner, palely illuminated by the lamp he still held aloft, now inside the garden and closer, but thankfully still a considerable distance away. He was moving his gaze slowly from one side of the garden to the other as he peered intently into the darkness. From their concealed position in the bushes, Anna shifted her focus to see if she could make out his hideous aura through the fog. To her relief she could not! 'That might just mean he won't be able to make out our auras either, at least as long stays at that distance,' she reasoned desperately.

The mist parting had coincided with a third wave of the prickling sensation, and then suddenly the figure let out a terrible, anger-filled growl as he swiped violently at the air around him with his cane, just as the fog engulfed him once more. Whilst the image had been but momentary, it had been enough to send a bolt of terror through Anna. But once it was gone, faint hope returned. Their enemy's anger might be born out of frustration at having lost track of Gillespie.

Anna focused desperately on holding Gillespie's aura entirely concealed within her own. Wave after wave of searching probing played upon her aura and another muffled roar of frustration reached their ears. Anna remained motionless, maintaining the positioning of her aura. At her side, Gillespie seemed to be breathing more easily, as though he were finally feeling some respite from Faulkner's continual presence, but he did not move and he did not lessen his grip on Anna's hand.

Several minutes, which felt like aeons, passed, and then they heard the angry growl of rage again – but if anything, the noise of their hunter sounded closer! Anna could not see anything through the fog now, nor could she make out anything of Faulkner's aura, but once again her fears began to get the better of her. She had visions of their nemesis wading through the long grass, snarling and thrashing at the misty darkness with his cane, seeking out their auras and hunting down his prey. If he were to find them, every instinct in her body told her that it would certainly spell their end. Once again she started to see images of the Beast in the fog, and she fought to maintain her grip on reality. There was no way they would be able to fight off that monster with its abominable essence. The prickling sensation on her aura intensified, becoming positively painful as it bore the brunt of the Satal's most penetrating search yet. Anna braced herself grimly for the final attack.

The longest snarling growl of rage reached them. As it continued though, Anna could have sworn that it was beginning to grow more distant, as though the face of their enemy had just turned away from them. Anna held her breath, hoping beyond hope that he was finally abandoning his murderous quest. Yes, as the moments passed there was no mistaking it – the sound of Faulkner's anger was definitely moving away! Not for one second did Anna let down her defences, however, the evening's experiences having taught her that any further lack of caution on her part might be the last mistake she ever made.

There came one more, angry growl, this time away in the distance, followed by silence. Perhaps most tellingly, the frequency of the prickling sensation on her aura also subsided, then stopped altogether. Anna remained motionless. The only sound she made was a brief whisper to Gillespie not to speak a word or to move a muscle until she told him. She would take no further chances and she would wait as long as it took to be certain that Faulkner was no longer around.

After a long time had passed, it became clear that Faulkner had indeed gone. Anna finally began to breathe normally again. The night was cold and both she and Gillespie had begun to shiver, for the first time more through cold than fear. She still dared not make the return journey across the lawn, but she was genuinely concerned for the condition of the shivering physical and mental wreck next to her. Continuing to surround Gillespie's badly damaged aura with her own, Anna first turned to face him, then very slowly gestured to him to sit down in the long grass beyond the bushes. He did so without hesitation, a model of obedience. Anna took up a position sitting cross-legged in front of Gillespie and started to look in more detail at the scars on his aura which had flashed such bright scarlet in response to Faulkner's probing. The gash-like openings on the surface of the aura were not so wide, but once again she could see how deep they ran. The effect brought to Anna's mind the damage that might be inflicted on physical flesh by the long claws of a mighty tiger or some other fierce animal. Then without breaking her containment of Gillespie's aura, Anna started to visualise her own moving aura gently over the surface of his, in what she hoped would once again be a soothing motion. Gillespie raised his head which had been bowed, and whispered, "Anna, yes, that's it. A bit of peace. Blessed peace at last, please don't stop..." He lowered his head, his dark hair falling over his face, and he rested his forehead gently on Anna's left shoulder. His breathing was now deeper and more regular.

Anna continued with the gentle, massaging motion of her aura on Gillespie's for several minutes, and she was able to see a very positive change in his aura. The black colouring around the wounds was gone, and the wounds themselves seemed much shallower. Anna felt sure that whatever Faulkner had done to Gillespie's aura to track him had been undone now, and he could be safe. After a while Gillespie's breathing became deep, and gradually his full seated weight became slumped against her. He had fallen asleep! And a blessed rest it must have been. Anna gave him a quick hug, wondering just how long it had been since the poor boy had actually had any such untroubled sleep.

Anna herself shivered from the cold; she decided the time had come to move. 'No point in escaping Faulkner only to freeze to death!' she thought. The fog had thinned enough to see across the garden, and with considerable effort, Anna roused Gillespie and led the stumbling form across the divide. Having been crouched and for so long in the cold her legs were stiffer than she could remember. They managed to make it across without incident. All the while, Anna continued to engulf Gillespie's aura in her own in case of any return by Faulkner, but she felt nothing more. They traversed the wall, and once again were on the pavement of the road beyond the garden.

"Well, I think Faulkner has gone. It's time we both left this place and got ourselves warm," said Anna, her voice quieter and harder to come by than she had expected.

Gillespie was still holding Anna's hand for grim life. "Anna, that sleep you gave me," he murmured, close to her ear. "It was beautiful, with dreams, but not terrible dreams... I can't remember the last time I slept like that. Anna, you make me feel like a different person. I knew you could do it, whatever it is you've done – I don't begin to understand any of what you and Faulkner can do, but thank you – I feel like I owe you my life and I will never forget it."

"Gillespie... Billy, you are really welcome. I just hope I have been able to help you. But please don't think about me and Faulkner having some kind of similar ability, or in fact anything at all in common, because we don't." Anna was telling herself this as much as Gillespie.

"Whatever you say Anna. I just want to tell you how real grateful I am."

"It's my pleasure, Billy," Anna replied. "Now I think you should leave here and go somewhere far away, somewhere safer, and get some proper rest." Then she found her full voice again as she said, "you've had quite a day – and night!"

"Right-oh, I'll be getting along then," Gillespie responded before taking a few steps, then stopping and calling back to her. "Thing is though Anna, I don't really want to be apart from you now. You've made me feel better tonight than I reckon I ever have and I don't want to leave you now."

Anna drew close again and said quietly, "Billy, we've been very lucky to escape Faulkner tonight, extremely lucky. I don't need to tell you to keep clear of him from now on, and please just steer clear of trouble. Then I think you're going to be all right. I am hoping you've turned a corner tonight. Anyway, we had better not stay here any longer, and there's no way you can come back to my home, which is where I'm going now, so you'd better get going to somewhere far away and safe for yourself."

"All right Anna, I'll do whatever you say. But thank you again for tonight – I will never ever forget it," said Gillespie, more of the volume and strength returning to his voice. Then Anna remembered the question that she had meant to ask him earlier.

"Billy, please tell me,' her voice once again lowered, "how you knew where to find me this evening."

"Oh, well, Lizzy who works in your house, she don't live too far from my place. So I caught up with her and asked if she could give you a message. I knew you weren't likely to see me just because I asked you to, I mean, not after the last time we met, and, well, we ain't exactly ever been best of friends have we? But Lizzy asked me where you usually met with your friends - I don't know why she wanted to know, and I told her I wasn't exactly sure, but it was somewhere near that stretch of canal - and she told me she would arrange something. Then later she came round my house to tell me roughly what time you'd be passing by that road where I met you. She said I might have to wait because she weren't sure exactly what time you'd be there, but if I was to wait she said I'd probably catch you. So that's what I did. I'm very grateful to her."

"Right, I see," responded Anna, trying to take in what this might mean. "Anyway, thanks for letting me know – and good luck!"

Gillespie turned and began to disappear into the retreating mist ahead. Anna watched his figure recede into the darkness, and suddenly felt a renewed pang of sympathy for the boy. He might have turned a corner, but into what kind of life was he now returning, all alone? Could he really escape Faulkner's clutches, even if he did flee far away? He was very much a marked man, and for certain his brother was in the most extreme danger. Whatever bad and mischievous things Billy Gillespie might have got up to in the past, and no matter how much he might have brought his own downfall upon himself, the receding figure was still just that of a boy, not yet fully grown, and yet he had already felt the full weight of the worst of what this world could inflict upon him.

"Billy," she called out after him. He had almost passed completely from sight by now, but he stopped instantly and turned back to face her. She did not speak, but simply opened her arms. Half stumbling, Gillespie retraced his steps to re-join her, and she gave him one last, big hug and whispered, "Don't worry Billy, I feel sure things are going to be all right for you now. Be brave, try to do the right thing, and I think everything will turn out to be fine in the end."

At that, Gillespie hugged her back so tightly that Anna almost started to worry – that he might start to get the wrong idea about her intentions, and also that she might not actually be able to escape from his vice-like grip! However as she lessened her own grip, he did likewise. Tiredness now being the overriding expression on his palely-illuminated features, he once again whispered his thanks, bade her farewell and moved off.

She started to walk in the other direction as briskly as she could manage. Suddenly, from the corner of her eye, she glimpsed a figure running away from her along the pavement ahead, on the other side of the road. It was no more than a momentary sighting and the figure was a long way off. All she could make out was the impression of baggy clothes and a cap pulled down low over the wearer's face. She had the sense that it might be another boy roughly her age. 'Surely not a trap now, not after all I've been through tonight?' she thought, her senses re-heightened. But the unidentified figure seemed to be running as fast as it could into the foggy night ahead of her, and in an instant it was gone. Her caution redoubled, Anna looked back in the direction of Gillespie, who was by now many yards away, at a point where his aura was only just visible. Suddenly she caught her breath. She was sure she had seen the aura change colour momentarily. Had there been a flash of scarlet? Then it happened again – another flash of bright red which was this time unmistakable. Gillespie was a long way away from her, too far to catch up with quickly.

"Quick, Billy!" she shouted in his direction, "I think he's coming back. Quick, run for it!"

Gillespie looked round briefly, just long enough to see Anna gesticulating frantically for him to run, then he bolted as best as his tired legs could manage. He had progressed to the edge of Anna's sight when it happened. From the swirling mist above Gillespie's head, a giant, hideous, swooping shape emerged. From its head rose two terrible horns, and below its wide, bat-like wings stretched legs tipped with long, deadly talons.

"No!" cried Anna, but the word stuck in her throat. She froze hopelessly to the spot. The giant predator closed on Gillespie like a massive, demonic bird of prey, took hold of him in its talons and carried him away! Anna was much too far away to do anything but watch. In a moment, both the beast and its victim were gone. She sank silently to her knees, powerless, as the horrific form disappeared into the misty night sky whence it had come. Then there was just a silent, empty road ahead of her.

Anna knelt motionless in the road, deep in shock. Gillespie had come to her for help, the only person he believed could help him. Just when she thought she had rescued him from Faulkner and given him new hope for the future, that hope had been viciously snuffed out in an instant, together with poor Billy's life. She thought she had healed his aura and broken the contact with Faulkner, but she had not done enough. She had failed him. Her shock turned to desperate tears. The world had become a crueller and more vicious place than she could ever have imagined.

Just a few months before, the Marylebone Gang and their older brothers had seemed to be their only enemy, and it had been their mission to stop them. But those enemies had turned out merely to be the puppets, and now the shattered victims, of the one who was their true enemy: Faulkner. He was the one they needed to stop, whatever it took. That would be a task infinitely more difficult than stopping the likes of Archie Knowles and Kenny Gillespie, but through bitter tears, Anna started to steel herself. Deep inside, that intuition about the future which sometimes spoke to her, told Anna that the day when she would come face to face with Faulkner in battle was now very near. With a steely determination forged out of that evening's tragic experience, she vowed that when that day came, she would end the evil brutality of this Satal, and rid the world of it forever. She had failed Billy, and her failure had cost the boy his life. Whatever it took, she would avenge his death and she would make sure that no-one else would ever again suffer at the hands of Faulkner.

Epilogue

Several hours deeper into that same, deadly night, many miles across the great city and its mighty river, Billy Gillespie's brother, Kenny, desperately stuffed into his battered old bag the meager possessions that came to hand, together with the hidden money he had come back to collect. He dashed down the stairs of the dilapidated building where his lodgings were housed, opened the back door and slipped silently into the unholy fog that had gripped the city that night. Escaping to the docks and finding a ship that might take him as far away from London as it was possible to go was now the only thought in his terror-stricken mind. In recent days he had witnessed things more terrible than he could ever have imagined, still less have explained, and he had spent every waking moment since in quaking fear for his life.

Kenny Gillespie had done many bad things in his time, some of them very bad indeed, but that road had now brought him face-to-face with evil in its purest form, and it had been far, far more than he could handle. It had taken until now for him to dare risk a return to his rented lodgings from his previous place of concealment, to pick up the small amount of money he had managed to save from his various 'work' assignments. He had known full well he could not afford to linger a moment longer than absolutely necessary. Gillespie was no stranger to London after dark - indeed, over the years, it had become his natural habitat - but the fog that night was denser and more sinister than on any he could remember. It seemed possessed of an eerie, almost living quality which sent shivers through him, more vigorous than could have been induced by the mere cold alone. Through wide, frightened eyes, time and again he was convinced he had made out a snarling ghostly face in the swirling mist through which he ran, dimly illuminated by flickering gas lamps. 'It's just the troubled state of my head... my mind's playing tricks on me... it's this damned fog... I'm seeing things because I haven't slept for days... it'll all be all right once I'm safely out at sea...' Gillespie rambled desperately to himself as he hurried down the cobbled back-street, past the yards of the terraced houses that adjoined his lodgings, sticking close to the wall for fear of losing himself forever in the haunted sea of mist that stretched away into the blackness.

Then he heard it. It was the sound that he had come to fear most in the world, the sound that had haunted the snatched moments of sleep he had managed since the awful events in the Marylebone warehouse. It was an inhuman, blood-curdling scream, completely filling his ears and echoing around his head. He could not tell from which direction it had come – it appeared to be from all directions at once – and his head span as the tricks played by his eyes in that infernal fog multiplied.

Gillespie stumbled once to his hands and knees on the freezing cobblestones, before immediately regaining his feet and lurching forwards into the foggy soup in front of him. By now he was seized by sheer, blind panic, and the most basic animal survival instinct was the only thing driving him forward. On he plunged, until his wits began dimly to return and he became aware he was approaching the better-lit main road which adjoined the backstreet he was on. A vague glimmer of hope and the remembrance of his plan to reach the docks re-entered his consciousness. There was no way to convince himself that he had imagined that terrible sound moments earlier – no way that his imagination could have conjured up such a sound – but maybe, just maybe, its owner had not yet spotted him through the all-consuming fog.

On reaching the corner, he scrambled around it... and there it was. Perfectly silhouetted against a bank of thick, ghostly white fog that was palely illuminated by a large gas street-lamp somewhere behind it, was the large black outline of a horned creature at least ten feet tall, with wings outstretched at either side, each tipped with long, deadly talons. Gillespie froze in his tracks, the final remnants of hope draining from his exhausted body, and for a moment neither figure moved. The thought of turning and trying to escape crawled across Gillespie's numb and shattered mind, but the futility of such an attempt was apparent even to him. All hope gone, he stood rooted to the spot as the monster before him slowly arched its head upwards, let out a scream that was to be the last sound he would ever hear, a sound so unlike anything from this world that it would be spoken about in the folklore of South London for generations to come, and then it struck.

The end for Kenny Gillespie when it came was mercifully swift, even if the damage inflicted on his physical body was truly horrific, shaking to the very core even the most hardened of policemen who saw it. 'Beast Strikes South of the River!' screamed the newspaper headlines the following day, stories of demons spread like wildfire, and London lay gripped in fear.

The End... of the Beginning

Lightning Source UK Ltd.
Milton Keynes UK
UKHW010809221019
352062UK00002B/53/P

9 781910 406748